Read what people are already saying about

Tall Oaks

'Clever, atmospheric and with **possibly the most diverse and divisive set of characters** found together in one book'
Liz Loves Books

'The best thing I've read in quite a while'
The Literary Shed

'This was a fun and **cleverly written book,** and I would recommend it to anyone who enjoys a good mystery with a hint of humour!'
Emma's Bookery

'Set in small-town America and filled with **some of the most exciting characters I have seen in fiction for ages**, this is a intriguingly twisty story that will net Chris Whitaker a TON of fans'
Reading Room with a View

'I had **the biggest laugh out loud moment I've ever had** from a book whilst reading *Tall Oaks*'
The Book Magnet

'I thoroughly enjoyed reading this; there are so many delightfully comic touches along the way, but all supported by a deeper sentiment and **characters you can't help but feel for**'
Buried Under Books

'Not only was this book, and it's many characters, **intriguing and thrilling to read**, it was also really funny'
Maureen's Books

'Chris Whitaker writes at a good pace and **the ending of the book took me completely by surprise**'
Dot Scribbles

'The reader is treated to a cast of **intriguing, quirky characters** and their stories all come together painting a great portrait of life in this small American town'
Portobello Book Blog

'Comes to a **dramatic and totally unexpected** conclusion'
It Takes a Woman

'**You seriously have to read this book**'
Lipstick & Lace

TALL
OAKS

Chris Whitaker was born in London and spent ten years working as a financial trader in the city. When not writing he enjoys football, boxing, and anything else that distracts him from his wife and two young sons. *Tall Oaks* is his first novel.

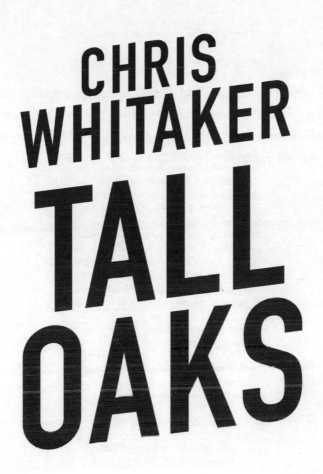

CHRIS WHITAKER

TALL OAKS

twenty7

First published in Great Britain in 2016

This paperback edition published in 2016 by

Twenty7 Books
80–81 Wimpole St, London W1G 9RE
www.twenty7books.com

A CIP catalogue record for this book is available from the British Library.

Paperback ISBN: 978-1-78577-030-2
Ebook ISBN: 978-1-78577-031-9

For Victoria, who after ten years still hasn't realised that she's too good for me.

1

Send in the Clown

Jim closed the blinds, unplugged the telephone, and put the tape in. He leaned back in his chair, took a breath, and pressed play.

The tape crackled, the sound familiar though no less unsettling, for he knew what was to come.

He skipped past the preliminaries, stopping when he heard Jess's voice.

"'The baby monitor is one of the new models. There's a small camera downstairs in Harry's room, and a base unit next to my bed. I was nervous about Harry sleeping in his own room, especially with him being two floors below: the lower ground floor. It's a long way down. The house wasn't really designed for family living. Michael loved it though."

He turned up the volume and closed his eyes. He heard her take a sip of water. He flinched as the glass touched her teeth.

"I liked lower ground floor over basement, like the realtor said. Basement sounds creepy, dark, and cold. Harry's room is nice though—there're animal stickers on the walls. We had the ceiling painted blue, like the sky."

She coughed lightly, shuffled in her seat.

"It'd taken a few weeks before I managed to sleep more than an hour without checking the monitor; seeing what position he was sleeping in; making sure he hadn't kicked his sheet off. The night-vision mode gives his room an eerie, green glow; makes his skin look so pale I felt sure he was freezing cold down there."

She laughed then, a fleeting, anxious laugh.

"I wasn't sure why I was sitting up in bed that night, why I was sweating, why my heart was pounding so hard. I remember reaching for the clock, seeing it was three-nineteen. Funny . . . the things you remember."

Another pause, another cough.

"I glanced at the monitor and fought the urge to check him. I drove myself mad, always checking. He's three after all, not a baby. I reached for my glass of water. My throat was dry and scratchy . . . I'm not sure . . . maybe I was getting sick . . . a cold or something."

She cleared her throat. *"Is this too much detail?"*

He heard his own voice, calm, reassuring, practiced. *"You're doing well."*

"I lay back and stared at the blank screen. He was fine. Harry was fine. It had been like this every night since Michael left. I was a wreck . . . I am a wreck: fucked. The person I used to be . . . gone . . . I'm not even sure I remember her. I wonder if I'll ever see her again . . . that person I mean. Do I sound crazy?"

He'd smiled gently, shaken his head.

"My mother said it will just take time, that I'll find my way again. But how much time? How much longer will I have to go on like this before it gets easier? She doesn't know, she can't tell me. I'm waiting for the day when I can stop thinking about him, flip a switch or something; dark to light. But at the same time I'm terrified of moving on, because I love him so much. Do you get that, Jim?"

He'd met her eye, offered a slight nod.

"I wonder when I'll be able to eat a meal and not think about who he's eating with, or worse, sleeping with. It's like an illness, it consumes you. I breathe him in, but never out. Is that fucked-up, Jim? It's unfair, you know. He just walked out. It's easier for him to find someone else. I'm the single mother now, the one with the baggage, the one that needs a small miracle to find someone decent . . . someone that wants to be a father to another man's child. And who does? I mean, really? I try to force these thoughts to the back of my mind. But lying there at night . . . that night . . ."

She trailed to a heavy silence.

They broke, this time for her to visit the ladies' room.

He thought about stopping the tape—he always did at this point. He traced his finger over the button, drawing it away when he heard her voice again.

"A long hour passed before I started to relax. My eyes grew tired and I started to drift. And then I heard it.

A whisper.

'Jessica.'

I opened my eyes wide, my breath caught in my throat. I stared at the monitor, the screen still dark, the green light still burning.

I must have been imagining it. That's what I thought, Jim: Get a grip, Jess. It was my mind playing tricks again, the way it did when Michael first left. It had been easier then because Harry had slept in my bed, as much for my sake as his. He didn't want to though. Imagine that. A three year old wanting to sleep on his own. So grown-up."

She cleared her throat.

"I sat up. My hand shook as I reached for my water."

He remembered her cheeks burning, her eyes darting up, around.

"I heard it again.

'Jessica.'

Still a whisper, but louder this time."

Her words tumbled out.

"I dropped the glass. I picked up the monitor and pressed the button. I calmed when I saw Harry, fast asleep on his back, with his hands above his head. He'd slept that way since he was a baby. I must have imagined it. Just a voice in my head. That's what I kept telling myself, because that's what you do . . . you rationalize. I watched him until the screen faded. I placed it back onto the nightstand and forced myself to lie down. I thought I was going mad, Jim. I thought I'd call my mother in the morning and tell her. Then maybe the men in the white coats would come and cart me off someplace.

I couldn't get back to sleep. I kept thinking, what if I hadn't imagined it? What if there was someone in Harry's room? The scan button. I had forgotten about the scan button. I reached for the monitor again. There're four arrows on the side of it, so you can move the camera around. I pressed the right arrow. The camera swept along his bed and past his toy chest, his rocking horse, and his ride-on car. I hoped that it didn't make a noise when it moved. He's only just started to sleep through the night, a big deal for a boy who used to wake every few hours."

He could hear her fingers clawing at the table as the panic began to take hold.

"The camera reached the far wall. I scanned back again. And then, just before it reached his bed, I saw something. The camera swept back to Harry's face. He looked so calm, Jim, so peaceful."

She spoke quietly, almost in a whisper.

"I pressed the arrow intermittently. It jerked slowly right.

Again, I pressed it. Again, it jerked.

Again and again . . ."

She paused, struggling for breath.

He'd wanted to break then, had moved to, then stopped himself.

"And then it settled on the rocking chair in the far corner of the room.

I saw a shape in the chair, but it was too far away to make out.

I knew that it shouldn't be there.

Every night I sit Harry on my lap and read him a story in that chair. I strained my eyes trying to see what it was.

I pressed the zoom button and watched as the shape slowly became something that I recognized.

A man.

A man in my son's room."

Her voice shook savagely.

"The man was wearing a clown mask."

He swallowed then, felt his own throat dry.

"I screamed, dropped the monitor, and grabbed the phone.

I put it to my ear. The line was dead . . . the storm outside.
I walked across the bedroom and stopped when I felt something
wet beneath my feet. I was about to scream again when I saw the
glass on the floor. Water. I had spilled my water."

The clawing was louder now, faster.

"I crept down the first flight of stairs, wiping the sweat from
my eyes.

I walked along the hallway and into the kitchen. I had left the
blinds up, could see the rain falling outside. I saw the knife block.
I reached for the largest, the carving knife. As I walked down the
final flight of stairs I stopped and listened.

My heart was pounding so fast, Jim, it was all I could hear.

Thump.

Thump.

Over and over.

I took a breath and ran for the door, pulled the handle down,
and burst into the room.

I hit the light switch and screamed, gripping the knife so tightly
that my fingers turned white. I looked at the rocking chair.

No clown.

And then I looked at my son's bed.

I dropped the knife and fell to my knees.

My son wasn't there.

He was gone.
Harry was gone."

Jim rubbed his eyes, his shoulders tight as he exhaled heavily.

He sat in the dark for a long time, listening to her cry, willing himself to stop the tape.

2

Pinstripes and Termites

It was hot out. Far too hot for the heavy woolen suit—a three-piece too. But seeing as it had been the only one with a pinstripe, Manny had insisted that his mother purchase it. The fact that it was half off had worked in his favor, so she had relented.

As he stepped out of the Ford Escape, he felt the sweat plastering his father's starched white cotton shirt to his back. He glanced down at his shoes—black wingtips, a shine so deep he could see the fedora wrapped tightly around his head reflecting back at him. The fucking hat was a medium though, and really starting to hurt. Mr. Phillips, in the gentleman's clothing store on Main Street, had told him that he needed an extra-large, told him this as he'd wrapped a tape measure around his head and let out a long whistle. They might be able to order one in, but it could take weeks, a custom job for a head of this size.

Manny turned back to the car, scowling as his mother pressed the horn and waved.

He'd begged her to buy an old Cadillac, or a Lincoln. But then the muscled Ford dealer, with his three-day stubble, and squint blue eyes, had started to flirt with her and she'd gone to pieces. He probably could've sold her the gum from his shoe by the time he'd finished his patter. She'd been like this since his father walked out: a dog on heat, and an old dog at that. As they'd walked the forecourt Manny had become resigned to the fact that his first car, which he would share with his mother, would be a Ford Escape. He'd reasoned that at the very least it would have to be black, with the privacy glass, naturally. But then the muscled squinter had led them to a duck-egg blue model. As his mother circled it the squinter had told her he could do her a good deal on it, winking as he said it.

"No shit. What other poor bastard would want the duck-egg?" Manny had offered, though his pleas had ultimately fallen on smitten ears.

As she signed the paperwork, Manny had tried mightily not to cry. But then the squinter had looked him up and down and asked his mother why her son looked like a 1950s gangster, and he had felt much better. People were starting to take notice. And it wasn't just the clothes; seventeen weeks of not shaving his upper lip had started to bear fruit. The mustache had finally arrived, though it was still the wrong shape. Genetics had dictated that Manny's mustache take the shape of an arrow. An arrow whose head, save for a small gap, met exactly at the center of his nose. He had tried, with great desperation, to encourage it to change direction, but met with little success. One time the overzealous use of a beard trimmer had led to the arrowhead being shortened too much, which had resulted in his classmates referring to him as "Adolf."

Manny sighed as the Escape disappeared from sight, the sun bouncing off of its duck-egg body as it went. He turned and walked toward the school gates.

"Looking sharp, Manny."

Manny turned to see his best friend, and future *consigliere*, Abel Goldenblatt. Not that he needed to turn to see who it was. Abe's voice was deep, ludicrously so. And when that ludicrously deep voice was paired with his ludicrously tall, and ludicrously thin frame, the result was . . . well . . . ludicrous.

"Shit, Abe. I told you to use my other name from now on."

"Sorry, I forgot it again."

Manny frowned, slowing his pace when he felt the sweat running down his forehead and onto the collar of his shirt, a shirt that was a full inch too tight around the neck.

"I told you a thousand times, just call me 'M.' Like Tony Soprano is 'T' to the guys closest to him."

"Right, sorry, M. Do I have to call you it in class too?"

"Of course. How else will it take? Have you thought about what you want to be called?"

Abe shrugged, his lack of commitment evident.

Manny glanced up at him and, not for the first time, lamented his friend's given name. "What kind of sick, twisted parents call their only son Abel? Sure, you're Jewish, but there are plenty of Jew names better than Abel."

"I think Abe is quite cool actually. Biblical names are enjoying a renaissance. My cousin just called his son Binyamin."

"You mean Benjamin."

Abe shook his head.

"You can't just take a perfectly good name and change a couple of letters."

"It's a real name. Binyamin . . . like Netanyahu."

"You know, half the time I don't know what the fuck you're talking about."

Abe laughed. "You sound just like my aunt Devorah."

Manny grinned. "You got me. Well played. *Touché*."

Abe frowned.

Manny pulled at his shirt collar.

"I can't believe it, man, not long until graduation. Then we're free," Abe said, pushing his glasses up his nose with his index finger.

"Did you ask your mom if we could paint the Volvo?"

"Not yet."

"And don't forget to ask about the windows too. I can get us twenty percent off the blackout sheets. You have to apply it carefully though, otherwise it'll bubble."

Abe looked at him, nervously. "My mom's not going to let us black out the glass. She won't be able to see out. You know how her eyes are."

Manny's mind ran to Mrs. Goldenblatt, who wore lenses thicker than her son's, with a frame so heavy it had left a permanent indentation in her nose.

"Fucking hell, Abe. How are we supposed to make collections if we don't look the part? And that reminds me, you're going to have to buy a new suit."

"What's wrong with this one? It's Brooks Brothers. I only got it last year for my nephew's bar mitzvah, remember?

I shouldn't really even be wearing it in this weather. It's going to be ninety degrees today. My mother said there's a real danger of me overheating."

"It's tan. Gangsters don't wear tan."

"It's not tan. The guy in the store said it's *Evening Barley*. He said it flatters my figure far better than a darker number would . . . gives me width."

Manny looked him up and down and sighed.

"Besides, who are we going to collect from? And when will we make these collections? My mother's fixed me up with a job with Mr. Berlinsky this summer, so we'll have to fit it in around that."

"Mr. Berlinsky? The Jewish butcher? He's on my list of people that need to pay up. You can't work there, Abe. No fucking way. People will laugh if they see me making collections with a butcher's boy. You'll probably reek of raw meat too. I feel nauseous just thinking about it."

"I still don't get it. I know that we're going to be gangsters, even though I'm Jewish. But why will these people pay us money?"

Manny fought the urge to scream.

"Firstly, it doesn't matter that you're a Jew. The Italians and Jews have worked together for generations. Just look at Lucky Luciano and Meyer Lansky. They fucking ruled shit."

"But you're not Italian, you're Mexican."

Manny bit his fist.

"My father's great-uncle married an Italian. Rosa. That means my cousins are Italian, which makes part of my family Italian, which makes *me* part Italian. And secondly, they'll have to pay up because if they don't then shit will get crazy around here. You think Mrs. Parker wants to see her Tearoom run out of milk? Or Mr. Ahmed wants his dry cleaners to get the power shut off? No, they fucking don't. So they'll pay up. They've had it easy for too long. It's time for someone to muscle them."

Abe put his skepticism to one side and pushed the classroom door open.

When the other kids saw them they burst out laughing. As did the teacher.

Roger felt his pulse quicken as he switched the computer on. The screen was large, the stand clear, and with no wires on show, seemed to float in the air.

He didn't have much use for an office, though the interior designer had insisted. His chair was leather, Herman Miller, and his desk a weighty oak. Bookshelves lined each wall, the books in neat rows, no gaps, an assortment ranging from classics to reference. All untouched.

As the screen flickered to life he glanced at the framed photograph beside it. They looked young in it. Their wedding day. Henrietta glowed. She'd fallen pregnant a month before, unbeknownst to him, to anybody else. They'd called their son Thomas. He'd lived for six hours.

He swallowed a lump of shame as he picked up the photograph and set it facedown on the desk.

The screen lit the room. With the blinds closed he squinted as his eyes adjusted. He opened the browser and navigated to the site.

Though certain he was home alone, he glanced at the office door repeatedly, his cursor hovering over the X.

He dabbed the sweat from his forehead with a monogrammed handkerchief, licked his dry lips, and tried to stop his hands from shaking. It was always like this for the first few minutes, until he calmed, until he escaped.

He smiled as he stared at the image, feeling shards of excitement begin to take hold and the guilt that would later suffocate him begin to lighten. He felt the muscles in his neck unwind, his shoulders drop, and his heartbeat slow.

He unbuckled his belt.

And then he heard the doorbell chime.

He stood quickly, his trousers falling to the floor. He pulled them up, then sat again and tried to close the browser. It froze on a picture; a picture that only a moment ago he had thought quite beautiful, though now a picture that terrified him. He clicked the X repeatedly.

He looked for a power button on the screen but could see nothing.

The door chimed again.

He'd leave it. It was probably just a delivery—something for Hen, probably shoes. More shoes.

And then he heard the key in the door.

"Darling?" he heard her call.

He swallowed.

He leaned down to the computer and pressed the power button once. Nothing happened. He pressed it again, several times.

She was unlikely to venture into his office, but he couldn't take the risk.

He picked up the screen, cradling it in his arms, and tried to pull it from the desk. It was heavy. He tried to wrench the wires out, but found they were screwed in. He tried to unscrew them, but his hands were slick with sweat.

"Darling?"

He set the monitor down and banged the side of the computer with his hand.

"Darling, what was that noise?"

"Nothing." His voice shook.

"Darling, where are you? I'm carrying a heavy box and can't bend to put it down."

Of all the excuses available to him, his panicked mind sought out the most absurd.

"I'm up a ladder."

"Why on earth are you up a ladder? You shouldn't climb ladders alone. What if you slip and fall?" she called.

He breathed again as the screen finally faded to black, then sprinted through to the kitchen and retrieved the stepladder.

He clambered quickly to the top.

He heard her sigh, make a production of placing the box onto the kitchen counter, and then there she was, standing beneath him, peering up.

In his haste he had picked up his glass of wine. He stood up there, his apparent nonchalance betrayed by his shaking hands, and took a sip.

He stared at the wall and, to his utter relief, noticed a small crack in the plaster just above him. He ran his finger over it and shook his head.

"What is it? Is it bad?" she asked.

He rubbed his chin. Had he had the faintest clue about anything remotely connected to plasterwork, or building work, or anything resembling manual labor, he might have come up with a better reply.

"Could be termites."

Luckily, Henrietta was even more ignorant of the work of the termite than him.

"Termites? I'll call Richard."

He swallowed, deflating at the mention of Richard's name. Richard was a builder to whom they had paid more money than he could remember to remodel the house. Richard was tall, and handsome, and muscular. A real man. The kind of real man that Roger regarded with quiet deference.

"No, don't call Richard. Leave it to me. I'll deal with the little buggers myself," he said, mustering the kind of conviction he hoped might see her drop the subject altogether.

"What do you know about termites, Roger?"

Having never been a proficient liar, he began to lose his grasp of the English language. "I know much . . . in actual terms. We had a place in the Cotswolds growing up; damn house was riddled with them. We had to fire them out in the end."

He arched an eyebrow, his own lie taking him by surprise.

"And what does *firing-out* entail?"

He coughed. "A blowtorch . . . and a little chemical substance called Termex. I'll call into the hardware store tomorrow and see if they have any."

She started to walk away, then turned back. "Be careful, darling. I don't like you drinking up ladders."

He closed his eyes and exhaled heavily, then took a liberal sip of wine.

He had slayed the dragon.

He heard the doorbell chime as he was descending, and then Henrietta leading someone along the hallway and into the kitchen.

"Darling, it's Richard. He's left one of his drill things in the garage. Might as well get him to look at the termite problem while he's here."

Richard, real man Richard, entered the room and raised a quizzical eyebrow.

Roger sighed. It had been a valiant effort, but it was over now.

Thalia frowned at her toy washing machine, banged the top with her small fist, then smiled as it began to spin again.

"Manny, I need you to wash the car. It's starting to lose its shine. Jared said to keep the bodywork clean. It'll hold its value better," Elena yelled, trying to make herself heard above the noise.

She looked up as her son walked into the kitchen.

"Jesus Christ, Manny. What happened to your head?"

Manny gingerly rubbed the thick, red groove that striped its way across his forehead.

"The hat, Ma. The hat is too tight. Who the fuck is Jared?"

His mother shot him a look. With Thalia at an age where she repeated all that she heard, Elena was trying hard to censor her son.

"Watch your mouth. I'm already mad at you, so don't make it worse."

Manny raised his hands in surrender. "What have I done this time?"

"You dropped Thalia off at preschool this morning."

"Yeah. We weren't late or nothing, so what's up?"

"And you remember that I said she has to take a piece of fruit in. All the kids do, and then they cut them up and share them out at snack time?"

He nodded, carefully, already eyeing the exit.

"So what did you give her?"

"An apple or something."

"Wrong, Manny. Try again."

He cast a furtive glance at the fruit bowl. "An orange?"

"You gave her a potato."

He looked over at Thalia, trying not to meet his mother's eye.

"Kids need carbs too," he offered.

Elena glared at him.

"I'm serious. All that fruit will give them the shits. I did it for the kids, and I was in a rush to get to class. Technically, it's your fault for leaving the potatoes out. Anyway, who's Jared? And why does he care about the duck-egg?"

He watched his mother open the refrigerator and pull out a thick cut of steak, wrapped in a Berlinsky's bag.

"Are you making the ziti? You know how I like it, with the Mortadella sausage ... little pinch of pepper flakes ... just enough to tease the palate."

His mother looked at him, wearily. "I don't even know what ziti is. I'm making *huaraches*. They're your sister's favorite. We're Mexican, not Italian, Manny. Accept that."

"I had ziti at Azzurro, remember? Last year, for my birthday. Who's Jared?"

"Jared is the nice man that sold us the car. He's taking me to dinner on Friday, so I'm going to need you to look after your sister."

Manny stared at her, horrified. "Fucking squint-eyed muscle man? You can't date him, Ma. He's young enough to be your son."

"Manny," Elena hissed. "Curse one more time and your allowance is gone."

She stared at him until he looked at the floor.

"Jared isn't that much younger than me, and I will date whoever I like, and *you* will wash the car and stay home on Friday. Do you understand me?"

He looked up at her and nodded, reluctantly.

"Good."

He watched her turn back to the refrigerator. She looked tired, she always did. The separation had been hard for her, for all of them. She worried, Manny knew that. She worried, but she tried to hide it from them.

"I'm sorry, Ma. I'm just looking out for you."

"I know."

"Jared looked like a dipshit player asshole type. Can't you just wait for Dad to come back?"

She sighed. "We've talked about this, Manny. It's been two years now. If your grandmother hadn't written to me I wouldn't even know where your father was living. And Jared is perfectly nice. It's not like I'm going to marry him anyway. I just want someone to go out for dinner with, maybe catch a movie. And for the last time stop cursing. Thalia is right there, and for some reason she looks up to you, so no more language."

Manny grabbed a bucket from under the basin and filled it with water.

As he was walking out of the door he heard his sister's washing machine stop spinning, mid-cycle, and then her sweet voice as she turned to their mother.

"Fucking batteries have shit the bed."

Manny dropped the bucket and ran out the door before his mother could catch him.

3

The Tiger

French John stepped back and gazed at the cake. He found it difficult to let go. He always did. He'd lost count of the number of hours that had gone into creating it. The icing was filigree. An intricate lace pattern covered every inch, very nearly invisible to the naked eye. The bride and groom figurines were hand-carved, the tier stands painted in gold leaf. It stood almost as tall as him. He circled it slowly, looking for imperfections, however minor.

It would have to be dismantled again, each tier specially packed for the short drive across town to the venue. He still had time, more than enough, to make any alterations the bride-to-be saw fit.

He glanced up at the board behind, at the sketches nearing a hundred in number. The kitchen was stainless steel, buffed and shined with a fervor that made those closest to him, of which there were few, question his sanity. He knew it was a necessary evil, perfectionism that bordered on obsessive-compulsive disorder: an affliction shared by many a master of their craft. He'd once dated a shoemaker in San Francisco who wept openly over each completed pair. It was a relationship that soured when the shoemaker had failed to summon as much passion for the other facets that made a life.

He turned when he heard the door open.

"Good morning, French," Elena said.

"Morning, Elena. How's life this morning? Manny still cursing? Thalia still cute as a button?"

"Yes, and yes."

He watched Elena circle the cake, look up at him, and smile widely.

She stepped in and hugged him tightly.

"Is it finished?"

"Quite possibly. Will you call Her Majesty and let her know she can view it?"

"Sure."

"Her Majesty" was Louise McDermott, an insipid beauty with a head full of air and a father that many speculated had a worth somewhere in the low billions. The wedding would be suitably lavish, the guest list suitably large. And French John had been tasked with creating the star of the show.

"I need her to see it soon, ideally. I hate it standing here like this. Anything could happen to it," he said, biting a nail.

Elena rolled her eyes, never one to indulge his neurosis.

She'd been his first, and only, hire: a rare find—someone with an eye for detail that very nearly rivaled his own, and a wit quick enough to keep him firmly in place. He guessed that she had honed her skills through years of back and forth with Manny.

"Are you still nervous about Friday?" he asked.

"Every time I think of it I get a pain in my stomach."

"You've dated before though. I know it's been a while, but it hasn't changed too much you know, except now you're expected to go Dutch, and the goodnight kiss has been replaced by a goodnight blowjob."

"I'm starting to understand why you're always so happy after a first date."

He laughed, picked up his icing gun, and attached a fine, closed-star nozzle to the end.

He took a step toward the cake before Elena snatched the gun from him and placed it back on the counter.

"The chance would be a fine thing. It's been a long time since someone took me out on a proper date."

"Maybe your standards arc too high."

He shrugged. "All I want is someone kind and funny . . . with muscles and a tan, of course."

"Of course."

Elena took the cakes from the fridge and began to set them out beneath the polished, glass counter, stopping when she saw French John's boots.

"Care to explain?" she said.

He followed her eye. "Hiking boots. I'm breaking them in. Fracap—handmade in Italy."

"Only you could make hiking so stylish. Though if I'm honest, I thought it was another fad, like racquetball."

"Racquetball was a touch intense. It's hard to look good when you're dripping with sweat."

She laughed.

"I saw Manny pass by yesterday, still pretending to be a gangster," he said.

"Yep, still pretending to be a gangster. It's been something new every few months since Danny left."

"I know. I remember the *Rocky* phase. How's his nose by the way?"

"He was lucky. The doctor said it was a clean break so it straightened out fine. I know it's funny for everyone else, but I worry about him. A boy needs his father, especially during the difficult teen years. Thalia is okay. She was just a baby when Danny left. She doesn't even remember him. She saw a photograph from our wedding the other day—you know, the one where Danny has his hair all long at the back and short on the sides?"

"I remember."

"Well, she looked at it and asked who the man was. Lucky Manny wasn't around to hear that. The air is blue enough in our house."

"So, he's still angry?"

"Sometimes, and then other times he speaks of Danny like he was a saint, like he gave a shit about him when he was around."

"He's young. It must be hard to see his mother dating."

"So you think I shouldn't go?"

"No, that's not what I meant. You deserve a break, Elena. You deserve to have some fun."

She nodded, tried to smile. "So why do I feel so guilty, like I'm letting them down?"

"You've been out a couple of times since he left."

"Yeah, and both times I told the guys I wasn't ready to get into anything afterwards. I mean, you should have seen Manny's face when I got home. He waited up for me, like I was the kid. And he looked so sad. It gets me just thinking about it."

French John switched on the coffee machine: a chromed behemoth that spluttered and coughed until it churned out coffee that very nearly tasted as good as it smelled.

"It won't always be like this. I think he just needs to get used to the idea that you're a person, and not just his mother."

"I didn't think life would take this turn, you know, French?"

"I don't think anybody ever does."

"I didn't think I'd end up alone, with a daughter that will never know her father and a son that thinks he's a gangster. What a mess," she said, sadly.

"But at least you're not forty yet, and you've got a great ass."

"That means a lot, especially coming from a known ass man like you."

He laughed, pulling her in for a hug as he did.

Manny walked across the flower bed, carefully avoiding the roses, so that he wouldn't have to walk around and onto the new neighbors' driveway. No one had really talked to the new neighbors yet. There was a daughter about his age, a mother that never left the house, and a father that drove a Porsche. He hadn't wanted to go and welcome them, but his mother had been on him again. Lately she hadn't stopped, all the time ragging on him: do this, do that, stop cursing, find a summer job, stop wearing a suit and hat every day.

He looked sharp. He needed to. Gangsters didn't wear shorts and a fucking T-shirt. Not only that, but he didn't look good in a T-shirt. The last time he'd tried one on, he'd stepped in front of the mirror and nearly cried. He'd gained weight since he'd stopped boxing, and now he had a decent set of tits: tits that some of the girls in his class would have been jealous of. His mother said that was alright though: he was still growing, it was just puppy fat, though he had never seen a puppy with a set of tits like his. They even showed through his shirt, so he had to keep the vest on.

He swallowed when he saw the girl, the daughter. She was hot. Majorly hot. Long legs and slim waist, dark hair, and full lips. She'd look good on his arm. Him in his three-piece, and her in her faded jeans and Rolling Stones T-shirt. He'd have to charm her first, though he didn't imagine that being too difficult—he was wearing a fedora after all.

"What's up, doll?"

She smiled, looked up at his hat, and then down at his wingtips.

He straightened his tie.

"Hello," she said.

"I'm M. That's my place next door."

"I'm Furat."

He extended his hand and she shook it.

"Furat. Tough break. Anyone ever call you Rat?"

"No."

"Well, that's something at least."

"Furat means sweet water. What's M short for?"

"Manny. Don't know what it means though. Probably something badass, like warrior or hero."

"Manny means he who walks with tiny penis."

Manny stared at her long enough to see the corners of her mouth begin to turn up, and then her half-smile turned into a laugh. He laughed too.

He walked into the garage, desperate to get into the shade, and sat down on the ride-on mower.

"Where are you from?" he asked.

"I was born in Iraq, but we moved here when I was very small. My father is a dentist."

Manny nodded, sagely. "A dentist? I know what that means, I've seen *Homeland*."

She frowned. "And what does it mean?"

"You know, he tortures people and shit, fucks them up to get information. Probably did train as a dentist once upon a time, but then Al Qaeda spotted his potential, started asking him to pull out teeth for them, except these people weren't patients—they were prisoners. So what, you left Iraq to come here, probably witness protection or some shit? Don't worry, I won't say anything. I'll look out for you. You're under M's wing now."

Her frown turned into a look of bewilderment.

They both looked over as a rusting, silver Volvo pulled up in front of the house.

"That's Abe. He runs this town with me."

"Runs it how exactly?"

They watched Abe climb out of the car, his long, thin legs proudly displayed in a pair of black, denim shorts; shorts that

Manny felt certain used to be jeans, until Mrs. Goldenblatt set about them with a pair of scissors after Abe outgrew them.

As Abe walked toward them the car horn sounded. He jogged round to the driver's side, showing more than a little ass cheek in the process, and kissed his mother through the open window.

She drove away much too quickly, holding second gear as she did. The Volvo's complaints could be heard long after she disappeared from sight.

"For fuck's sake, Abe. Where's your suit?"

"I'm sorry, M. My mother took it away. She said it's much too hot out for a suit. She's worried about me, said I'm too thin to lose body moisture. I've still got the shoes though."

Manny and Furat looked down at Abe's spindly, pale legs and were both surprised to see black and white Oxford Brogues on his feet. He wore them with black socks that reached his knees.

Manny held his head in his hands, sighed, and then introduced Abe to Furat.

"I've seen your father in town. He's got that sweet Porsche. What does he do?" Abe asked.

"He trained as a dentist back in Iraq and now he's taking over the practice in town."

Abe looked at Manny, his eyes wide.

Dentist.

Iraq.

Manny closed his eyes and nodded solemnly.

Jess gently, very, very gently, tried to open her eyes. The right opened without too much trouble, but the left seemed to be welded shut. She brought a hand up to her face and rubbed it gingerly, dislodging dried mascara.

She licked her lips. The skin was dry; a putrid taste filled her mouth.

She saw that she wasn't in her bedroom: the bedroom in her mother's house that she now called her own.

She could see her bra on the floor, her skirt beside it.

The pounding in her head would last most of the morning.

She glanced at the nightstand, at the empty vodka bottle that sat on it. She brought a hand to her mouth, fighting the urge to retch. Her fingers smelled of cigarettes. The varnish on her nails was chipped and faded. She still wore her wedding band, though on the ring finger of her right hand, in case it scared the more upstanding men away, though she conceded that these men were unlikely to frequent the kinds of establishments she had been favoring of late.

She saw a freestanding clothes rail against the far wall. Shirts and suits hung from it. A step up from the McDonald's uniform she'd seen on the floor of another shitty apartment a few weeks back.

There was no drape at the window, just bare pane with stark lines of sunlight streaming in. She found the light hard to take.

She felt movement behind her, a kick, a roll, the sheet pulling tight against her body. She could hear his breaths, thick and rasping. She felt a leg brush hers, the hairs tickling her skin. She moved away, toward the edge of the mattress.

She noticed a small, wooden shelf trying desperately to hold up a myriad of empty wine bottles and deodorant cans. On the far corner of the shelf sat a lone bottle of cologne. The label was striped orange and black, the word *Tiger* emblazoned across it. So that's what the smell was: a smell that she could well believe belonged in a zoo.

The Tiger began to snore, each breath a choke and splutter. She didn't look round. There was little point. He was there to serve a purpose, to fulfill a need.

She scoured her mind for the name of the town she had driven to the previous night, the bar she had drunk in, or even what the Tiger's name was. She could find nothing.

She was about to risk sitting up when she saw a framed photograph on the nightstand. She moved the bottle to the side and stared at it. It was of a man crouching down beside a small boy. The boy was holding a catfish, his fingers pressing into the scales. She could see water behind them, and a cloud-topped mountain in the distance.

What stood out most to Jess, even more than the giant catfish, was the look of pure happiness on the boy's face: the kind of happiness only a child can possess—singular, undiluted by the distractions that age brings.

She remembered that look from her boy's face. Her Harry.

As she fought to make space for his beautiful face in the dark depths of her mind, she saw the Clown appear, tearing into her thoughts, without warning, as it so often did. The Clown that no one had believed existed, until the forensics team had found a long, green hair that had buried its way into Harry's road-map rug. They had first thought it might have come from one of his soft toys, but a detailed analysis had not yielded a match in his room. And so they grudgingly—and she wasn't sure why it was grudgingly—started to believe her.

The Clown grinned at her. She shook her head violently, but it clung on, its claws sinking deep into her thoughts. She pulled at her hair, tugging out a fistful and gasping at the pain.

As the Clown began to laugh and then snarl, its face twisting with burning rage, she started to relive that awful night when she had run into the street barefoot and crying, clutching a carving knife. Just as she felt the scream building in her stomach and rising up to her throat, she felt the Tiger's hand on her hip and his body pressing against hers.

Just in time.

She hooked her thumb into the waistband of her underwear and slid them down, closing her eyes as tightly as she could, forcing the scream back down into the pit of her stomach.

4

Rumors and Tumors

At six foot nine, and closing in on 500 pounds, Jerry Lee was used to the staring and whispering. He was used to the laughter too, though that came when he opened his mouth. With the height, the weight, a list of allergies as long as his arm, and a mind his mother said often took a beat too long to form a coherent thought, life might have been difficult enough. But with a voice that soared to the highest of pitches, he really didn't stand much of a chance.

It was a gift, the voice, a gift from God. That's what his mother said. A gift that was far better received when he was younger and he took the reluctant lead in the St. Mary's choir. But now, at the age of thirty-five, it was a gift he wished God had given to someone else.

He opened the PhotoMax store a full hour before he was supposed to, like he did every day. His boss, Max, wouldn't show up until lunch, if he came in at all. Monday mornings were never good for Max. He usually went out partying on Friday night, leaving Jerry alone on Saturday, their busiest day. How this made him late on a Monday, Jerry didn't know, and certainly wouldn't ask.

He stepped behind the counter, set two stools side by side, and carefully mounted them. They creaked and groaned. He sat perfectly still until they acclimatized to the strain.

He checked his Death Watch, a gift from his mother for his last birthday. He'd die on March 15th, 2040. That's what it told him, though he hadn't updated it lately, and he'd gained even more weight. He watched the minutes tick down. He did that often.

The door had a bell on it. He flinched as it sounded.

"Good morning, Jerry."

Jerry climbed down, walked round the counter, and took the mail from Mel, the mailman. He didn't say hello to Mel. He never did. He tried to speak as little as possible.

"Looks like it's going to be another hot one today," Mel said.

Jerry nodded.

"See you tomorrow."

Jerry set the mail down on the glass counter, mounted the stools again, and opened the only item addressed to him.

He studied the magazine and gently traced his finger across the title. He had been subscribing to the *National Amateur Photography Magazine (NAP)* for thirteen years. Though Max deducted the six dollars from his paycheck every month, and he had to work almost a full hour to cover it, it was worth every cent.

With the deadline approaching for the annual *NAP* competition, Dawit's photograph sat on the front page again. Dawit had won the previous year. Jerry had read all about him, how he lived in a slum in India, had found a disposable camera in the mountains of rubbish he scavenged each day, and then used it to take a last photograph of his sister as she lay dying in the bed they shared. A local newspaper had printed it and one thing had led to another.

To Anam.

That's what it had said on the inside cover. The winner got to dedicate their photograph. Dawit's sister had been called Anam. Anam meant blessing. Jerry had looked it up online.

He frowned at the photograph, wondering if his was better. They were difficult to compare: Dawit's, unflinchingly emotive; but Jerry's . . . Jerry's was special too. He knew that when he'd shown his mother. She'd spent a long time staring at it before she'd made him promise not to send it, even made him promise to delete it.

The door chimed again.

Jerry flinched again, though when he looked up, he relaxed.

"Hi, Lisa."

Lisa smiled at him, a smile that flushed his cheeks and made his shirt cling to his back. She handed him the paper bag—his mother's medication. Lisa worked for Hung, the pharmacist.

"How is she?" Lisa said.

"Okay. She's still in pain. The pills aren't working."

She nodded, sympathetically. "Maybe you could speak to her doctor. There're others she could try—maybe Prelone. Is she taking them with food?"

"She doesn't eat much anymore."

"With milk then, Jerry. It's important."

"I'll try."

She glanced at the magazine. "That the new one?"

He nodded.

"Dawit again?"

He nodded.

"When are you going to enter, Jerry? I've seen some of your stuff. You've got a great eye."

He looked down, blushing furiously.

"I'm not sure about that."

Lisa was one of the few people he felt comfortable talking to, one of the few he could call a friend, even though he still struggled to meet her eyes. They were far too blue, far too pretty.

"Is Max about?"

He shook his head.

Lisa was engaged to Max.

She checked her watch. "Too early for him, lazy shit. When he shows up will you remind him that we have an appointment with the realtor at five?"

Jerry nodded.

Lisa perched on the stool meant for customers.

"So what do you get this year, if you win?"

"First prize is a Nikon DX950."

"Oh."

"A vacation to Aruba, wherever that is."

"That's more like it."

"And your photo printed on the front cover of the magazine."

"Wow. That's the big one, right? What you've dreamed about. Do it, Jerry. What have you got to lose?"

He shrugged, the stool creaked. He tried to cough, to mask the sound, but he was too late. His mind struggling again to keep pace, like it always did. His mother said it was because he was starved of oxygen when he was born. The cord had got wrapped around his neck. Dad said he'd come out blue.

"I'll think about it," he said, quietly.

"Are you still camping out every weekend? Still looking for the red-billed cuckoo?"

He shook his head.

Lisa had first told him about the bird, about how her father used to take her bird-watching when she was small, and how they used to hide among the tall oak trees that gave the town its name, looking for the red-billed cuckoo. It hadn't been seen in America since 1913, and most thought it extinct, though Lisa's dad claimed to have seen one in Tall Oaks. He'd said it was the most beautiful thing he'd ever seen. Lisa had smiled when she'd told Jerry about it, smiled and cried. Lisa's dad had died when she was young.

The coffee wasn't mixed well. Jim could see black sludge lining the bottom of the cup.

"It's funny, you wanting to talk to me now. Didn't want to know last time, when I couldn't get any sleep," Mrs. Lewis said.

Jim smiled. He looked around the room, tried not to appear appraising.

Mrs. Lewis kept her eyes fixed on him. She was old, Jim guessed eighty, but could've been a decade out either side as she wore so much makeup.

"So they've left town."

"Who?"

"The cavalry. The Fibbies," she croaked, lighting another cigarette.

He noticed a bookcase in the corner, each shelf bowed under the weight of a pile of crime novels.

"Come on, Sergeant. The FBI. We all know they were here. Saw the black sedans. No need to be embarrassed. They bring 'em in for high-profile cases like these. Small-town cops haven't got the experience—they make mistakes, jeopardize the case."

Jim glanced at the window, longing to open it.

Mrs. Lewis blew a cloud of smoke up toward the yellowed ceiling. A fan spun above—noisy, but too slow to clear the fog.

He looked down at his notebook, had underlined the word "crackpot" several times.

"So, back to the complaints you made."

"Lot of shouting. Crying sometimes . . . think it was the lady, the pretty one. Jessica Monroe. I never really spoke to them. Like to keep myself to myself."

He took another sip.

"I notice you called about them several times a few years back as well."

She coughed loosely.

He noticed her fingernails were so long they had started to curl.

"That time it was the baby crying. Harry. Kept me up all night. I knocked. They didn't answer."

Jim wrote "crying baby" on his pad and then crossed it out and underlined "crackpot" again.

"You've called us forty-three times in six years."

She blew a jet of smoke from her nose, then reached for her coffee and gulped it down.

"I hear noises, I call the cops. The time I don't will be the time someone breaks in, mark my words. I don't have John here to look after me anymore." She crossed herself. "So it's just you working the Harry Monroe case? Everyone else has packed up, moved on. Too many crimes, not enough cops. You're looking for something they didn't see, something they missed? Solve the case on your own? I like it."

"You read all of those?" he said, nodding in the direction of the bookcase.

"Oh, sure. More than once."

The house was large, like Jess's. Though this one hadn't been touched in a long time. Mrs. Lewis would die soon enough. Jim would get the call, from her mailman, or from the gardener. They'd say they hadn't seen her in a while. He'd break the door, find the corpse. He got calls like that a couple of times a year— a generation dying off. Her kids would sell the house, pocket half a million and the developer another half once he was done with it.

"You any closer to finding him?"

He drank the last of his coffee, setting the cup down before the sludge reached his lips.

"Bad news, this long, Sergeant. Don't need to tell you that. Poor kid. What was he, five?"

"Three."

Mrs. Lewis shook her head. "There're a lot of rumors ... whole lot of nothing. Someone knows something."

He nodded.

Someone knows something.

Jerry sat in his dark room. It wasn't really a room, more of a closet, a big closet, on the ground floor, next to the kitchen. The house was too big for them, had been even when his dad was alive. Jerry's great-grandparents had built it.

He rubbed his stomach. It hurt. His mother had never been a good cook, but since she got sick she'd gotten even worse. She forgot recipes when she was right in the middle of cooking them, then she added ingredients that really didn't go. Tonight she had cooked him sausages, though they were charred on the outside and frozen solid in the center. She liked to watch him eat, hated it when he didn't finish everything. She'd baked a pie, too. Apple and something he couldn't quite place. He was afraid to ask what it was. A pint of what he'd thought was custard to pour over it had turned out to be cheese sauce.

Dad used to love her pies. He was big. Mom too, though neither as big as Jerry.

He looked at the photographs splayed out on his desk: some of Lisa smiling, some of her frowning, some where she didn't know she was having her photo taken.

He picked up his favorite, taken on Valentine's Day. Max had taken her to Yosemite and they'd stayed in a log cabin. To the untrained eye it was a fairly unremarkable photo, but Jerry stared at it, sometimes for hours on end, lost in her eyes. He could see something in them—kindness maybe—something that made him want to hold her, to love her and for her to love him back. Max didn't know Jerry had made copies for himself. He would have been mad. But Max didn't even like printing them; he only did it because Lisa made him. She liked to put them in albums. Jerry didn't ever take copies of the really private ones, the ones where Lisa wasn't wearing many clothes, even though a part of him wanted to. He just copied the ones that Max probably didn't linger over, that Max probably didn't think were special.

He heard the bell. Though the sound was nothing more than a tinkle, Jerry heard a clanging so thunderous he fought the urge to place his fingers into his ears.

He stood, switched the light off and closed the door, then slowly made his way up the stairs.

He walked into the bathroom and opened the cabinet, taking out three candles. It was Monday, and Monday meant sandal-wood and ginger.

He set them down in a line along the edge of the tub and lit each in turn. Then he ran the water.

He poured in the bath oil—geranium and orange—and watched it turn the water cloudy. He swirled it with his hand, wetting the sleeve of his shirt as he did.

"Jerry."

He walked into his mother's bedroom.

"Hi, Mom."

She stared at him.

He walked over to the window and closed the drapes.

"Are you feeling any better today?" he asked.

"No."

The tumor was aggressive. He knew that much. She wouldn't let him go to any of her appointments, said he wouldn't understand anyway.

"Did you take the pills? The new ones? All of them?"

"I don't know why they make them so big. I'll choke one of these days."

"And the pain?"

She shrugged. "Are you praying for me, like I asked?"

"Yes."

She reached out. He took her hand.

"Ready?" he said.

"Ready," she said.

He helped her stand. Her feet were swollen, her ankles vast.

Together they panted and wheezed toward the bathroom.

She dropped her robe. He looked away.

5

Mayor of Despair

"You can't go out dressed like that, Jess."

Jess looked into the small mirror and finished putting on her makeup. She applied it with a heavy hand. She didn't want to be recognized. Her knee bounced, her hands shook. She had drunk what was left of the vodka bottle hidden in her closet, but still she couldn't stop the movement.

Hiding vodka and living with her mother. She was seventeen all over again.

"Leave me alone, Alison."

It was Alison, not Mom anymore.

"I'm worried about you, Jess. It's too much—the drinking and staying out all night. I can't sleep; I don't know where you are half the time."

"Yeah, well, that makes two of us."

Jess looked up at her mother and saw the worry in her face, saw it in the bags beneath her eyes, in the lines that streaked her forehead.

"Where are you going tonight?"

"Out. Out of town. Away from Tall Oaks."

"Why don't you go down to the country club if you need to get out? They have a nice bar there. I'll come with you."

She could hear the pleading, the desperation in Alison's voice.

"I can't go out in Tall Oaks. Everybody knows me here. They all know what's happened."

"And why is that a bad thing? You have friends here, Jess, people that care about you."

Jess turned back to the mirror, painting the anguish away with each stroke of the brush.

"Jess, are you listening to me? Let's go to the country club. I'll buy the first round."

Jess stared at her. She could see traces of Harry in her mother's face. Not always, mercifully, but sometimes. It made being around her all the more difficult.

"You took his picture down," Jess said, staring at the wall behind Alison.

Alison swallowed. "I didn't know if . . . I saw you staring at it during dinner . . . you're not eating . . ."

Jess nodded. A week had passed since Alison last mentioned his name. Jess could remember a time when her mother had spoken of little other than her grandson; a time when Alison had hovered over her as she changed his diaper, watched every spoonful of food she fed him, called night and day whenever Harry was sick. It had gotten to the point where Jess had to tell her Michael was tiring of her visits.

"I can put it back," Alison said quietly.

Jess snapped her mirror shut and looked for her keys. She'd left them on the hook by the kitchen door.

She looked at the empty hook, at the plaque behind it. THERE'S NO PLACE LIKE HOME.

She used to like that saying. Before that night. Before someone switched the color off in the world. Now it was just dark, the words looking more like a threat than a promise.

"Where are my keys, Alison?"

"I'll call us a cab. Then we don't have to worry about having too much to drink. I'll get us a bottle of that wine you used to like; I forget the name . . . the pink one. We can talk, or just sit there and drink. Whatever you want."

"I just need my keys. Please give me my keys."

Jess kept her voice even, though she wanted to scream. She could feel it now. She needed to go.

"Or we could have a gin and tonic. You used to beg me for a taste when you were younger. Then when I finally relented you'd purse your lips from the sharpness, but you'd always say that you wanted another sip a few minutes later."

Alison tried to laugh. It sounded wrong, forced.

"Please, Alison. My keys, give them to me now."

"Tell me why we can't go to the country club."

Jess took a breath. "Because people look at me. People I thought I knew. People that I thought were friends. They look at me and they whisper to whoever they're with. *There goes Jess Monroe. Still no news about Harry. Terrible thing that happened, wasn't it? She's falling apart. Look at her. She's a fucking mess. She should be home, sitting by the phone. She should be doing more to find him.'"*

"No one thinks that, Jess."

Jess stood and paced the kitchen, opening cabinets and slamming them shut.

"And then, if I look at them, let them know that I know what they're thinking, they turn their heads or pretend to look at their phones, or in their bags, anywhere but at me."

"They're just worried about you, Jess. Everyone worries because everyone cares."

"Maybe. But they want to do it from a safe distance. They don't want any of the shit that I carry around to be passed on to them, like some fucking disease. God forbid I might stop and chat for a while, or worse, ask if I can join them. Then they won't be able to smile, or laugh, or talk about their own problems, because their own problems are so fucking small and trivial compared to mine."

Jess opened kitchen drawers, tossing the contents to the floor.

"They'll wonder why I finish my drink so quickly, and then wonder if they should offer me another, or will that loosen my tongue too much and make me start to tell them what my life is really like now."

Alison flinched as Jess knocked a glass to the floor, watching it shatter around her feet.

Jess stood still. She could feel the tears begin to blur her eyes. She looked up at her mother.

"Please," she said, in a whisper.

Alison reached into her pocket and handed Jess her keys.

It was only when Alison heard the engine start and the car pull away, and she was sure that the door was locked and the windows closed, that she allowed herself to cry for her daughter and for her grandson.

Jim watched Jess pull away. He made no move to follow her, though he felt the urge.

He reclined his seat. She might be back tonight, might be back sometime tomorrow. There was no set pattern.

He opened his window and breathed in the warm night air. He thought of Harry often; more as each day passed. He thought that funny. When the calls stopped coming in, when the urgency was beginning to ease, when people had no choice but to carry on with life, he'd stood still. Stood still beside Jess.

He kept a photo of Harry in the glove compartment. He didn't need to show it anymore. Everyone knew who he was.

He leaned back, closed his eyes and tried to get some sleep.

The shit-hole bar was in a hick town called Despair. Jess smiled when she saw the sign, thought she might be the perfect candidate to run for Mayor.

She parked in the gravel, between two pick-ups.

She reached for her phone and dialed Michael. He didn't answer. He never did. She listened as his answerphone clicked on. He hadn't recorded a greeting. She longed to hear his voice.

"It's me . . . I'm not sure if you listen to any of these. I hope you do. I'm out. Not sure where really . . ." She cleared her throat, surprised by how quickly the tears formed, by how warm they felt

as they rolled down her cheeks. *"Do you think about him? You must. Do you think about me? Do you sleep well? Do you sleep at all? I was thinking back to when we brought him home for the first time. He had that fluffy hair. You kept kissing his head . . ."*

She choked back her words, held the phone to her ear until she heard the click.

She took a moment, wiped her eyes, put her phone in her bag.

She sat still for a long while, waiting. She looked down at her hands, then up at the sky. The moon was big, full but dull.

As she walked into the shit-hole bar with the equally shitty name, The Squirrel, she felt every pair of eyes in the shitty place look up from their beers and find their way either to her tits or her legs.

The floor was wooden, her heels clicked across it. Smoke swirled above the pool table, empty glasses lined up on the torn felt.

She kept her head up, her eyes fixed straight ahead.

As she made her way to the bar, with its flickering neon signs, its sticky coasters and elbow dents, she felt the eyes leave her tits and her legs, and focus on her ass.

She ignored the stares. She wouldn't later, but for now she was content to drink alone.

The bartender was tall and heavy. He reached for one of the pumps, pulling it down and revealing yellowed sweat stains that hung low beneath his pits.

He smiled at her—a warm smile, though missing a tooth here and there.

"Be with you in a minute."

He turned back to the pump, leaned down to collect the glass. Strands of greasy hair fell from behind his ear. The rest was tied back tightly, highlighting a misshapen head. His sleeves were rolled up, exposing meaty forearms. Tattooed, naturally. The left bore a scantily clad lady, and some illegible writing; the right, a large splodge of gray black.

He turned to her.

"I'm Rex, but everyone here calls me Guns."

She glanced at his flabby biceps, fought the urge to roll her eyes.

"Well, Mr. Guns . . ."

"Oh, it's just Guns. We don't go in for all that formality here in Despair."

She glanced at the photographs tacked to the back wall, all of unsmiling men, mostly shirtless and barefoot.

"That's my dad, second from left, with the hair."

She smiled, unsure of what to say.

"His name was Guns too. Used to bench three-fifty."

"So you're Guns Jr."

He shrugged.

"Well then, Guns Jr, I'll have a vodka, please. No water, no ice."

He free poured a misted glass halfway to the top.

As she reached for her bag, a large, calloused hand slapped a ten-dollar bill down in front of her.

"This one's on me."

She looked up. The guy was tall, broad. Might once have been good-looking but the years had taken their toll.

"Thank you –"

"Billy. Billy Brooks."

She drank her vodka in one quick and impressive gulp, her throat long since numb to the burn.

Billy nodded at Guns to pour her another, told him this time be generous with the measure.

She saw the look that passed between them, conspiring to get her drunk. She wondered if Billy's pride would've been hurt if he'd known that tonight she was anyone's, literally anyone's at all: anyone that might take her away for a night, even if it was to some place awful, where the sheets were stained and the walls crawling with mold. Where clothes lay on the floor and you needed a tetanus shot after using the bathroom. Wherever it was, it couldn't possibly be as bad as the place she had come from.

After her seventh, or maybe eighth, vodka, she felt the knots unfurl, her shoulders drop, her hands stop shaking and her mind begin to swirl. The bar wasn't as shitty. Billy had gotten better looking.

His hand was on her back, kept slipping to her ass. She pretended not to notice. Billy kept telling her about his business, like she gave a fuck. He owned a farm, or a mill . . . something like that.

They'd been joined by some of his friends. Guns had locked the door, poured himself a whiskey and put some money in the old jukebox next to the pool table. And then one of Billy's friends, could've been Duane or Bobby, or some other name you gave a kid to make sure he never got a white-collar job, lifted her up onto the pool table and she started to dance. As Donna Summer sang about "Bad Girls," Duane or Bobby jumped up onto the table and started grinding her from behind, and then Billy was rubbing her leg as she danced, his hand inching higher and higher. He wasn't smiling anymore.

She knew she was in trouble, especially when he pulled her down and started trying to ram his tongue into her mouth. His breath smelled sour, his tongue felt rough. She tried to push his face away. He just laughed—a wheezy laugh tinged with desperation.

Billy was breathing hard as he grabbed her breast.

She lay back and closed her eyes, saw the Clown grinning back at her, and so opened them wide.

And then the men were all on her, hands going everywhere, clawing at her clothes as they laughed and shouted.

This is what you wanted. You're not a victim if this is what you wanted.

But as she caught a blurry glimpse of Billy pushing another man away, and opening his belt, she knew that it wasn't really what she wanted. It was what she deserved . . . because she didn't protect him. And now he was gone.

She tried to sit up.

Billy punched her in the mouth, hard.

She fell back, her head hitting the felt and her mouth filling with blood.

She licked her front tooth and felt it loosen.

"Now lie still, or I'll really hurt you."

She met his eye.

"Hurt me?" she whispered.

He glared at her.

She began to laugh. "Hurt me?"

She laughed again. It was a loud laugh, high and manic.

The song ended.

She kept on laughing.

Duane or Bobby stopped whatever it was he was trying to do with her arms and stared at her. She sat up, her laugh now hysterical.

They took a step back.

She held her stomach, laughing so hard she thought she might die.

She caught a glimpse of herself in the mirror behind the table. As she laughed blood spilled down her chin and onto her chest.

She turned to Guns and spat at him, thick lines of stringy blood that landed on his face.

He backed away, panic in his eyes.

That made her laugh even harder.

The other men stepped back too.

She stood up, lopsided, missing a shoe. She pulled her skirt down.

Her eyes were dark, darker than Billy's, and when she stared him down she saw his desire fade under a torrent of more laughter and another bloody smile.

She limped to the door, turned the key and felt the air on her face as she walked to her car.

"Hurt me?"

She laughed again. To hurt her she would have to feel something. But there was nothing left inside of her, not after what she had been through.

Nothing at all.

6

The Trick

It was dawn when Jim made it home. He'd fallen asleep in his car. His neck hurt. He'd seen Jess's car in the driveway when he woke, relaxed a little, then driven back to his apartment. It was on the ground floor, cramped, though the small yard made up for it.

He walked into the living room. It was sparsely furnished: a leather sofa facing a television, a couple of bookshelves, a few books on each.

He reached for a tape from the stack, slotted it into the machine and pressed play.

He stayed standing, yawned and stretched.

He thought back to the day, two weeks after Harry got taken. He could see Jess in his mind, her eyes bloodshot as she set her bag down on the floor and sat on the plastic chair. He remembered leaving the door open—she'd asked him to, after that first time, when she'd gotten freaked out talking about the Clown. She said she couldn't breathe, that she felt dizzy, trapped when he closed the door.

He skipped forward.

"Where The Wild Things Are. *That was Harry's favorite book, except he used to get scared when I read it to him. He'd ask for it, every night he'd ask for it. But then as I soon as I turned to the first page he'd cuddle up close to me. I'd be trying to read and he'd be asking questions, asking if the monsters were going to eat the boy. We'd read it maybe a hundred times, but he'd still ask. He wanted a wolf suit.*"

He remembered her smile, beautiful, under different circumstances.

"*Seriously. I'm glad he didn't tell my mother otherwise she would've tracked one down and bought it for him.*"

He paused the tape. There were lots of tapes, the original copies at the station. He'd listened to them all a dozen times; the interview with Michael two dozen. They'd asked Michael to come back in again, to help them out. His lawyer said that unless he was under arrest then he wouldn't be coming back. There wasn't much Jim could do. He didn't need to ask Jess twice. She'd said if there was anything they needed to just ask. And he had. They'd spent hours talking. He wasn't sure if it had been necessary, they had enough background. But he liked seeing her, knowing where she was, seeing how she was holding up.

He walked into the small kitchen and grabbed a drink from the empty refrigerator. He was becoming one of those cops. He hadn't wanted to. It had sucked him in, before he knew what was happening he lived the case: the case and Jess. Nothing else.

He sat down, pressed play.

"*Are you getting anywhere, Jim? Have you found anything at all?*"

"*We're doing all we can.*"

She didn't have anywhere else to go, no one else she felt she could talk to. He wondered how much longer she could go on.

He skipped ahead again.

"*He loves his father so much. I mean, I know boys and their fathers have a special bond, but you should've seen him when Michael stopped by. His face lit up. I never told him when Michael was coming though, in case he didn't show.*"

"*Did he see Harry much?*"

"*No. Only if he needed something from the house. He'd usually stop by after Harry was asleep; he said he didn't want to confuse him. But Harry always woke up. It was like he had some kind of sensor that told him when his father was in the house. He'd climb the stairs and walk into the living room, his hair sticking up and his eyes all squinted. He had these cute pajamas, with letters and numbers all over them. So he'd stagger into the room, his legs wobbly, and then he'd see Michael and break out the widest smile. Then he'd make him stay and read to him, even though Michael said he had to go, and made eyes at me to help him out.*"

"*So he didn't want to spend time with him, read to him, stick around until he fell asleep?*"

"*I could smell her on him.*"

"*Who?*"

"*Whoever he was fucking. He smelled like her. Probably that whore from his office.*"

"*Cindy Collins?*"

"*I saw lipstick on his shirt once. Fucking cliché. He didn't bother hiding it by then.*"

"*When did he leave?*"

"He drifted from my life, Jim. He started working longer hours, staying in hotels, not coming home. There was no one time where he said that's it, it's over. We'd argue over the phone. He'd say he'd had enough, shit like that. I thought it was just a fight. Then he packed some bags when I was out with Harry. I came home and saw some of his clothes were gone. I thought it was a rough patch . . . that we'd work things out."

"Even though he was cheating?"

"Yeah, even though he was cheating. I can imagine how that sounds, but what if you just know?"

"Know what?"

"That there's nobody else out there for you; that you've found the only person that will ever make you happy. What do you do? You can be strong, kick them out, never be happy again. Or you can hold on, take the rough with the smooth. Because at least there're some good times, some chance that one day he'll see how nice you treat him and stop fucking around. He'll love you. And then you get everything."

"So you'd do that to keep him? You'd put up with it, with how he treated you?"

"Yes, I would. And I did. But it still wasn't enough. He still left."

He stopped the tape and opened the blinds, watching the town slowly come to life.

Abe climbed into the car, a broad smile on his face.

Manny looked at him and frowned.

"Well?" Abe said.

"Well, what?"

"Check it. You said get a new suit. I found this number in my father's closet."

Abe straightened his lapels, fired his cuffs.

"It's the same as the old one."

"No. This one's double-breasted. Gangster."

"It's the same color."

"Wrong again, M."

"Well what color was the old one?"

"Evening Barley. I told you."

Manny sighed. "What color's this one?"

"My dad says it's *biscotti*."

"What the fuck is the difference? They're both fucking tan."

Manny stepped on the gas, shaking his head as he did.

"This one has a buttercream lining," Abe said, opening the jacket.

"Well, I think it's nice," Furat said, from the back seat.

"I think it's nice too," Thalia said from beside her.

Manny slowed at the lights.

He glanced to his left, saw an old man staring back at him.

The man was driving an Escape, same year as the duck-egg, but his was black.

The old man smiled and motioned for Manny to open his window.

Manny did and the old man leaned out. "You went with the duck-egg. She's beautiful. I wanted her for myself, but the wife made me go for the black."

Manny fumed silently, then turned to Abe. "You see. This is what happens when you drive a fucking duck-egg blue

Escape. Old men think it's okay to start conversations with you, even if you're a gangster wearing a three-piece and a fedora, and might very well have a Smith and Wesson tucked into your belt."

Manny heard the old man whistle his appreciation.

"Your wife made you go for the black?" Manny said.

"Yes, sir, said she felt the duck-egg would be harder for a man to drive. But you look wonderful in yours, especially with the hat and the suit. Just dandy."

Furat leaned forward and gripped Manny's shoulder tightly. He could feel her willing him to keep his mouth shut.

"Well, they do say that once you go black you never go back. Ask your wife about that."

Manny closed the window.

Furat tried desperately not to laugh.

As they pulled into a space on the wide, tree-lined Main Street, Manny shut the engine off and tried to ignore the sparkle of the paintwork as he walked round to get Thalia out.

"M, some of the bandage is showing," Abe said.

Manny adjusted his hat until the thick, white bandage was hidden.

"If the wind picks up and that hat blows off you're going to look ridiculous," Furat said.

"One, it's not windy today; I checked the weather report. And two, the hat's so fucking tight that your father, plus all of his Al Qaeda brethren, couldn't get the thing off, even if the fucking CIA undercover operative list was hidden inside."

They walked slowly up Main Street, the Don holding hands with his three-year-old sister; a sight that made Furat smile.

Roger sat by the swimming pool and closed his eyes. It was hot again. Too hot for golf; too hot for tennis; too hot for anything at all.

Henrietta was working in the Tearoom, which she ran with her sister, Alison. Though given the circumstances, Alison spent much of her time with Jess now.

He thought of Jess often.

Hen would be gone all day, which was why he'd felt confident enough to wear the trunks. He had ordered them online, though struggled with the sizing. He had an old pair, from his days as 100-meter, freestyle champion at Trinity College, and they were a medium, though a little baggy on the seat. So he had ordered a small. But they were so skimpy they bordered on indecent. Were he to wear them to the public pool he felt certain he would be arrested. All it would take was a strong kick of the leg, or an attempt to swim butterfly, and one of his testicles would break free and announce itself to the hordes of teenage girls that flocked there of a weekend.

He breathed deeply. A sickly smell of coconut filled the air: tanning lotion, also surreptitiously ordered online. It wasn't the kind that Hen bought, the kind that protected. He reached for the bottle. *Tropical Heaven.*

He frowned at the label. Though far from convinced that the scientists at Tropical Heaven had indeed succeeded in unlocking the secrets of the sun, he'd slathered it on liberally.

From his limited understanding it would basically turn his body into a solar panel.

Just as he was beginning to drift, the scent of burning flesh, combined with that of the noise of the bolt on the side gate sliding across, woke him.

He opened his eyes wide. Someone was coming in.

He stood quickly, then launched himself into the pool.

The water was cold.

He sank deep and stayed under until his chest burned, staring back at the surface, hoping that the figures approaching might turn and leave again.

When he could hold his breath no longer, he surfaced, gasping for air and staring straight into the handsome face of Richard—real man, Richard—and two of his men.

"Henrietta asked us to call round and finish painting the back of the house. You remember Chuck and Eddie?" Richard said.

He did—he had trouble forgetting them. Eddie had the chiseled body of a Greek god, and so rarely wore a shirt, and Chuck had a tattoo on the back of his neck that read "*made in the USA, 1980,*" as if he were some kind of doll, produced for housewives that had tired of the far less virile models they had married.

"I thought you were finished? It looks good enough to me," he said, hoping to flatter them away. He smiled at Eddie, who looked away quickly.

"It needs another coat. Otherwise, come winter, it'll start to fade."

"Righty-ho."

Hen had told him that no one said "righty-ho" anymore, especially not in America. An ass. That's what she'd called him. An ass. At that moment, in his tiny trunks and reeking of coconut, he could do little but agree. He was an ass.

"If you don't need me, I'll just be relaxing in the pool," he said, eyeing his towel.

"Could you open the garage for us? The paint's in there. And while we're at it we'll take a look at the termite problem," Richard said, smirking.

Chuck and Eddie laughed.

Roger felt the humiliation as the three *real* men walked back out of the gate, still laughing.

With little time to waste, he climbed out of the pool, ran to his lounger and started to unravel his towel, quickly discovering it was a hand towel.

A very small hand towel.

He glanced at the gate and saw them untying the ladder from the roof of their truck. He contemplated running for the house. It was a long way. He cursed the Americans, with their abundance of land. In London, had he wanted to put a pool in the garden of their mews house, he would have had to sacrifice the living room and most of the kitchen in the process.

He wrapped the towel tightly around the front of his trunks and then waddled toward the house, just as the real men walked back through the gate.

He caught his reflection in the glass doors and winced. From the front, he resembled a cheap hooker with a skirt so short that it barely covered the source of her income. And from the rear, unbeknownst to him, but clearly apparent to the real men as he passed them, his robust exit from the pool had caused the thin expanse of material to disappear into the crevice of his bottom.

Richard turned to Eddie. "I thought the Brits were more reserved."

Eddie shook his head, dropped his paintbrush, then began to walk away. "I'm not working here again. Just get one of the other guys to come over."

"What's up with you today?"

Eddie shrugged.

Richard glared at him.

Eddie gestured in the direction of the house, clearly agitated. "I could nearly see his asshole."

"Oh shit, man, nice shirt," Manny said, as Jerry stood to greet them.

Max had given Jerry the shirt, then insisted he wear it. They were to begin printing T-shirts, and Max said that wearing the shirt would be the perfect way to advertise. It was a little tight, like most of his clothes, and Jerry felt very self-conscious wearing it.

Though he didn't really understand the writing—LADIES, THIS IS WHERE IT'S AT—or why the red arrow beneath pointed down to the ground, he was certain that it was a joke made at his expense. Max liked to play jokes on him; jokes that Jerry didn't find all that funny if he was honest.

"Hey, Jerry. Did you see NAP this month? That new Sony is something else. Did you see what it does in low light?"

Abe was one of the few people Jerry knew that shared his love of photography.

"Yeah, I've seen it. I bet it's heavy—nice heavy, not like the Minoltas."

"You should get Max to order one, replace that Hasselblad that got stolen. Any news on that yet?"

Jerry shook his head.

"Is Max still pissed about it? Did he get the insurance money yet?"

Jerry shook his head again. "I mean, he's still mad, but he hasn't got the insurance money."

Jerry felt his cheeks begin to burn. His dad used to laugh when Jerry got nervous or embarrassed, used to say he looked like a beetroot.

"You going to enter the competition this year? I've seen some of your work, Jerry, it's awesome. You should get Max to put your photos up again."

"He likes the ones of the girls instead," Jerry said, glancing up at the framed photos, most of models in various states of undress, all black and white, all masquerading as art.

"Well, I think you'd have a good shot at winning. I mean, Dawit's was good, but a bit . . . point and click."

Manny turned to Furat when the conversation moved on to the merits of last year's winning picture. "It's like listening to Barry White talk to the guy on that YouTube clip. You know, the one that's had his nuts removed."

Furat nodded in agreement. "They should switch voices."

Manny walked over and interrupted them.

"Thalia is here for her pictures. We got that voucher from the newspaper."

Jerry checked the diary then smiled nervously at Thalia.

Thalia hid behind Furat's leg.

Max usually dealt with the kids. He had a trick to get them to smile.

Jerry picked up the phone, dialed Max's cell phone and listened. He glanced down at Thalia again, then up at Manny and the new girl. The new girl smiled at him. He looked away quickly. He prayed Max would answer, his heart sinking when he heard the voicemail.

"Max isn't answering. He always deals with the kids. I'll try him again in a minute," Jerry said, quietly.

"I'm not going home again, Jerry, just because that lazy prick hasn't bothered showing up. Can't you just do it?" Manny said, pulling at his collar again, trying to stretch it, if only for long enough to allow him a proper breath.

"Max taught me how to do the portraits once, but that was six years ago."

"She's a kid. How hard can it be?"

Jerry led them reluctantly through to the small back room they used as a studio.

The floor was polished white. Max made him clean it every day—he liked it to gleam. The walls were white too, and there was a box full of props that they sometimes used.

Jerry didn't ever do the portraits. Max said he wasn't a people person so was better off sticking to the technical stuff. That and he might frighten the kids, him being so big and them being so small.

Jerry picked up a tiny, wicker basket and asked the little girl to get into it.

"Jesus, Jerry. That's for newborn babies. She's three."

Jerry placed the basket back into the box, his face burning bright as he felt their eyes on him. He hated people looking at him. Even nice people like Abe. In his experience they didn't stay nice. He'd thought the school kids were nice. They'd come in, smiled at him, and then asked him lots of questions about photography. He'd thought they were interested, but really they just wanted to hear him speak, so that they could laugh at him. They'd come into the store in big groups, boys and girls, only ever when Max wasn't there. The boys would stare, point and laugh so hard that they turned red too. The girls didn't laugh; they'd just stare, and sometimes whisper. He could always make out what they were saying though, always something about his weight.

He tried desperately to diet. His mother said it was genetic, that he shouldn't fight it, but Jerry knew that all the food she cooked didn't help. Food that she piled high on his plate, food that she said would make him feel better. And it did, when he'd come home from school in tears, the chocolate brownies had made him smile again.

For a time Jerry had been doing better, skipping lunch, losing weight. He even tried jogging, after dark, so his mother wouldn't see. He'd lost thirty pounds. But then she'd gotten sick, and he'd needed the brownies again, the pies, the cakes, all of it.

After some not-so-subtle cajoling from her brother, Thalia climbed up onto the small armchair and stared down the lens of the camera.

"Big smile, Thal," Manny said.

Thalia sat perfectly still, stone-faced.

Abe grinned at her and poked his tongue out. Thalia glared back.

"Please, Thalia? We'll take you for ice cream after," Furat said.

Thalia shook her head.

They all turned to Jerry.

Jerry knew that Max blew on the kids and they smiled back at him, but he didn't know if that was just the babies, or if it worked for the older kids too. Something about the breeze on their faces made them smile.

He took a deep breath and blew. Hard.

Thalia drew back and put her hand up to stop the onslaught.

"What the fuck, Jerry? She's not going to smile with you blowing your dragon breath all over her," Manny said.

Manny crouched beside Thalia, who appeared to be on the verge of tears.

Jerry drew an even deeper breath. He sucked the air deep down into his stomach and then blew with all of his might.

Manny took the brunt in his left ear.

"Shit, Jerry," Manny said, doubling over, a hand to his ear. "I think you've damaged the drum."

Manny looked up and caught Furat frowning at him. He raised his hands and took a step back.

Jerry crouched low, which wasn't all that easy, raised the camera and peered through the lens. The little girl stared back at him, and then began to cry.

"What's the matter, Thal? He's not going to blow on you again," Manny said.

Thalia pointed at the wall behind Jerry, at the line of framed photographs showing the most photogenic of children.

"It's Harry," she said.

Jerry turned, following her gaze, and then felt the sweat creep down his spine when he saw Harry Monroe's angelic face smiling back at them.

7

Gradual Retreat

Jess sat across the cluttered desk from Jim: a weekly ritual that both were growing to hate, though neither would soon let go of it. Three months had passed since Harry had been taken; three long, dark and agonizing months; months that ran together into the kind of nightmare from which Jess wondered if she'd ever wake.

The pain came in ebbs and flows, the stress more constant, unbroken. She often traced her mind for a time when he was with her, when she was happy, but she was finding those times harder and harder to locate. If her mind were a story, it began the last time she'd seen his face. Of course she could recall other periods: her wedding day, Harry's birth, Harry's first day at pre-school. They didn't seem connected though; there was no life between them. They were the blips on a radar. If she tried to relax, didn't drink, didn't seek distraction, the Clown needled his way into those blips too, taking the face of Michael, sometimes even Harry. He sat at the back of the church at their wedding; he held her hand as she gave birth.

She had seen a psychiatrist, the family shrink, a man retained to help cure or bury. She'd seen him off and on most of her life.

Dr. Stone. The most apt of names for a man that, she often felt certain, was actually made of stone. When she broke down and cried, he stared back at her, his gaze dismissive and his face stoic. When she told him stories about Harry, stories that made her lip tremble, he nodded impassively. A man that had seen it all before.

She knew that she needed help. She also knew that Dr. Stone wasn't the man to help her. She needed Michael. He would help her. He was the only one that could help her.

At the beginning, those first few days after Harry went missing, her mother had said it was the not knowing that was the hardest cross to bear, the thing that she most struggled with. Jess thought that was bullshit.

A couple of weeks into the case they'd stopped getting newspapers through the door. Jess had caught her mother reading a piece that informed them that if a child wasn't found in the first twenty-four hours then the chances of finding them alive grew slimmer by the day. She wondered if it were really necessary to share that information, if it really helped anyone at all. Perhaps it lit a fire under the cops to begin with, and then, once the golden window passed, it forced the case to the backs of their minds.

No. Just looking at the man across from her she knew that wasn't true. So the not knowing wasn't the worst part. The worst part, and the part that she lived in fear of every time her phone rang or there was a knock at the door, was that the police might one day tell her that they had found a body. But until that day, a day that might never come, she sought distraction wherever she could, to keep her mind from running the downward slope to that night.

"So, here we are," Jim said.

"Here we are," Jess said.

"What happened to your face?"

Jess shrugged, seemingly irritated.

He looked at her arms, noticed the red marks and the yellow bruising.

She stared back at him.

He looked down at his coffee cup, at the red letters scrawled across it.

Keep Calm and Carry On.

He looked up at Jess.

The past three months had devoured her.

They'd gone to the same school, everyone in town had. She was in the grade below; he doubted she remembered him. He remembered her though. She wasn't easily forgotten, and not just because she'd gotten into so much trouble.

Back then she'd had something about her that made you stare. Not now though. Now she wore a cloak around her. A dark cloak, all thick and heavy, that told you she was a woman drowning.

Things like this didn't happen in Tall Oaks.

They had the usual stuff—break-ins, vandalism, the occasional fight. Most people in the town were well-heeled and silver-spooned with a name to protect. He could still remember back when he was a boy and his father had been a cop. There'd been a stabbing outside a bar on Main Street. The local news lit up like a firework. And that had been just a stabbing. The abduction of a child had hit the town like an avalanche. News vans arrived, State police convened. The four roads that led in and out of the town were closed, with blockades quickly set in place. A police helicopter circled above, fixed in the sky until the storm got too bad, its noisy rotors waking up half the town before they even had a chance to switch the television on and see the reporters standing in front of Jess's house. The media invaded like locusts, filling the coffee houses and restaurants and taking over the two small hotels owned by Francis McDermott.

Jim had been impressed by the way the town had closed ranks, much to the annoyance of the reporters who sought out rumors as if they were fact.

The following morning, in the pouring rain, an army of locals had convened outside the small police station on Main Street. It was a show of force the media ran with and "THE TALL OAKS TAKE" became the most talked about crime of the moment. The newspapers ran a picture of Harry alongside a picture of the mob lined up to find him on their front pages. Jim and his team focused on the woods at first: The tall oak trees that started on the edge of town, then ran into the Black Lake National Forest, and its fifty thousand acres. They'd searched as best they could, though as the hours passed the storm had worsened. The winds were strong, the ground unforgiving. Before long, vast swathes of woodland were flooded. They waded through, knee-deep. It was grueling. Daniel Fischer, a local lawyer, had slipped and broken his leg. The weather made bringing a helicopter in impossible. It had taken six hours to get him out. As night fell Jim had had little choice but to halt the search. Three days after that the rain had finally stopped.

State police had set up in Jim's office, alongside his own men. All were quickly overwhelmed with the number of sightings, and crackpots that claimed to know something. When she left her mother's house, Jess was greeted with the kind of hysteria normally reserved for a flavor-of-the-month actress who had forgotten to put on her underwear.

It was as they had gathered once more, as Jim and his team lined up to enter the woods again, that they received their first decent tip. A lady had called the hotline, said she'd seen a boy being led into Aurora Springs, a luxury lakeside retreat a hundred miles or so to the west of Tall Oaks. It could have come to nothing, another possible to add to the pile, but then the lady had said the boy had been holding a red cloth. Harry's comforter. A detail they hadn't released. A small team stayed back, helped coordinate the search of the woods. Jim headed west, siren blazing, helicopters overhead. They'd searched: for two weeks they'd combed every inch of the place. It was half-finished, a retreat for the wealthy, with much of it still a building site. The houses fanned out around a lake, two miles across. The divers had gone in. All were relieved when they found nothing. Frustrated, but relieved, Jim had headed back to Tall Oaks with more questions than answers.

And then some twelve-year-old psychopath, in another un-assuming town a hundred miles away, had taken a gun from his father's unlocked cabinet and opened fire on the group of bullies that had made his life a misery, and a few of the teachers too. No sooner had it arrived than the circus left town again.

Harry was relegated to the local news.

Though all of this had been a distraction, it didn't alter the fact that Jim had nothing else to go on. Other than the single green hair, forensics had found nothing of interest. Nothing. And there were no witnesses. No neighbor had heard anything—no screams, no car engine starting. Nothing. Granted, with the rain so fierce prints could have been washed clean, noise drowned, but still, it troubled him. But not nearly as much as the clown did. Jim had no doubt that Jess was telling the truth. Why had the clown called her name? Why wake her? Why dress as a clown? It could have been the work of a pro, a serial killer, but searches on the national database, and the heavy cooperation of the FBI, yielded no similar cases. Again, nothing.

"So, I remembered something new about the night he was taken. It's probably useless, like everything else was."

Jim sat up a little straighter, more to show that he was interested than because he thought she might have remembered something relevant. His eyes pleaded with her to give him something more to go on, to remember something he could use, something that would help him make some progress.

"You know what I said, Jess. It all matters. All of it. Every single strand of information that you give us might eventually be something we can tie together."

"My last words to Harry, I remembered what they were."

He waited for her to continue, though didn't reach for his pen just yet.

"I used to sit on the eight steps that ran from his floor up to the kitchen. At first I sat by the door in his room, so he could see me. Then I moved just outside the door. Then it was the first step, and then slowly I'd climb up a step at a time, until a month or so after I started I was at the top. I read about the technique in a book, it's called gradual retreat. And it worked. He started sleeping through the night and became able to settle himself if he woke. I used to keep the video monitor with me. I'd sit there and watch him fall asleep. It's funny how kids are. We lie down, close our eyes and then drift off. They lie there with their eyes wide open. And they keep them open, like they've got matchsticks holding up the lids. And then, when they can't keep it up anymore, when they're so tired that they can't even focus, they start to blink. And then the blinks get longer, and every time that they do those long blinks you wonder if they'll open their eyes again. Until they don't, and then they're asleep."

He watched her speak, the way her lips moved, the way she ran a hand through her hair.

"The week or so before that night he had started to bite his nails. I don't know why. Maybe he fell out with one of his friends at the park, he wouldn't say. That night I was tired, really tired. Michael had phoned and we'd had a huge argument. That's when he said that I had changed since we had Harry. I was no fun anymore. That all I did was talk about Harry and all the cute things he did. He said that I stopped being Jess, the Jess that he fell in love with, and I just became a mom. Like that was the worst thing in the world."

Jim nodded again, waiting for her to tell him something he didn't already know. That the whole town didn't already know. The phone call with Michael had been leaked and Michael hadn't come off well.

"So I was tired, and I was in a bad mood. And I was sitting on the top step watching Harry start to long-blink, willing him to go to sleep because I just wanted to get into the tub with a glass of wine and try to relax. And then, just as I stood up and started to creep toward the kitchen, he opened his eyes, brought his hand to his mouth and started to bite his nails." She was talking faster now, starting to struggle for breath between each word. Jim hated to watch her like this, had to fight the urge to take her into his arms and tell her that everything would be alright. That Harry would turn up soon, and he'd be fine. That if—and it was a big if—he turned up alive he wouldn't be all fucked-up from the months he had spent away from his mother.

"I wanted to scream at him to go to sleep. I wanted to walk away and pour my wine and run my bath. But I knew that if he called out for me and I wasn't there it would break the trust. And then I'd have to go back to sitting in his room, and then climbing the steps one night at a time. And I couldn't go back. So I called out to him. I said that only dirty little boys bite their nails. And then I saw him quickly snatch his hand away from his mouth and bury it under the sheet. Then his bottom lip started to shake. And I said, *'Don't you dare start crying. Go to sleep.'* And then he did the thing that kids never do. He closed his eyes tightly and tried to sleep. Tried to sleep even though there were tears streaming down his face. But he didn't make a sound. He didn't sob like he normally did. He was too scared. What if the Clown had been in the room then? What if he was biting his nails because he knew that the Clown was coming for him?"

Jim walked around the desk and put his arm round her shoulders.

She leaned forward, doubled over, her head down as she sobbed.

8

The Act

Manny passed by the window for the fifth time, and then decided that he must have the gun belt in the window of Selwyn Antiques. Though it was part of a World War Two display, and wrapped around the torso of a mannequin dressed as a soldier, it was exactly the kind of thing that a gangster, like he was, should wear beneath his three-piece.

He grabbed a table outside the Tearoom opposite, and sent Furat and Thalia inside to get drinks.

"What do you want?" Furat called, from the doorway.

"Milk . . . the ulcer," Manny replied, holding his stomach.

She rolled her eyes.

"Better make it chocolate," he called, then turned to Abe. "I want that belt, Abe. It's a gangster's belt, and old man Selwyn's got it on an army doll, fucking idiot."

Manny looked at Abe. It was time to go to work.

"Go in there and feel him out. Let him know that we're the new muscle in this town and that we're going to start collecting real soon. He might get a pass, for a while at least, if he were to give up that belt."

Abe scratched his head, then took his glasses off and wiped the lens on his shirt.

"I don't know, M. He's a tough old guy. Can't you go?"

Manny closed his eyes and exhaled slowly. "I'm the Don. The boss. *El Capitan.*"

"Isn't that a mountain?"

"I can't go in there and try and get a free belt. It'll fuck up our credibility. You think Joseph Colombo stole the furs with his own hand?"

Abe met his eye, looked down and shook his head.

Abe took a deep breath and stood. "What should I call myself?"

"I've given it a lot of thought," Manny said, his fingers steepled.

"And?"

"Skinny Goldenblatt."

Abe frowned. "What about Joey Merlino? He's called Skinny Joey."

"Yeah, well, I've seen his photograph and you're much thinner than he is."

Abe walked slowly toward Selwyn Antiques.

"Where's Abe going?" Furat said, setting the drinks down.

Manny reached for his sunglasses and put them on. "Business. Doesn't concern a civilian like you."

Furat shook her head.

Manny sipped his chocolate milk, then crossed his legs and smoothed his tie down.

"Thalia's inside, she's playing with Mrs. Parker," Furat said.

"So, how you settling into Tall Oaks?"

"It's nice enough. Quiet though, after living in the city."

"My mother says that."

"What's the school like?"

"Full of assholes."

"Like most schools then."

He laughed. "No, it's not too bad. Well, it won't be for you."

"How come?"

"You're pretty."

She tried not to smile.

"How come you left Chicago? Long way to move," he said, suddenly embarrassed.

"My father wanted to leave."

"And you?"

"Not really. My sister is still there," she said quietly, looking away.

"Oh."

She stood. "I'll check on Thal."

Manny turned to see Abe walking toward him, without the belt.

"What happened?"

"He said he didn't want to sell it. But if he ever did, it would cost twenty dollars."

"Did you tell him about the protection money?"

"I started to, and then he looked at me real funny so I walked out."

Manny lifted his sunglasses and rubbed his eyes. Abe needed a pep talk. Manny took another sip of chocolate milk.

"It's tough out there, Skinny. These people have had it easy for a long time, their whole lives, really. They don't want to pay up, nobody does. But if we don't get in there first and claim this town then someone else will. Like those fuckers from Blossom Creek, or the animals from Pleasant Hill. They've got their own gangsters there, people like us that saw what they wanted and had the balls to take it: visionaries. It's virgin land. Like Bugsy Siegel saw Vegas when he looked at the desert, I see an empire when I look at Tall Oaks. And you know who's sitting on top of that empire?"

Manny slapped Abe's cheek gently.

"We are, Skinny. We are," he whispered. "Now walk across the street and make old man Selwyn an offer he can't refuse."

Ten minutes later, Abe returned with the belt in his hand and a smile on his face.

Manny grinned back at him.

"How'd you do it?"

"I made him an offer he couldn't refuse," Abe said, looking deep into Manny's eyes and seeing the pride reflecting back at him.

Manny stood, pulled him in for a hug, and then kissed both his cheeks.

Gangsters.

"By the way, you owe me thirty bucks," Abe said, "for the belt."

Jared thought of the evening ahead and felt nervous: stomach-flipping and dry-mouth nervous. He always was before a date. The nerves clawed at his stomach, marched down his spine and shook his knees. He tried to control them, found that sometimes a drink or two helped. He couldn't risk any more than that, in case it loosened his tongue. He hated the nerves. They served as a tacit reminder that he was just an actor, that it was all just an act.

He hit the gym four times a week, always following the same routine. Twenty minutes on the running machine, trying desperately not to look at the spandex-clad ass of the woman in front of him—he didn't want to be *that* guy. Twenty minutes of free weights, and then a final twenty minutes in the pool. He didn't lift heavy weights, he didn't want bulging muscles like some of the guys he saw in the locker rooms. Guys that enjoyed being stared at.

He got his hair cut weekly at the salon in town, unisex, though he had yet to see another man in there. If he was honest, the cut was exactly the same as the one he used to get in the barber shop in Echo Bay, though double the price. It was as if replacing the word "barber" with "stylist" gave them free rein to add ten bucks to a simple trim. He paid it nonetheless, more fool him.

Then there were his clothes. He had spent years cultivating a wardrobe to be proud of. He owned two sports coats; neither fitted, but close enough. He wore those on top of a polo shirt, Ralph Lauren, tucked into navy jeans, Hugo Boss, and always with Gucci loafers, which he purchased online. The result, to the untrained eye, was of a man of means. A man who took care of himself—someone confident, outgoing and stylish. The kind of man you could take to meet your friends and not be embarrassed by, a man equally at home in a fancy restaurant or sitting on your sofa with a glass of wine watching a movie.

Then came his pitch, the way in which he conversed. All carefully worked on. Movies had been studied, endless books read.

And, so long as people didn't get too close, which they rarely did, his act held up just fine. But that also meant that he could never get too close—a certain distance had to be maintained. Ladies that took a shine to his polished act, which happened often, were taken out two or three times, so that he could practice, and then for reasons they would never know, unceremoniously dropped. The nice young man that they were starting to really like, the one that they had already told their mothers about, the one that might be, well, *the one*, all of a sudden became much too busy to return their calls, or take them out, or see them ever again.

So he had to keep moving. No ties. No close friends. He couldn't walk down Main Street and find the sidewalks littered with girlfriends from days gone by. He might start to get a name for himself, or worse, they might start to talk about him. He tried to select with care, seeking out the kind of women that dated often, that wouldn't make too much of a couple of dinner dates, which was why he found it all the more puzzling that he had chosen to take Elena out. He didn't like the way that her weird son had looked at him. Still, there was something about her. Something that made him want to ask her out, and not just as a way to practice and polish his act. He liked her. And he didn't like many people. He had seen something in her eyes, something that he recognized. Toughness, steely determination, maybe. She had been hurt but she was too strong to crumble and fall. He was strong too. So he would take her out. Two strong people having dinner together.

Henrietta stood in front of the door. It was locked. Only she had a key. Roger rarely ventured up to the top floor of their home. The maid, Teresa, was under strict instructions to leave it well alone. Roger thought it was Henrietta's office. She had even less need for an office than he did.

She took a moment before she went in, a moment to remind herself of what she had done, of what was going to happen. It would come out soon enough, all of it. She found the thought didn't frighten her as much as it probably should have.

She still felt nauseous though. Nauseous enough to vomit.

She blamed him for it. He had driven her to it. Driven her mad. Not guilty by reason of insanity.

She needed to be a mother again. They'd tried for years and years after Thomas had died. Then the doctors told her that her body repelled Roger's sperm. It did that to protect her, they'd said. She had thought it an apt metaphor for their relationship from that point onward.

Roger took the news well, stiff upper lip; moved swiftly on, as was his way.

She closed her eyes, pressing her head against the door. She could remember their last discussion about it vividly.

"We could adopt?" she'd said.

"I hear there's a waiting list for Western babies as long as my arm. We'll be much too old by the time a suitable one becomes available."

"How about an older child?"

"They'll be too set in their ways, and I'm much too set in mine. We might clash."

"We could look abroad?"

That always got his attention. "A Chinese might be nice. Superb intellect and inbuilt subservience. You know, the children in China start the school day by raising their flag and reciting the national anthem? Can you imagine the English doing that? They wouldn't know the words. And the ones that did certainly wouldn't know the second verse."

"Darling, no one knows the second verse."

He'd cleared his throat and taken a sip of water. She'd raised her hand to stop the singing before it began.

"I read an article about Russia the other day. We might be able to get a baby there, a white one too. We could say it was our own," she'd said.

"I'm not sure about Russians. Blunt, serious, and mostly chain-smokers. Corrupt too."

She banged her head against the door gently, the memory alone enough to sap her energy.

That's how all the conversations had gone, in one form or another. Every time she'd brought up a serious subject, he'd reduced it to something silly. Over the years it had become perfectly obvious, if never voiced, that he didn't want children. He was too selfish, too busy and too . . . *uncaring* wasn't exactly the right word, but he most definitely wasn't paternal. No, she couldn't imagine him cooing over a baby, or chasing after a toddler. He wasn't a bad man, far from it, he just wasn't the man for her. And she had known that almost from the day they had met.

On paper they were a good fit: offspring of the wealthy, wanting for nothing. It soon became apparent it was the only thing they shared, the glue that held the fragments of their relationship together. The glue had been like cement at first, with their parents so pleased and their future so effortless. But with the passing of each unpropitious day, the cement had been chipped away, until they were nothing more than polite strangers sailing toward a darkening sky.

She closed her eyes and turned the key, stepped inside and shut the door behind her.

He was in bed, where she had left him. His hair was light, like hers. She wanted to wash it. She would do later, when she was certain Roger wasn't around.

She stood there for a long time, watching him sleep.

She'd spent nearly a year preparing his room. She'd painted it blue, with doves above his bed. She wasn't a particularly skilled painter, but with the option of outside help precluded, she'd done her best.

Though he was light, she could see the mattress dip under his weight.

Sometimes she spent hours with him, other times only minutes, whatever time she could spare. She drew comfort from being near him. Roger wouldn't understand that. Not many would.

She couldn't keep him for too much longer though. She knew that. But letting go would be difficult. So very difficult.

She crept over to him, her bare feet sinking into the plush carpet.

She leaned down gently, then kissed his head, always dismayed by how cold his skin felt against her lips.

Jerry turned the key in the door, rattling it so that he wouldn't startle his mother. He wondered if she were awake, and if so what kind of mood she would be in. There was no telling anymore.

He stepped into the hallway Dad had decorated thirty years ago. The house hadn't been touched since then. Jerry liked the wallpaper—the flowers and the spots, the browns and the yellows. He reached out, running his hand over it. It was textured, bumpy in parts, smooth in others. He could hear noise in the kitchen.

"Hi, Mom," he called.

He hung his jacket on the peg, next to Dad's winter coat. His mother had told him to wear Dad's winter coat when it was cold out. It was far too small though, and he had felt funny the one time he'd tried it on. It smelled of tobacco and cologne. And a little of mothballs.

Jerry liked moths. He liked how they were drawn to the light. He'd watched a movie about them once, or at least about a creature that looked like a moth. Dad had rented it from the video store on Main Street before it closed down.

"Mom, I'm home."

He put his keys on the side table, next to Dad's car key. Dad's car sat in the garage. Jerry couldn't drive. His mother said that he lacked spatial awareness so would most probably be involved in an accident. Dad had driven the same car for twenty-four years. A 1976 navy blue, Chevrolet Caprice Classic. Sometimes, when he was sure that his mother was asleep, Jerry would creep into the garage and sit in it. The car smelled of tobacco too. Though not of cologne or mothballs.

He unclipped his name badge. The badge was shiny. JERRY, ASSISTANT MANAGER. He'd been assistant manager since his first day. Max took the money for the badge from his paycheck. Jerry didn't mind, the badge made him feel important.

He'd applied for the position after seeing it advertised in the local newspaper. He'd applied for lots of jobs, though until that point had never been asked to come in for an interview. Dad had said it was because he didn't have any qualifications. But there wasn't much Jerry could've done about that as his mother had told him he wasn't college material.

Dad had driven him the seventy miles to the High & Mighty store at the outlet mall by Pleasant Hill, to purchase a suit for the interview. The coat and pants hadn't matched. It didn't really matter though because Max said that he was the only person to respond to the advert so he had gotten the position by default. Mom had baked a cake to celebrate. She baked cakes for all sorts of occasions, even minor ones, like the time Jerry had won a goldfish at the carnival. The kids at school had said his mother was even weirder than him. He supposed Dad was weird too. He collected birds' eggs. Jerry had once seen him get attacked by a blue jay. It didn't do any real damage, but Dad was shaken enough to spend the next few days recuperating on the couch.

Jerry walked over to the kitchen door. He could hear sizzling. He could smell bacon. His stomach growled as he placed a hand on it.

He opened the door gently.

Mom stood with her back to him, facing the stove. She was naked.

Jerry blushed.

He hadn't seen many naked women in his life. Last year, for his birthday, Max had given him some photographs of a girl he was seeing. A girl he was seeing even though he was engaged to Lisa. The girl wasn't nearly as pretty as Lisa, and she was doing things to Max that he couldn't imagine Lisa doing. Jerry had blushed when he'd seen those too. Max had laughed. Jerry kept the photographs in the drawer in his dark room. He'd wanted to throw them away, wanted to rip them up and throw them away. But something had stopped him. The same something that had stopped him leaving the room when Dad had rented *Basic Instinct*.

He looked at Mom. A spider web of veins bulged from the backs of her knees. Her skin was mottled, blotchy; stretch marks crept from head to toe, creases and folds as deep as caves.

He cleared his throat.

Mom span around, startled. Her gold crucifix nestled between her sagging breasts.

She screamed.

It was a piercing scream.

He held his hands up, his face stricken.

Mom reached for the pan and threw it at him. The oil splashed over his stomach and legs. He could feel the heat begin to sear his skin.

He stepped back.

Mom reached for a knife.

He tried not to scream himself.

"Mom. It's Jerry," he said, trying to keep his tone soft.

She clutched the knife tightly, fear in her eyes.

His skin was burning.

She took a step toward him, raised the knife.

And then he opened his mouth, and he sang.

He sang "Ave Maria," like he used to when he was in the choir and Mom used to sit on the front pew and cry.

She stopped.

She stopped still and listened.

And then she dropped the knife, and she looked down at his legs, and at the pan on the floor. And she started to cry.

She fell into his arms, and he started to cry too. But he didn't stop singing, because she loved it so much.

9

SomAli

"How do I look? Honest answers only, please," Elena said, spinning round slowly, trying to get a read on the four sets of eyes staring at her.

"Hot," French John said, lying back on her bed, quite exhausted from all the excitement.

"I like it," Furat said, as she dusted some lint from Elena's black dress; the dress that Danny had bought for her when he'd first made his money.

"You look pretty, Mommy," Thalia said, while trying to balance in the sparkly shoes she had found in her mother's closet.

"It's too short. Like . . . whore short," Manny said, wrinkling his nose in displeasure.

French John groaned. "She looks great, Manny. Try to be objective."

"No offense, French, but you can't really tell whether she looks hot or not."

"And why's that?"

French John braced himself for the answer, as did Furat, Elena, and even Thalia.

"Because she doesn't have a cock."

French John laughed.

Elena did not. She picked up the nearest object to hand, her lipstick, and threw it at her son.

"Jesus, Ma, that could have hit me in the head or something."

"Good. Maybe it would have knocked some sense into you. Apologize to French. And what about your sister? She's heard enough of your language to last a lifetime."

Furat picked up a small, framed photograph on the dressing table, beside a dizzying array of powders and creams.

"What's this? It looks like Manny, only he's thinner and wearing boxing gloves," Furat said.

French John snatched the photo before Manny could, smiling as he looked at it.

"Manny took up boxing. He got obsessed with the *Rocky* movies, you know the ones? Sly Stallone plays a mentally handicapped boxer."

He looked up just in time to see Manny's mouth fall open and a fire ignite behind his eyes.

"Shit, French. He wasn't mental. He just spoke funny. You try getting your head caved in two thousand times and see if you can still function properly. He always won though. Fucking tough that kid."

Elena ushered Thalia out and toward the television in the living room.

"So what happened? Why did you quit and gain the weight?" Furat asked.

"He trained hard for two months, lost about ten pounds . . ."

"Twenty," Manny said.

". . . And then he thought he was ready to fight, so he found this boxing roadshow you could enter online. He chose this little Indian boy as an oponent . . ."

"He was Somali."

"The morning before the fight he tried to get all the local kids to come out and run with him, like that scene in the movie."

"Lazy fuckers wouldn't get out of bed. And then Mr. Walters, in the grocery store, he wouldn't throw me an apple as I ran past. I had to stop and pay for it first," Manny said.

"So we all drove to this church hall just outside of Tall Oaks, and the place was full of red necks baying for blood. This Indian boy . . ."

"Somali."

". . . he showed up with his dad, and just as he was getting warmed up the lights shut off. We all thought there had been a power cut, and then we hear the theme music from *Rocky*. And Abe shines a flashlight . . ."

"It was a spotlight."

". . . on the door, and we see Manny jumping up and down, draped in an American flag. This poor Somali boy looked terrified."

"No shit he looked terrified. I was all ripped-up and sexy. Had my hair set all nice with curls on the neck, black shorts with gold trim, fucking deadly. I had Abe in my corner, he was supposed to be like Mickey, all motivational and shit. But the kid knows nothing about boxing. I would've been better off with French in my corner, if he could've torn his eyes away from all the muscle-bound hunks fighting that night. I had these sweet boots too, cost like two hundred dollars but we got them half off because my feet are so small."

"So, what happened?" Furat asked.

French John went to speak, but Manny held a hand up to silence him.

"Turned out this kid was some kind of wizard in the ring. Like Ali or some shit. I'm trying to hit him but he just keeps dancing around. When I read his profile, and saw that he was from Somalia, I thought he'd be all skinny and weak, you know, because their water's full of shit particles. But then, just as I got a read on his rhythm and was about to hand his ass to him, Abe must have pressed the spotlight or something, because for a second I was dazzled. And then this sneaky fucking Somali, who probably had some weights in his gloves, not that anyone checked, saw that I was effectively blind and cracked me on the nose. It was a dirty shot. I thought, fuck this shit. I'm not fighting a cheat. So I ducked out of the ring and walked out. The crowd knew he was dirty, they were booing and cursing."

"Were you hurt?"

"Nah, small break in the bone. Wasn't nothing."

"He was hurt. My heart broke when he cried in the car on the way to the hospital," Elena said, catching her son's hard stare in the mirror.

French John bit his lip hard enough to draw blood, though still couldn't rein in his laughter.

"I didn't cry. You get hit in the nose and your eyes water. Everybody knows that."

"Poor Abe was shaken too. We had to get the doctor to take a look at him. Seeing all that blood made him feel faint."

"So you just quit? I think you looked good with the weight off, and without that mustache. Why is your mustache that shape by the way?" Furat said.

French John turned away from them, now biting his fist.

"I had to quit. She wouldn't let me fight anymore. Probably would've been champ by now, regional at least. And it's this shape because it's gangster," Manny said, smoothing the arrow down.

Elena stood and spun round again.

French John whistled. Manny glowered.

Jim played the interview tape again. He could repeat it *verbatim*. After hearing Jess's latest revelations he hadn't been able to sleep, hadn't been able to eat. It was like the beginning all over again. He rubbed his eyes, then his neck. He felt tired, worn to the point of ruin. He could only imagine how Jess felt. He'd have to stop sleeping in the car, his body couldn't take it.

He opened the Harry Monroe case file, felt the familiar sense of dread. It was heavy, full of interview transcripts, forensic reports, possible sightings and leads. There were photographs of Harry inside, too many to count. Jess had dropped them in. He didn't need them all, had the kid's face seared into his mind.

He thumbed through the pages. There was nothing new in it, nothing he hadn't looked at a hundred times before. He saw snippets now, just snippets, all blurry, the words streaming together into nothing.

They had run down every suspect that they had, starting with Jessica and her estranged husband Michael.

Michael was a prick. No doubt about it. He'd had everything given to him on a plate. He was good-looking, smart too. It was like God had said, 'I've made enough average Joes so here comes a special one.' He came from a loving home and had a good job, a beautiful wife and a really sweet kid for a son. It would have been easier to be nice . . . to try.

A little bit of digging found that he had been cheating on Jess almost from the day they were married.

"Men aren't built for one woman. Marriage is tough. I mean, it's suffocating. Jess should have known. I didn't hide who I was. When I met her I was with someone else, she knew that. And then she expected me to change overnight, to be a person I'm not. Just because you stand up in church, you say a few words . . . it doesn't mean anything. Not in the real world. Look at the stats."

His voice was smooth, even on the crackling tape.

He was calm, far too calm for a man that had just been told that his son was missing. Like he knew something. That's what Jim had thought at the time—this guy knows something we don't. He's not worried enough; he's not surprised, not frantic.

Jim had searched his face for something, anything—fear, panic. He'd found nothing. It was clear that he didn't give a shit about his son, about his wife. Jess said he did the minimum, played with Harry only to keep him quiet. He didn't change diapers, didn't stay home when Harry was sick. He could turn it on though for birthday parties, social occasions; he could be the perfect husband and father in front of their family and friends.

They'd questioned him for near three hours. He'd had that air of confidence that Jim only saw on suspects with watertight alibis. And his was watertight. He had been in the sky at the time, in a 787, 40,000 feet above the earth. He lawyered up too, even though there was no need. Smart.

Jess had been entirely different. She was distraught, beside herself, just as he would have expected. She was like a caged animal in there that first time, desperate to get out and look for her boy. Although among it all, through the tears and the panic, the worry and the pain, he still saw the love she felt for Michael. He still saw the longing there. She still wanted him, despite what he said, despite the things he had done.

It bothered Jim. But he got it. He'd studied enough cases of domestic abuse to get it. You can't help who you fall for.

If you could, then Jim wouldn't have fallen for Jess.

Not in a million years.

Jess ran fast, her legs a blur, her body on fire, sweat dripping. She maintained the pace for as long as she could, miles and miles, flat out. She ran to the point of exhaustion, often arriving back at her mother's house on the verge of collapse. She didn't run to stay fit or to lose weight. She ran because she couldn't sit still. She couldn't relax, not ever. She used to be able to. She used to lie in the tub, or watch a movie, or read a book and be able to block out the outside world ... the noise. But since that night she hadn't stopped moving. Even when she was sitting down, she was moving. Her leg would twitch. She'd look down and see that her foot was tapping on the ground, or that her fingers were clawing at the table.

The doctor had said that it was anxiety. A real revelation. He'd refused to medicate her, worried what she might do. It was for the best anyway. She still needed to be at her sharpest. The drink was okay, because it wore off. Jim had said himself that any day she could reveal something crucial, something that might lead them to Harry. He said that sometimes, when people went through the kind of trauma that she had that night, their minds tried to block out the pain, and then slowly, over time, when the threat had died down, they started to piece it back together again. She could remember though: she could remember everything. That was the problem, because she remembered the Clown's face so vividly.

Sometimes she snatched an hour or two of sleep, before the nightmares dragged her back into the world, but only when she was truly exhausted, which was why she found herself running through the tall oak trees, a long way from her mother's home. Too far to keep it up.

She stopped by a clearing, lay back on the grass and fought for breath.

She could smell last night's vodka seeping from her body. She stared up at the sky, watching the light clouds drift above.

The woods reminded her of her father. He'd liked to hunt. He'd drag her along, thinking that they were spending quality time together: his kind of quality time, the kind where he didn't have to utter a word to her. It had been her job to carry the compass. Her grandfather had taught her how to navigate the land. She'd get a signal from her father, stand perfectly still and watch as he raised his gun and shot deer. He didn't do it for the meat; he didn't seem to enjoy the thrill of the chase. She'd asked him why he did it once and he'd ignored her. It could have been for the same reason that he worked himself into an early grave, even though he had millions in the bank. It's just the way he was.

She'd wanted to be there when they searched for Harry—she could have helped coordinate, but Jim told her to stay home, in case someone called. She'd wanted to follow them up to Aurora Springs too, to see where it had happened.

Jim thought he'd been kidnapped; it fit, with her family being so wealthy. But no call had come.

She reached for her cell phone. She kept it with her, still waiting for a call.

She dialed his number, listened to it ring, heard the click.

"Sometimes I can feel him. Like now. I can feel him. Do you think he's dead, Michael? That's what they all think. That he's dead. They don't say it, but I can see it in them. And I fucking hate them for it. Because they don't know, they're all just guessing. I can't go on for much longer. It's too hard, without him, without you. I'm so alone. Will you call me? Just once. Or leave me a message? I need to hear your voice."

10

Equally Gray

If the first and second glasses of wine did little to settle Elena's nerves, then the third told her to take a breath and just enjoy herself. To relax and stop worrying about everything, stop worrying about the fact that she was sure that the maître d' had seated them at the same table where she'd sat with Danny on her birthday three years ago. It also told her to stop over analyzing Jared. To stop looking for reasons why it wouldn't work out between them.

So far he'd done everything right. The compliments were sincere, he was a gentleman, had pulled out her chair and opened doors for her, though stopped short of standing when she got up to use the ladies' room—that would have been too much. His clothes were perfect; he had avoided that just-come-from-the-office look by wearing a polo shirt beneath his sports coat, and smart jeans instead of suit pants. His hair had the smallest touch of product in it, certainly not enough to leave a mark on your pillow, or for fellow diners to lament the fact that they had left their umbrellas at home. He had ordered a beer, which she liked.

Wine might have said he was too prissy for her. Spirits said hard drinker, the kind of man that reaches for the Scotch each night, just to take the edge off.

But was it all too perfect, too engineered to get her into bed?

The third glass said that it wasn't, that she was thinking too much.

"So how come you haven't settled down?"

She smiled at him and he smiled back. Nice teeth, white but not scary white like the receptionist at her dentist.

"I had a couple of close calls, but if I'm honest I guess I haven't found the right person yet. I don't buy into the whole soul-mate thing, but I still think you have to really click with someone to commit long term."

"I'm not sure I agree with the whole meant-to-be thing either. I used to, but not now."

He smiled. "Is this the part where we talk about our ex-partners?"

She laughed. "It's a *faux pas,* right? Especially on a first date."

"I think it's better to just get everything out there. You have kids so their father must have been a big part of your life."

"Sometimes I wish he wasn't. I mean, he left me. There, I said it."

"Feel better?"

She finished her drink, shook her head and laughed. "Not really."

She glanced around at the other diners. She wondered who else was on a first date, who else felt the pressure of trying to impress weighing on the desire to just be open and honest.

"I can't imagine having children, all that responsibility. I mean, I love kids, it just seems too . . . forever."

The waiter appeared and topped up her drink.

"And then you must worry about being a good parent," he said.

"Just stick around and you're halfway there, Jared."

"I'm not sure that's true," he said, quietly.

"You don't have a good relationship with your parents?"

She saw him swallow, and his eyes drift. "It's hard being a son too. It's tough, the family dynamic. Was your ex-husband a good father?"

"He was and he wasn't. He was there for the fun stuff. He preferred Manny when he was a toddler to when he was a baby. Babies are difficult—they scream and cry and need changing, and then get sick on your clothes. Doesn't matter if you're wearing your pajamas or a two-thousand-dollar suit, they'll ruin it regardless."

"I couldn't have that," Jared said, smoothing his jacket. "I'd have to wear an apron."

Elena laughed.

"I like my sleep too."

"Oh, that's the worst part. We'd hear Manny begin to cry and Danny would start cursing, asking me how was he expected to get up for work in the morning. He blamed me. Stupid as it sounds, he blamed me for Manny crying, like I was doing something wrong. It got better as Manny got older, but then I fell pregnant with Thalia and I knew that he wouldn't be able to go through it all again. It was around this time that Danny realized he was still a young man. Even when he made all the money he still felt that there was more out there, that we were holding him back. He even told me one day that he thought he got married too young and felt trapped. What was I supposed to do with that? What could I say?" She exhaled heavily and rubbed her eyes. "Shit."

"What's the matter?" he said.

"Look at me, spilling my guts. You can leave if you want."

He laughed, reached out and touched her hand. "Elena . . ."

She looked up at him.

"I'm having a nice time."

"I am too. Thanks, Jared."

Manny sat down, crossed his legs and rested his hands on his stomach. He wanted to take the hat off, felt that he should, but without his mother to help him, and with the bandage still firmly in place, it wasn't a viable option.

"You know it's hard for me to come here. To reach out to you like this," he said.

Jim sighed, wearily. "How many men has your mother been out with since your father left?"

Manny took a moment, counting in his mind.

"Three."

"And how many of these men have you reported to me?"

Manny sipped his coffee. "Is this instant? Tastes like shit. You want me to get Skinny to run across the road, bring back some of the good stuff? He's right outside."

Jim rubbed his eyes and yawned. "I'd love to humor you, Manny, to take the piss a little, too, but I just don't have the time."

Manny leaned forward. "There's something off about him, Jim. Seriously. He looks at me funny."

"The hat?"

"Please, Jim. I know all the shit you're going through with Harry Monroe, but I got a feeling about Jared."

Jim sighed again and finally nodded.

Manny stood. "If anyone asks why I was here, could you tell them you brought me in for racketeering?"

Jerry looked through the perfectly polished window of the PhotoMax and squinted at the sun. The boys were out there again, laughing. He didn't know why they did it, only that the leader was named Dylan. They might have been easier to ignore if he hadn't just finished working on the glass. He cleaned the glass weekly. Not because he enjoyed it, but because the boys kept throwing eggs at it. They were meant for him, the eggs. Sometimes the boys followed him home. They walked behind him. Sometimes they made *boom* noises when he took a step; other times they called him a freak. They didn't throw eggs when Max was inside, because Max had big muscles. Jerry sometimes wished that he had big muscles too. He'd seen an infomercial once, late at night when he should have been asleep. The men had gotten big muscles just by jumping up and down on a trampoline. Jerry had ordered the trampoline, but he jiggled so much when he tried to bounce on it that his mother had laughed at him. It was in the attic now, gathering dust with his rollerblades.

He had a good system for getting the egg off of the windows, one that didn't leave streaks and smears. He used paper towels, one square at a time. He could see most of Main Street through the window, from Wells Fargo at one end to the small police station at the other. He found himself watching the station more and more of late.

He felt tired, really tired. The previous night, after he had finished his dinner, and brushed his teeth and washed his face, he had pulled his sheets back, the blue set with the moon and stars, and seen that Mom had emptied the trash can into his bed. It had taken him a long time to pick up all the leftover food and bits of plastic and card, and then he had noticed that Mom must have put some kind of liquid into the trash can, maybe soup, because it had left a big stain on the sheet. So he had changed all of the bedding. He had to put on the set with the birds, because he had only just changed the set with the dolphins and they weren't even washed yet. He hated the bird set. They weren't friendly looking birds, like cartoon birds with cute yellow faces and smiles. They were real birds, with sharp beaks and beady eyes.

When he finally got into bed, and lay his head down on the sharp beaks and beady eyes, that's when he'd noticed the smell. His bed smelled like trash.

He looked up when the bell chimed, then quickly back down when he saw Jessica Monroe walk into the store.

Jess walked up to the counter.

Jerry didn't look up, not until she made a noise with her throat.

She licked her lips and still felt the swelling.

"I need some more posters. Max did them last time."

Jerry nodded, and then turned to the computer.

Jess watched him work, wondering why he wouldn't meet her eye, why he never met her eye.

He was big, really big. He had a funny voice. Harry used to like him. He used to say that Jerry was a giant, like the giant in *Jack and the Beanstalk*.

"How many do you need?" Jerry asked, still not looking up from the screen.

"Fifty."

She watched him type, watched his hand shake. His shirt gaped at each button, his stomach barely contained. She could see red marks on his skin, angry red marks that were starting to blister.

She didn't enjoy coming into town, but it couldn't be avoided. She'd see people, people she knew. They'd be doing something, buying something, going on as normal.

She watched Jerry hit a few more keys, then heard the copier begin to print.

She moved from foot to foot.

"What on earth have you got in your mouth?" Henrietta said.

Roger raised a hand to his mouth, self consciously. "It's called Invisalign . . . to straighten my teeth."

"What's wrong with your teeth?"

Both were acutely aware of how crooked they were.

He cleared his throat. "Not too much really, but I've always suffered with migraines and the new dentist, Doctor Al-Basri, said that it might be because my teeth sit slightly out of alignment."

She frowned, placing a lid on the Styrofoam cup she was holding.

"Where did you get that awful running vest?"

He glanced down, folding an arm across his chest. "I'm headed to the gym."

"The gym? You hate gyms. And your arms . . . that tan."

"I just thought I'd get into shape. You know, watch the old waistline."

"Well, I don't think you need to worry too much. You're not overweight and you play tennis, and golf."

She handed the tea to him.

"I saw Jess just now, heading into the PhotoMax," she said.

He nodded, glancing out the window.

"And?" he said.

"And nothing. Still nothing."

She turned, fiddled with the coffee machine and placed the milk back into the small refrigerator.

"So you spoke to her?"

"Who?"

"Jessica," he said.

"No, just Alison. I wish there was something we could do. Do you think I should go over there and ask how things are?"

"No," he said, quickly. "Best to leave her be. She might get upset."

Roger leaned forward and kissed her cheek.

She watched him walk out, and then noticed his shorts. They were silky, cut high at the sides.

She felt the bile rise quickly. She made it into the bathroom just in time to vomit.

"Are you okay?" Jim said, finishing his coffee.

He reached over, pulled out a chair.

Henrietta sat down, heavily. "Just a bug I think."

He smiled.

"Refill?"

"No, thanks. I drink too much of the stuff."

"How's it all going?" she said, though she could read him well enough to see it was a silly question.

"It's not."

She saw the file. She reached over to touch his hand.

"He's such a sweet boy, Jim."

"But you weren't that close?"

"We tried. I tried. She can be difficult, Jess. You know that. I've said it before. She's something of a closed book. She had her family, her life. I couldn't impose . . . it's hard enough for Alison, and she's Harry's grandmother."

"I see Alison. It's tough on everyone."

"You too."

"Yeah, me too."

"Harry deserves a good life. Separation is hard for children. Alison thought he was too young to understand, but I could tell he was troubled by it. They feel stress, they feel anxiety. Just like us really."

He nodded.

"Some people don't deserve to be parents. Michael . . . he doesn't deserve Harry," she said.

"At least he has a mother."

Henrietta nodded. At least he has a mother.

"You don't talk about Chicago much," Manny said. "Or about your sister."

Furat tugged at the grass with her fingers.

"How come?"

"My sister got pregnant."

"Oh."

"I'm not ashamed," she said. "My father is. She wasn't married. The guy's not Muslim."

"Oh."

"She's great. My best friend."

"You'll be an aunt."

"I'll be an aunt."

"Makes you sound old."

She punched his arm.

"Will you go to the prom with me?"

She noticed him look down at her shoes, then up at the sky, anywhere but into her eyes.

"Wow," she said.

He finally looked at her.

She saw the usual look of defiance in his eyes. But behind the defiance, a long way behind it, right at the back of the long line of other expressions he managed to convey with his large, brown eyes, she could see that he was nervous.

"Wow, what?"

"Wow, you managed a whole sentence without cursing. I'm going to tell Elena when I see her. Damn, I wish I had it on tape. She'll never believe me."

She stretched back on the grass and looked up at the sky. It was blue, brilliant blue with the lightest wisp of cloud. Away in the distance she saw a plane moving slowly, leaving a trail of its own white, wispy cloud behind it. She wondered where it was headed, if it was some exotic, sun-kissed destination. She liked to think so. But then there was every chance it was headed to Connecticut, or Detroit, or someplace equally gray.

"I'm being serious. You want to go or not? If you do, you need to let me know 'cause there's a whole bunch of broads I have to disappoint, and they'll need time to try and find a replacement for me. And that won't be easy—powerful men are hard to come by."

She laughed. She'd laughed a lot since she'd met Manny, but never more than when he'd first met her mother, who'd introduced herself as Mrs. Al-Basri. From then on Manny had called her "Al," as if that were her first name. Furat had been surprised, and a little relieved, when her mother had found it amusing.

"So is it a yes or a no?"

"I'll go with you on two conditions."

"A spirited filly, I like it, laying down the law already." He sat up, leaning on one elbow, looking down at her. "Name them?"

"One, you have to shave off the mustache. It looks awful, Manny, seriously . . . awful."

He ran his forefinger and thumb along the lines of the arrow.

"Skinny will be devastated if I shave it off. You know, he grew his own back when I mentioned the gangster thing to him. Four days in he looked like Tom Selleck. It was a work of art, all thick and lustrous. It was a privilege to walk the streets with him. And what with his height, he looked a good five years older—beautiful, especially in our line of work. My baby face is a curse at the moment. I know one day it'll come in handy, like when we're fifty and you're all dried up and shit, all dead skin and gray hairs, and I'll still be getting carded when I buy a bottle of liquor. Still partying with college kids and banging nineteen year olds."

"Yes or no? Will you shave it off? You can always take Abe to the prom if not—hold his hand and lead him to the dance floor."

"Jesus, okay, okay. Yes. It's a shame though, it really is."

He looked off into the distance, very much in a state of mourning.

"What else?"

"The three-piece, and the hat."

He looked at her, his eyes wide, slowly shaking his head.

"You have to wear a dinner suit, black tie, white shirt, no hat. Just for one night, for me. I've always dreamed of going to senior prom, but in my dream my date didn't have to wear a bandage around his head. That, or you can head to the after-party with Abe, maybe even try and kiss him at the end of the night."

She could see him thinking about kissing Abe.

He nodded.

She watched him glance down at his shoes and stifle a smile.

"Normal shoes too," she said.

He sighed. "That's the problem with women."

"What?"

"They always try and beat the gangster out of you."

11

Every Last Drop

"I need something stronger," Jess said.

She wore sunglasses. She moved from foot to foot, occasionally drumming on the glass counter with her fingers.

"There's nothing stronger without a prescription," Hung said. "Have you spoken with your doctor, Jess? I'm sure he'd give you something, if you just explain to him."

"I can't."

She ran a hand through her hair, every now and then glancing back over her shoulder.

"Have you tried Sominex?"

She waved him off brusquely. "It's all shit. Fucking weak shit."

He swallowed, not knowing what to say. He could see Lisa hiding in the back office. He didn't blame her. The last time Jess had come in she'd reduced Lisa to tears when she'd refused to sell her the Zaleplon she'd asked for.

Jess took her glasses off and rubbed her eyes, then put them back on again.

He thought of suggesting some herbal supplements before quickly changing his mind as he watched her scanning the shelves.

"How about painkillers? What's the strongest I can get?" Jess said, leaning over the counter.

Her top gaped low; he looked away.

"Can I ask what you need them for? Where's the pain exactly?" Jess stared at him, her lip trembling. "Please."

He reached out and took her hand. It felt thin in his, more bone than anything else.

"Talk to your doctor, Jess."

She snatched her hand away, then turned and walked back out into the sun.

The town was called Echo Bay, although it sat miles from the nearest beach. The ocean could be glimpsed on a clear day, so calling it a coastal town had seemed a good idea to the developers.

The drive there had taken Jim a little over two hours. It was hot in the car so he got out and stood in the dust. He glanced around, arid plains on all sides. He wondered who'd want to build a house here, and who'd want to buy one.

He wasn't sure why he had made the trip, could've probably got all he needed from a quick call. He was reaching, he knew that, but Jared had something to hide. Jared Martin. He worked in the Ford dealership on the edge of town. Jim hadn't been to see him yet, hadn't wanted to spook him. It was probably nothing much but Jared's Social Security number belonged to a man named Frank Tremblay, who'd died a couple of years back. Jared was Canadian. Lots of people outstayed their visa. Jim wouldn't bust him for it. Not if that was all it was.

He crossed the street, expected to see a tumbleweed float by. A light breeze whipped the dust around his shoes.

The construction site was quiet; ten guys maybe, most of them standing around. One of them pointed him in the direction of a small cabin. He strolled over to it, the sun fierce on the back of his neck.

He banged the door, heard a gruff voice beckon him in.

The man stood. He was short, round, messy. Droplets of sweat beaded on the thick hair that carpeted his forearms. He had little hair on his head, much more on his face.

Jim introduced himself, shook the man's outstretched hand then fought the urge to wipe his own on his pants.

The man's name was Clifton.

"Hot out there," Jim said.

"Ain't much better in here," Clifton said, pointing to a fan that stood in the corner of the office. "Been broke for eighteen days."

Clifton cleared his throat, hocking up something awful and then swallowing it back down again, whatever it was leaving some kind of residue on his dry lips. A residue he wiped onto the back of his arm.

"I wanted to ask you about Jared Martin."

"Who?"

"Jared Martin."

Clifton took a moment, then nodded. "I remember. Don't get many that ain't Mexican. What about him?"

"When did he work for you?"

Clifton rubbed his chin. "A year back, maybe more. Build's taking too long—ten units should be finished by now. Fucking Mexicans out there. Lazy. Permit's been delayed too."

"How long for?"

"Who knows with the fuckers they got running the place. I submitted a year back."

Jim shook his head. "I meant how long did Jared work for you for?"

"Months . . . a year. I don't remember. They come and go."

"You don't keep records?"

He shrugged.

"Anything you can tell me about him?"

"I get a lot of guys passing through."

Jim nodded and began to stand.

"You could try Arturo. I think Jared was sweet on his sister. You should see her, with the ass. I tell you . . . worth paying her a visit, if you know what I mean."

Clifton winked, his eye so red and sticky that there was a very real danger the lid would glue down and he'd have to open it manually again.

"You should get your eye checked out. Looks infected," Jim said.

Clifton shrugged. "I got another."

"Which one's Arturo?"

"The Mexican."

Jim stepped back outside, the sound of Clifton's laughter muting as he shut the door behind him.

He found Arturo by the cement mixer, leaning on it, smoking a cigarette and drinking a can of Coke. His skin was dark, his hands calloused. He took his hat off and wiped the sweat from his forehead. The other guys were watching, didn't look away when Jim stared back at them.

"You a cop?"

Jim nodded.

"This about the car?"

Jim shook his head.

Arturo took another drag.

"I wanted to ask about Jared Martin. He used to work here."

Arturo smiled, started to laugh then checked it.

"What?"

"Nothing. Nice guy. Quiet, worked hard. He had experience too. Knew what he was doing. Came from some other site. Not like the rest. You see them all watching? They think you're here to bust them, 'cause they don't have papers."

"But you do?"

"I do. Been here twenty years. Got kids, a wife."

"A sister."

"Yeah. Jared took her out a few times. She liked him. Said he was different."

"How?" Jim said, squinting into the sun.

Arturo shrugged, still smirking. "Good different. Nice. Treated her well."

"And?"

"And nothing. He skipped town. Most people do. They like the name. Echo Bay—sounds beautiful. Then they see it." He laughed.

Jim laughed too.

"Can I talk to your sister?"

"If you can find her. She took off with some guy."

Jim nodded, thanked him and then walked back toward his car.

"He do something?" Arturo called out.

Jim turned, shook his head.

The Ferrari roared. Roger gripped the side of his seat tightly, his face ashen. He glanced at the man sitting beside him. The dealer. The vulture.

The vulture glanced back, smiling, seemingly oblivious to the speed they were traveling at.

"Once you get her past eighty she really starts to sing," the vulture said, flooring the accelerator.

Roger emitted a strange noise, part squeal, part howl.

"Are you okay?" the vulture said.

"Yes, she's really lovely," Roger replied, his hair blowing into his eyes.

He wondered how the vulture could have deduced that the beast they sat in was female.

"I'll pull over in a second and you can take over."

"No, no. I'm quite alright here, thank you. You know how to handle her better than I do. She might not like the feel of my hand."

Jesus. He sounded like a pervert now.

"Roger, you can't buy her without driving her," the vulture said, as he brought the car to a stop and jumped out.

Roger spent an age ensuring that the mirrors were correctly aligned and his seat in the correct position. When he could delay no longer, he gently pressed the accelerator and the car promptly stalled.

"It's in full auto mode. I didn't even know that it could be stalled in full auto mode," the vulture said, as he looked at Roger with what Roger liked to believe was awe, but conceded might well have been pity.

"She wouldn't be the first girl that's recoiled under my touch."

Again, the pervert.

Twenty minutes later, as they passed through a bustling Main Street, the Ferrari drew many a lingering glance, though that might have been because Roger was driving it so slowly.

He ducked low when he saw Henrietta in the window of the Tearoom.

And then he saw that she wasn't alone.

She was with Richard: real man Richard. They were laughing and she touched his hand as they laughed. He was drinking a cup of something, most probably coffee, most probably black. It wouldn't be tea, not for a real man like him.

It wasn't that he was flirting with Henrietta that particularly bothered Roger. It wasn't the way she touched his hand, or the way she threw her head back and laughed at something he said. It was more the feeling he got when Richard glanced over at him, then turned back to Henrietta, not even offering a wave, a smile, an acknowledgment that he was there. He did that often during the building work—ignored him and went straight to Hen if they needed something. Real man Richard, always looking down on him. It was then that he noticed Eddie, one of Richard's men, standing outside, smoking a cigarette. Eddie looked up. Roger smiled. Eddie also looked away.

Roger felt the anger building in his stomach, boiling over and spilling its way down his legs. He wouldn't be ignored any longer. As he came to pass the Tearoom he floored the accelerator, heard the engine roar, and plowed straight into the back of a duck-egg blue Ford Escape.

"Motherfucking cocksucker. You got this Ferrari and you can't drive for shit," Manny said.

As Roger sighed and offered to pay cash for the damage, to try and keep the fallout to a minimum, he regarded the smartly dressed young man in front of him. From his polished shoes to his rather tight looking fedora, he looked far out of place on Main Street.

"Jesus Christ. It's not enough that you fucked up my car, now you're checking me out too."

"God, no, I'm married," Roger said, as he turned to the Tearoom and, aside from the stares of passersby, noticed that his wife and real man Richard had disappeared. "I just thought that you looked good. A little like a gangster, but in a good way."

Manny could scarcely suppress his smile. "It's not so bad. Maybe we'll have to get the whole car resprayed."

Jim sat on the small deck and watched the sun dip low in a cloudless sky. The temperature didn't drop much at night. He drained the last of his beer then stared into the empty bottle. There was a small drop left inside, painting a clear track on the glass. There always was, no matter how long he left it upturned for.

He tipped it up again, watching as the droplet ran to the top and stopped still. He blew into it, trying to coax it out.

Jess had been waiting for him when he got back to the station. She'd wanted to know where he'd been. He hadn't told her. There was nothing to tell. She was wearing a skirt. He'd noticed the bruising on her thigh. Fucked-up Jess with her fucked-up life.

He thought of Harry. He picked up the case file and opened it again. He took it home every night, ate with it on the table, slept with it on the bed.

It was quiet. He looked around, wanted to see a bird or something, anything.

He tried to escape, but never could. No matter what he was doing, who he was talking to, his mind never strayed far from Harry and Jess. A kid had been taken, in his town. And he couldn't find him. A three-year-old kid, with blond hair and big blue eyes. Three was a tough age. He wasn't a baby who would have been oblivious to what was going on. At three he'd have known. He'd be scared, and worried.

Jim clung to the tip, the sighting at Aurora Springs. It meant something. It helped him get to sleep at night. Harry was still alive. He believed that, he needed to. But time was passing. Weeks had turned into months in the blink of an eye.

He wondered how Jess ever got to sleep. The drink, that's how. And who could blame her? Why shouldn't she drink? She had a better excuse than most. She could drink. She could pop pills, or fuck every man in a 100-mile radius if that made her feel something, or feel nothing. She could do it because there was nothing worse, there could be nothing worse than having your child taken away. It was worse than when kids got sick, poor kids that got struck down with cancer or some other disease that adults couldn't even get a handle on—it was worse because there was someone to blame for Harry, someone other than God.

Someone knew something.

Someone had done it to Jess, to Harry. They'd said "Fuck the consequences, I want him, so I'm taking him. And when you can't find me, when you can't find me so that you can blame me, you can look in the mirror and point the finger at yourself. Because you should know by now that the world is a fucked-up place so you have to always be watching. Because I'm always watching."

But Jim knew there was someone else Jess could blame.

She could blame him.

Because it was his town. He hadn't kept it safe, and now he couldn't bring Harry back. He had failed at the one thing he was supposed to do. And it killed him knowing that.

He looked down at the bottle again, at the drop of beer left in the bottom. And he threw it at the wall and watched it explode into shards and dust.

12

The Formative Years

Jerry stared at the photograph, holding it carefully. He wanted to send it. More than anything he wanted to send it, because he knew it would win. The bird was beautiful—its bill bright red against the night sky. When he looked at it he saw only a shot so rare, so unfeasibly difficult to obtain, that it had to win. His mother saw something else entirely . . . every weekend for seventeen months. That's how long it had taken him to capture it. An eternity when you're sitting in the cold, trying to balance, trying to ignore the chill in your fingers and the rumble in your stomach.

He placed it back into the *NAP* competition envelope, then the envelope back into the file cabinet.

Then he turned back to Lisa. Lisa standing in front of the mountain. He studied the photograph carefully. He wondered what it was like to be Max, to get to be with Lisa, to kiss her. Jerry had never dated before, never kissed a girl, never even held hands with one. His mother said he'd meet the right girl soon enough, one that would love him for who he was, not for what he looked like. He'd need someone like him, "a little slow," she'd said.

He froze when he heard the knock at the door. Mel, the mailman, had already been. They never got visitors. It must have been the nurse again.

"Jerry," Mom whispered, from the kitchen.

"Mom," he whispered back.

"It's the nurse," Mom said.

They didn't answer the door to the nurse. Mom said that she'd want to take her away, put her in a special home where they'd be cruel to her and not let Jerry see her.

"Don't answer," Mom said.

Jess could hear the voices inside. She could see the man through the glass in the door. It was Jerry, from the PhotoMax. He was standing perfectly still. Like a statue.

She knocked again, this time harder.

She took a step back and looked up at the house. It was old, weathered, might have been nice if they threw some money at it. There were few houses like this left in Tall Oaks, houses that had been allowed to fall into disrepair, to embarrass the neighbors. She liked it.

In the past month she had covered serious ground, miles around the perimeter of Tall Oaks, and every street within the town too. She had knocked on hundreds of doors, and shown them all the same picture. The picture of Harry. In it he wore a red shirt with a tractor on the pocket, and blue jeans that made him appear both old and young at the same time. She glanced at it quickly, then away. Lingering would see the panic build, the tears fall, the urge to run overwhelm her. She wondered how she and Michael could have created something so completely pure and perfect, something so utterly pristine and delicate.

She wondered if all parents felt that way about their children, or if it took something so dire to make them realize what they took for granted.

When she showed the photograph, to the elderly couples or the mothers, or the maids or the strange men, she searched their faces. She didn't really know what she was looking for. What she found, more often than not, was suspicion. For a few moments they'd wonder what she wanted. Perhaps it was money—it was usually money—or maybe she had found God. Maybe she had been taken in by a group of determined well-doers who saw an easy scalp to claim, and then been sent back out to spread their prosaic word. But when they realized who she was, they softened. It always took a while: she kept her hair tied back, her face hidden behind large sunglasses. They asked questions, moot questions given the circumstance. They'd invite her in for coffee. On occasion she accepted. And on occasion she answered their questions, she indulged their curiosities. It helped to be doing something productive, something other than just waiting for his return.

And that's how it went, the search that consumed her, the merry-go-round she daren't step off.

She knocked on the door once more, this time hard enough to rattle the glass.

"I can see you," she said.

He didn't move.

She turned and walked away.

Elena saw Jared before he saw her. She found herself smiling. She'd called him about the dent in the car, and he'd told her to bring it in whenever she had the time. She was surprised to find that she had made the time, as much to see him as to get the car fixed. Though on the first date she had been nervous, and had drunk a little too much, and talked about Danny far too much, she'd enjoyed herself. Jared was different from how she had expected him to be, from how Danny used to be. She found it refreshing.

And now, when she saw him glance up and smile back at her, she felt something in her stomach, a flutter maybe, not the full blown jump-my-bones that she'd felt when she'd first met Danny, but it was definitely something. And it was a nice feeling, a feeling that she had denied herself for two long years while she made sure that her children were okay, that the separation hadn't done them too much damage. Thalia seemed okay—she was young—but the jury was still out on Manny. She worried about him. He'd always been a little odd, and was once painfully shy; the kind of boy that stood on the sidelines, watching the others with the kind of detachment more often seen in a teenager. It hadn't bothered her; he was just quiet, finding his way. But Danny, with his Latino male pride and love of sports and everything else that the young boy inside of him clung on to, found it much harder to take. He spent years taking Manny to games, only to glance down and see his son reading a book instead of watching the action unfold, or to play sports that Manny never really committed to.

Those years, the formative years when a kid is still trying to find himself, Danny was all over his son. Not bullying, but not exactly subtle in his desires either. She'd lost count of the number of times she had heard him berate Manny for a dropped catch, or call him a wimp for pulling out of a hospital pass. Manny wanted to please his father; she could see it in him, that need to please Danny. He just didn't really know how to. Before long Danny simply gave up; gave up on taking his son to games and movies and fishing; gave up on asking him what he wanted to be when he grew up, and getting frustrated by the fact that the answer was never one he wanted to hear. It was never fireman or football player. Never anything that Danny deemed masculine enough. Rather it would range from pianist—something Elena had encouraged ever since Manny started at Tall Oaks High and got involved in the music program—to artist, another hobby the school said he showed real promise in, but that fell by the way-side when Danny walked out.

"Elena, good to see you," Jared said.

"You too, Jared."

She leaned forward to kiss him on the cheek.

She noticed his slight flinch as her lips brushed his cheek.

Jared walked round to the rear of the car and crouched down to look at the damage.

"It's not too bad really. It looks worse than it is because of the red paint. I'll get the boys to hammer it out and respray it."

"Manny did it. Said a Ferrari ran into him on Main Street."

"Wow. If you're going to get rear-ended, might as well do it in style."

She laughed.

She noticed how good he looked, how handsome.

She could see a couple across the lot, taking a look at a black pick-up. They were holding hands. The guy said something, the lady laughed.

"Are you in a rush to get it back?"

"No, not really."

"I'll fix you up with a courtesy car in the meantime. Any preference?"

"No," she said, and then thought of Manny as Jared led her to a canary-yellow Fiesta.

"Perfect," she said, smiling.

Jared looked down at the ground, rubbing the back of his neck.

"I could bring the car back myself. Maybe we could go out for something to eat or catch a movie?"

"That would be nice, Jared."

She kissed his cheek again.

She climbed into the car and felt his eyes on her legs. She looked up and smiled.

"Busted," he said.

She laughed.

French John waited for tears that never came. Louise McDermott was a tough one.

"It's okay, I guess."

He tried not to wince. "Okay" was what you said when you tried on a pair of jeans in Gap and the cute sales guy asked you how they fit. You said okay because you both knew they didn't fit like a pair of Dolce and Gabbana Sixteens, which were better than okay . . . which were divine. And his cake was pure Dolce and Gabbana Sixteen, not fucking Gap.

"Why is it just okay, Lou?"

She circled the cake, scratched her head and pouted.

"It's just a bit . . . you know . . ."

He nodded, though he didn't know. He also didn't know how a half-million-dollar education could render her so inarticulate.

"I mean, it's exactly what I asked for. I just expected a bit more."

"A bit more than you asked for?"

Her eyes lit up. "Yes, a bit more than I asked for. Exactly right, French John. Could you maybe do something a bit more with it? We'll pay the extra of course. Daddy said whatever I want."

He thought of offering her a lobotomy, before conceding that no one would notice.

Her phone rang. He watched as she frantically searched through her Birkin.

She fished out a diamond-studded case and flipped it open, then promptly cut the call off.

"Shit. Pressed the wrong button."

Again, with the education, rubbing it in his face.

"Leave it with me. I'll try and add a bit more than you expected," he said. *And a lot more to Daddy's bill,* he thought.

Jess stuck the poster to the streetlight. Harry stared back at her, his smile wide, his hair messy. The sun was beginning to set; lights were beginning to flicker on. She felt weary. Her hands shook as she reached for another poster. She wore her wedding band. It was plain, platinum but understated. She wasn't showy.

The street was wide, flowering trees lined the sidewalk. A town lifted from the pages of a glossy magazine. She'd spent hours walking its streets, knocking on its doors and peering through its windows. She'd seen things she shouldn't have. Snippets of lives far removed from public projection. Sometimes they saw her and jumped up—caught. She bottled their secrets, far too focused on the task at hand to pay them mind. She wondered if everyone was fucked-up in their own way. *Quirks*. That's what Michael liked to call them. People had quirks.

She stuck another poster to another streetlight. She'd cover the whole town soon enough, then she'd start over again. She could feel them watching, the drapes twitching, the whispers deafening.

"You need a hand?"

Jess turned, snapped back into the world.

"Sorry, I didn't mean to startle you," Manny said.

Jess stared at him, then shook her head.

"It'll be quicker if I help. I'll do the other side of the street."

She looked down at the stack, then up at his hat.

"Thalia misses him. She talks about him all the time."

Jess tried to smile.

"Will you say hi to her from me?" she said, quietly.

"Yeah."

Jess turned away as the tears fell. She tried to hold them back, to wipe her cheeks clean, but they fell so fast.

She could hear laughter in the distance, smell barbecue in the air. Life going on.

He put a hand on her shoulder.

They stood there for a long time.

When she calmed, she reached into her bag and passed him a handful of posters.

He took them from her carefully.

They worked in silence for two hours, until moonlight colored the streets blue and the sounds of the town died in the humid night.

They stopped outside an old house and sat on the curb. Both tired.

Manny heard the voice first. He glanced over his shoulder, up at the open window.

Jess followed his eye.

He knew the song well, from church. 'Ave Maria.'

It sounded like a recording. So perfect.

They sat together, listening.

On such a beautiful night Jess couldn't help but feel the smallest sliver of hope deep within her, hope that he might come back. It kept her from giving up.

But as the night grew quiet once again, and as the clouds gently floated in front of stars, she knew it was a hope that rescinded with each passing day.

13

Hitting the Hut

If the duck-egg was bad for business, the canary-yellow Fiesta was a fucking disaster. Had Furat and Abe not been standing either side of him, Manny might well have cried.

"I like it," Furat said.

"You would. It's a fucking girl's car."

"It's not too bad," Abe said, avoiding Manny's eye and smiling at Elena.

Manny turned to him and hissed. "Fucking, Judas." Then he turned to Elena. "Why couldn't you have got black? Or even dark blue? Are you trying to piss me off? Do you want to see me cry? Is that what you want? To see your only son cry? 'Cause I'll fucking do it. Except I'll wait until that squint-eyed fuckface comes to collect you on Friday night, and then I'll cry and hang onto your leg. Might even shit my pants while I'm at it. Then we'll see if he wants to stick around, see if he wants to help raise a fucking adult baby. Stop fucking with me, Ma. You don't know what I'm capable of."

Elena grabbed Manny tightly and kissed his cheek.

"What the fuck are you doing?"

"You look so cute in your suit and hat. How's your head by the way? Have you changed the bandage lately?"

Manny glared at her. "We're going now. I don't know what you're so happy about but I don't like it. You should be in mourning for your son's lost balls. Fucking canary-yellow Fiesta."

"Where are you going? Can you pick up some eggs?" Elena asked.

"No, I can't. We've got business to attend to. We're gonna shake down Pizza Hut."

Elena turned to Furat. "Try not to let him get arrested."

"I'm on it," Furat said.

"Where's your suit, Abe?" Elena asked. "I don't think Pizza Hut will take you seriously in those cut-offs."

Abe frowned, then nodded, his glasses slipping down his nose as he did. He pushed them back up with his index finger.

Manny shot him a look.

"My mother said it's going to be ninety degrees again. My cousin Ebenezer contracted heat stroke a few weeks back, and I've got twenty pounds on him."

"*Ebenezer?* What the fuck is wrong with your family?" Manny said.

"Until the heat dies down a bit she's taken the suit away from me. I have to wear this cap too, keep the rays off my face. I'm wearing factor fifty, but I might need you to help me reapply later on. I can already feel the backs of my legs burning."

Manny stared at him, suitably horrified.

"Well, okay, you kids have fun. Get in the car now. Manny's starting to sweat—it's much too hot for a three-piece."

Elena waved them off and headed back inside.

"It's not fucking sweat, it's hair lacquer. I'm trying to get some waves going. Like Pesci in *Goodfellas*. I can't believe I have to explain this shit over and over."

When Jess saw Jim at the door she started to feel her legs buckle, and the bile rise up in her throat.

He held his hands up.

"I haven't heard anything. I just wanted to check in on you."

She exhaled heavily, the relief washing over her like an ice bath. But she still felt the tingle in her fingers, a reminder of what he might have said . . . that they had found a body. Always a body, never a name, even when they knew who it was. It would be too hard to say they had found Harry. That made it too painful even for the cops to deal with. They needed some kind of separation, otherwise how would they go home, eat with their kids and tuck them in, fuck their wives and fall asleep? How would they do that if they had found Harry and he was dead? "A body" was better. A body reminded them that we're all just a collection of blood and bones.

"Come in."

The entrance hall was grand. She led him past a sweeping staircase, through the galleried kitchen, and out into the sunshine. The backyard was vast, the terrace raised so they could see for miles. There'd once been a swing hanging from the largest of the Atlas cedars that dotted their land. She wondered what'd happened to it.

She could see the gardener striping the grass with a ride-on mower, so far away she could barely make out the whine of the engine. She struggled to remember the gardener's name. He used to let Harry ride with him sometimes.

She glanced at Jim. He stood awkwardly, staring at the trees, at the flowers and the pool.

She left him alone as she went back into the kitchen to fetch them some drinks.

When she returned she found him sitting on a cushioned chair, one of ten, and watching a cat creep across the grass, stalking a bird it had little chance of catching.

"Hot one today," he said, taking a beer from her.

"It always is."

"Nice place."

She shrugged.

Jess drained half her beer in one, long sip. Water compared to vodka.

"You going to see that shrink again?"

"No."

"Your mother wants you to."

"Talking to my mother about me?"

"She's worried."

"She always is. It's in her nature."

He sipped his beer.

She looked down at her leg, saw it bouncing up and down. She didn't try and fight the movement anymore, it always won, so she just let it ride over her, shaking her muscles and tightening her neck, exhausting her already weary body.

"You ever buy a Ford?"

She looked up at him, shook her head. "Why?"

"You ever go to the Ford dealership, maybe to get the car serviced?"

"No."

"Did Michael?"

"Michael drives a Range Rover," she said, certain he knew that already. "Why?"

"Just checking something out, probably nothing."

She inched toward him, sitting on the edge of her chair.

"Did you find something?" she said, wondering what it could be.

"No, nothing. Forget about it."

They sat in silence for a long while, the sun beating down on them.

He lit a cigarette. She bummed one.

She looked at Jim and thought about Michael. The two were cut from the same perfect mold. All flawless skin and long eyelashes, smiles that made women push their tits out and suck their stomachs in. Michael wore his gift like a second skin, well aware of his effect on the opposite sex and never afraid to use it. Jim tried to dress it down. He kept his hair close-cropped, his face unshaven. Like he didn't want people to think he gave the slightest shit about his appearance.

"Why'd you become a cop? I know you went to Harvard, studied law. Was it because of your father?"

"Yeah."

"That simple?"

"I guess so. I still look at the job like it's noble or something. People used to look up to him. He deserved that—he was a good man. People came to our house and talked over their problems with him, even if it was nothing to do with the law. And he always listened. They left feeling better, because they had someone to go to when things got tough and they needed help. That's why I studied law. I wanted to be one of those do-gooder lawyers, standing up for the people and all that bullshit. A pillar of the community, like my old man."

She crossed her legs, smoothed the hair from her eye. "So what changed?"

"There were too many other people with the same ideals. That cheapened it for me. Sounds stupid I know. But I wanted to really make a difference, change someone's life for the better or something. But then I met a hundred other people like me and saw the way they changed. By the end of the course ninety-nine of them went on to big-city law firms to collect their fat salaries and work twenty hours a day."

"What happened to the other one?"

Jim laughed. "He dropped out."

"So you came home again, took over from your father?"

"Not straight away. I joined the Boston PD for a couple of years, worked some of the nastiest cases you could imagine, shit that still haunts me now. I wasn't cut out for it though. I grew up around here and Boston started to kill me. The parts I liked about myself, they were getting lost. The last case I worked was a double murder, two ten-year-old girls. We got the guy, the stepfather of one of them, had him all wrapped up and ready to send to Cedar Junction. We got to court and I saw one of the guys I used to room with at college—he's not arguing, but he's sitting at the defense table making up the numbers."

"So what happened?"

"They walked him: got some of the evidence thrown out on a technicality, and the judge ordered the jury to find him not guilty. The stepfather smiled at me as he walked out—a real shit-eating grin that I can still see now, clear as you are in front of me."

"So you packed up and left?"

"Something like that," he said, watching the smoke from his cigarette swirl up toward the sky.

"And you thought you were done with all the tough cases. Then Harry."

She felt strange saying his name. Like the collection of letters no longer fit together.

"Everything felt different when I got back. My father was old, my mother too. The neighbors, people that I had grown up knowing, were dying off, making way for the children. They weren't bad kids, not around here, but values changed, lies came easier. My father's generation wore their honesty like a badge, like it was something to be proud of."

"Maybe it was you that changed."

"Maybe it was. I couldn't see it anymore."

"What?"

"The good. The thing you need to see, especially in my line of work. I think of those lawyers. They'll do what it takes to get a murderer off because if they do then they get a bonus, or a promotion, or a pat on the back from a partner. What's noble about that? What's to be proud of?"

"They do what they're told. That's what most people do."

"No questions asked. Just close your eyes to the outside world."

"Yeah."

"What a mess. What a big fucking mess."

"Well, I'm glad you came round to cheer me up."

He laughed then.

It was the first time that she had heard him really laugh. And it was a nice laugh, the kind of laugh that made her want to laugh too, and she very nearly did. And then she thought of Harry. She rubbed her eyes. She felt her arms beginning to burn, the sun too fierce above.

"You okay?" Jim said.

She nodded.

"We'll find him, Jess. We will."

"Go get a slice, doll, and don't worry about the tab. By the time we're done we'll own a piece of this place."

Furat ignored Manny and sat on the wooden bench by the door, watching the parking lot and wondering what she was going to wear to prom. She shouldn't even be going really, seeing as she was a full year younger than the seniors and wasn't due to start at Tall Oaks High School until the new semester began. But Manny said that it would be fine, and besides, she wanted to go, and wanted to go with him. After all, one thing was certain, they'd have fun.

She watched a family walk in, smiling at the little girls holding hands. She thought of her sister. She wasn't allowed to call her or even write to her. With only two years separating them, they were close. Her sister was smart, smarter than her. She was going to be a veterinarian. Now she was going to be a mother.

She turned as a harried-looking man came out from the kitchen and ushered Manny and Abe to an empty table in the corner of the room.

Manny looked at the guy in front of him. His name tag said STAN and that he was the general manager of the Tall Oaks Pizza Hut. He looked tired, as if the constant noise of the kids' parties, and the groups of teenagers that shared a small pizza and a small Coke just to have somewhere to hang out, were starting to wear him down. Tired, but wired too. Maybe too much coffee—he was jumpy and twitchy.

"Stan. I'm M. This is my associate, Skinny."

Stan looked at Abe. "I know your father. We used to play Pontoon down at the club. How the hell is old Mort? Still a card?"

Manny saw Abe tense up as he looked around the Hut nervously. He knew Abe was fighting the urge to get up and bolt out the door. He'd been nervous as soon as they entered the parking lot. He could see the sweat beginning to run down Abe's head, heard Abe's stomach churn.

Manny watched a young girl come out of the kitchen door carrying a Meat Feast with rubbery cheese spilling out of the crust. Then he turned back to Abe and watched him lay his head on the wooden table. He knew what was coming.

Abe vomited.

It was a silent vomit—no coughing, no retching, just the appearance of a thick layer of it on Stan's newly polished table.

Stan groaned.

"Jesus, are you okay? If it's some kind of bug I'll have to ask you to leave the premises. I can't have a hygiene scare in here. We barely turn a profit as it is. Head Office is all over me."

Abe turned to Manny, his head dipped in shame. "I'll wait in the car."

Manny shook his head and followed Stan to another table.

Fucking chicken shit Abe.

"Must have had a heavy night. I told him to lay off the 'Buca," Manny said.

"So what can I do for you, M? Nice hat by the way. Is that a bandage underneath?"

Manny nodded yes, a fucking bandage. "I'm here to offer you my services. A lot of shit has been going down around here lately. Graffiti, trash cans being turned over, cars being scratched. Real bad for business."

"We haven't noticed anything," Stan said, eyeing the parking lot nervously.

Manny frowned, realizing he had forgotten to tip the trash cans over the previous night. Thalia had asked him to help her build a fort. He'd gotten too involved, ending up collecting wood from Furat's yard. He'd used his father's nail gun, then spent the best part of an hour trying to manipulate it into fitting onto his gun belt.

"Well, you heard about that camera that got stolen from PhotoMax? The Hasselblad? Expensive shit."

Stan leaned forward. "I tell you what. I have noticed some kids smoking the odd reefer down at the end of the parking lot."

Manny tried to suppress a smile.

"And you want that shit to stop, right, Stan? Imagine some poor little kid arrives for her birthday party and some fucking dirty pothead offers her a toke. The next thing you know, you got a fucking screaming parent saying you got her eight-year-old daughter high, calling the fucking cops. Probably end up on the local news. *Pizza Hut manager gets eight-year-old girl high.*"

Stan rubbed his temples. "If Head Office visit and there's a pothead in the parking lot they'll be even further up my ass."

Manny nodded, solemnly. "They'll crawl up inside your asshole and pitch a fucking tent. Probably send out for pizza from in there too, and then they'll taste the shit that you serve, all that fucking salt to keep the kids paying for drinks, and they'll know this place needs a new manager, someone that has the foresight to keep the junkies away."

"So you can do that?"

"I can. I know people. Once the potheads find out M is running this shit-hole they'll back the fuck off."

"How much will this cost us?"

Manny reached into his pocket and pulled out a piece of paper, then slid it across the table.

Stan glanced at it.

"I can't authorize any expenditure over fifty dollars. You'll have to speak with Andre Shelton. He's the area manager, covers six Huts. Real hot stuff too. Drives a Mitsubishi with HUT1 vanity plates."

"Nice . . . committed."

"Company pay for the fuel too, and not in Hut vouchers like they did my last bonus. Cold hard cash . . . by way of bank transfer of course."

"Of course. And how do I reach Andre Shelton?"

"You'll have to put the proposal in writing, make it formal. Have you got a company? It should be on headed paper. Maybe copy in Head Office. Have you got access to a fax machine? Are you registered for sales tax?"

"Shit, Stan. I can't make it all legit. I'm offering a back-street service here. I only deal in cash."

Stan shook his head. "I'm sorry, M. I'll have to decline your services; I'll take my chances with the potheads."

"You sure about that, Stan?"

"I'm afraid so."

Manny stood, looking Stan in the eye. "That your Pinto outside?"

Stan nodded.

"I heard about those cars. The gas tank can rupture easily. Used to call it the *rolling bomb*. Take care, Stan."

Stan watched him leave, and, when he was certain that the canary-yellow Fiesta had left the parking lot, he telephoned the police.

14

Skanks and Skunks

"We agree that Michael's hiding something," Jim said.

"Yeah," Adam said.

Adam had joined the Tall Oaks Police Department straight from high school and had started out working the front desk before slowly climbing the, admittedly short, ladder. He was now a fully fledged police officer, and a competent one too. His quiet demeanor sat well with Jim, who had grown to like him over their five years working together.

"And we agree that he's an asshole."

"Yeah," Adam said. "But he's got an alibi."

"Doesn't mean he didn't do something. Might not have done it himself, but he could have planned something. And that sighting . . . Aurora Springs. He used to take Cindy Collins there."

Jim stood and walked to the window, opened the blind and peered out. He could see part of Main Street, the American flag waving in the summer breeze, and a line of cars parked at an angle facing the stores. The sidewalks were spotless, the roads newly painted. There was a new store just opened up, sold organic

produce. It was popular already. He could see a short line forming outside. He'd stopped by, said hello to the owner, a wire-thin
lady with waist-length hair and a dream catcher hanging from
each ear.

"Why?" Adam said.

"Why do something to his own kid?"

"Yeah. I mean, the kid already lives with the mother, he
doesn't make much effort to see him, he doesn't seem bothered enough."

"Money." Jim said, without conviction.

"Kidnap his own kid?"

Jim shrugged.

"There's been no ransom call."

"Maybe it went wrong."

"How?"

"Maybe he took Harry, wanted to keep him holed up in Aurora
Springs until Jessica's family paid up. Maybe Cindy Collins was in
on it. Maybe she got cold feet and made the call to us."

"Lot of maybes. And we didn't find anything. Not a trace.
And Michael had an alibi for that night too."

"His alibi was Cindy."

"We talked to her and got nowhere."

"Yeah, got nowhere because she brought along Michael's
cocksucker lawyer."

Jim sighed, opened the window.

"I just don't see Michael Monroe for this. He's too . . . smart.
I mean the guy's a dick, don't get me wrong, and it's not that he
doesn't deserve it, all this shit. The press . . . all those ladies . . .

they've savaged the guy. But I just don't see it. And the Clown mask, it's fucked up."

"So what do you think?"

Adam swallowed, then looked down at the file.

"Adam?"

"Someone planned it: watched the kid, knew the house, knew they didn't lock the back door."

"No one locks their doors in Tall Oaks."

"They do now."

"Yeah, they do now."

"Why the mask?" Jim said, running his hand along the window edge, sweeping the fallen leaves from it and watching them float to the ground.

"Nut job. Gets off on scaring kids, the mothers too. Luke Conway, 1996. Killed four kids before they caught him. Used to paint his face yellow with a big fucking smiley face. I still get the creeps when I read about that guy."

"Yeah, but there's nothing anywhere else about a clown mask. We searched."

"Maybe Harry's the first."

Jim rubbed his eyes. The case was taking its toll—the guesswork, the fact they were sitting in his office talking about Harry as if he weren't real, as if he were nothing more than a problem that needed solving. Jim picked up the photograph, one of the thirty or so that Jess kept dropping by. She thought they'd forget about Harry—that they needed constant reminding. That might have been the case in the city, where serious crimes rained down relentlessly. But not in Tall Oaks.

"If Harry's the first . . ."

"I know," Adam said.

"Shit." Jim said, crushing his paper cup and throwing it into the trash can. "Okay. So this guy, the Clown, he grabs the kid, then what? Jess called us, we got the roadblocks set up quickly."

"Not quick enough. Could've been long gone by then."

"Let's say he didn't have a car. No one heard anything."

Adam shrugged. "You saying someone would've heard a car engine over the storm?"

"Let's just suppose. He's got the kid. Then what?"

"My best guess would be that he headed for the Black Lake."

Jim nodded. "Mine too. But we searched."

"Fifty thousand acres."

"The dogs didn't pick up a scent."

"You're assuming Harry's still there," Adam said.

"So he's not?"

"You know the woods. There's a million ways out. He could've left a car parked on the other side, on the East Ridge maybe. And from there he could've headed west."

"To Aurora Springs."

Adam shrugged.

"Guesswork," Jim said.

Adam nodded.

Jim turned back to the window. The organic store had opened up and he could see people through the window, sifting through dates, and chard, and handmade pies, scratching their heads as they tried to work out what the fuck was in the aloe cocktails that cost ten bucks a bottle.

"We could try and bring Michael in again, see if he'll talk to us?" Adam said.

"He won't."

"You could speak with Judge Abraham. See if he'll give us a warrant."

"On what grounds?"

"He likes you. Wants you to take his daughter out."

Jim laughed.

"Throw her a pity date, for the greater good. I know she's big, but you don't have to take her out to eat, just to the movies or something."

Jim glanced at the photo again and stopped laughing. He kept the photographs everywhere: in his office, in the hallways, in his car, in his apartment. Harry's was the last face he saw at night, the first in the morning. He had one of Harry and Jess together—they were on vacation somewhere. Harry was younger, his hair shorter and his skin lighter. He tanned easy, that's what Jess said. He only had to look at the sun and he started to brown. He liked dolphins; she'd wanted to take him to swim with them. Jim liked it when she talked about Harry, it was the only time she forgot to frown, to hunch her shoulders and drum her fingers. When she spoke about Harry she changed. She got lost in him, in the things he said, the things he did. She'd shown him a card Harry had made her once, when she was feeling low. It was a mess of color, some glitter glue stopped it from opening. She carried it in her bag.

"Anything on that camera, the Hasselblad?" Jim said.

"No. Fucking Max is a ball-buster. He forgets to set the alarm and now he's got shit with the insurance company. He calls every day. He did even at the start, when Harry had just been taken. What sort of guy does that? I mean, I get that it's an expensive camera, but once he'd reported it to us and the insurance, there was nothing else to be done."

"Did he come in?"

"Yesterday."

"Did he get in your face?"

Adam waved him off. "He forgets I'm the one with the gun."

Jim laughed. "Send him to me next time."

"You think you can take him, boss?" Adam said, laughing.

Jim thought of Max and smiled. Max with his tight T-shirts and bulging muscles. It was all for show, Jim could see it when he looked into Max's eyes. He wasn't tough, not underneath it all. Jim was, though not many people knew it. He looked too pretty to risk getting messed up. He liked to fight though, enjoyed the simplicity of it. It felt natural, like he was built to do it. It set him apart from other, softer men. He didn't even know it until he got into his first fight in high school. The other kid, much bigger than Jim, had misread the smile on his face, thought he was trying to make friends, to get him to go easy on him. But Jim was smiling because he was jacked, seeing all his classmates form a ring around them, cheering and hollering when Jim knocked the big kid flat onto his back and climbed on top of him like a lion at the neck of a gazelle. They soon stopped cheering though. They soon stopped hollering, instead settling into an uneasy silence as Jim beat the big kid long after the fight was over. Beat him so bad the girls turned their backs and hurried back to class.

Adam drank the last of his coffee and stood.

"I saw more of the posters up. There's one right outside my place now."

Jim nodded.

"You got to admire her. The way she keeps looking, must be exhausting."

"She calls the local newspapers and the TV station every day."

"It's something," Adam said.

"Yeah. It's something."

Henrietta was sick. She was stomach-heaving, couldn't get out of bed or be more than five feet from the nearest toilet sick, though she forced herself to get up when she heard Roger slip out the door. She didn't know where he went, and she didn't much care. She sometimes heard him creeping out in the dead of night, wearing his running shorts and headband. His father had died young of a heart attack. She knew it played on his mind.

It had been a struggle to climb the stairs, but it was worth it, as she felt slightly better now.

She held him tightly, rocking him back and forth in the chair. She smoothed his hair down. It felt soft, wispy. He stared up at her, through her.

He wore expensive clothes, all chosen by her. She shunned designer names, instead opting for only the finest of materials— cashmere, merino wool. As long as it was soft, she thought he'd like it.

He felt cold. She reached for his blanket. She'd knitted it herself in preparation.

She closed her eyes, leaned back and tried to quell the nausea.

The blanket was an odd shape, not at all similar to the pattern. She wasn't good at knitting. She'd never been very good at anything really. She worked incredibly hard at everything she did, despite what Roger thought, though had never achieved anything of significance. She'd found school challenging, managing only to eke mediocre grades. Of course, she had gone on to study at Cambridge, but that had more to do with who her father was than anything she could bring to the table. She'd studied theology, the most arbitrary of choices. Though her mother was as deeply pious as any you were likely to meet, she found that she herself had little time for God. She imagined he'd have even less time for her after what she had done.

After Thomas had died, barely six hours into his life, Henrietta had turned her hand to many a failed project. There was the failed catering business, the failed party-planning business, the short-lived career as a writer of trashy romance novels, novels that turned out to be more trash than trashy. She always gave them her all, working her fingers to the bone until finally, when she was sick of swimming against the tide, she folded them and added another small notch to her post of failures. Dr. Stone said she was trying to compensate for her perceived failure at motherhood. She wasn't sure about that, just that each notch took a little something out of her. Something that had never been put back.

She heard the car pull into the drive. The ghastly red car that Roger had bought.

She leaned down, closing her eyes and kissing his head. She carried him gently to his bed, set him down and covered him.

"You smell funny," Jerry said, wrinkling his nose as Max staggered past him and collapsed onto the leather sofa meant for the customers.

Max brought his shirt up to his nose and sniffed it.

"It's probably the booze. I drank a shitload of Tequila. It really messes me up. And then I went back to some skank's house. She had this cheap, nasty perfume on. You know, the kind you find in a drugstore marked down to five bucks. Some of it must've rubbed off on me."

Max sprawled out, his arms above his head.

"Why are they called skanks? Because of skunks? They do smell bad, skunks. Dad ran over one once and I got out to check it. My mother wouldn't let me in the house when we got home that night. I had to stand in the backyard while Dad hosed me down."

Max laughed. "Yeah, a skank is a little like a skunk, 'cept a skank is a lady. Nah, not a lady, a woman. A woman of loose morals."

Jerry thought of Lisa. He wondered if Max ever did.

"Get me some water."

Jerry walked out to the small kitchen and poured Max a glass of water, then came back and set it down on the table beside him.

"You all set for Saturday night? We're meeting at my place at seven and then got a limo to take us to that strip club in

Crandall. You might have to jump in a cab though. I can't have you taking up two seats. There's about fifteen of us to squeeze in. You know the strippers work overtime if you got a few extra bucks for them? Might finally get you laid."

Max took a sip of water, then lay back down.

"I don't think I should go to your party, Max. My mother won't like me staying out late."

"You're thirty-five years old."

"I don't have anything to wear."

"I'm printing T-shirts for all the boys so don't even worry about it. Have we got any Advil back there?"

Jerry already had it in his hand, running his fingers over the small bumps on the side of the box.

He handed the box to Max.

Max swallowed the pills and rubbed his eyes. "My fucking head."

"Do you want me to close the blind?"

Max nodded.

Jerry closed the blind, then carefully climbed back onto the stools.

"I spoke to that cop about the Hasselblad again," Max said.

"Oh?"

"Still nothing. And I found out the insurance ain't gonna pay out."

Jerry swallowed.

"I'm taking the money from your paycheck."

Jerry looked down at his hands. They were big, the knuckles hidden beneath a wall of fat. He hated his hands.

"The insurance guy said the alarm wasn't armed. You close up every night."

Jerry could feel the heat in his cheeks, the sweat on his collar. "That's ten thousand dollars."

"Eleven."

"I can't afford that, Max. My mother . . . her medication."

"She's got insurance."

"It doesn't cover it all."

Max shrugged, his eyes still closed. "I'll take half your pay-check until it's cleared. I'm trying to run a business here, Jerry. Not a charity."

Jerry could feel the tears blurring his eyes. He wiped them away.

Max glanced out the door. He sat up quickly when he saw Lisa walk out of the pharmacy across the street.

"Fuck. That's all I need."

He stood up, still rubbing his eyes. "I'm heading out the back way. Just tell her I haven't turned up. Say I called in sick or something."

Max breezed past him.

He heard the back door close just as the bell chimed.

Lisa smiled as she walked over to the counter.

"Hey, Jerry."

He tried to smile back.

"What's the matter?"

He kept his eyes fixed on the counter, afraid that he might cry.

Lisa walked over and gave him a hug.

Her hair fell onto his face. It smelled nice, like strawberries.

"Is it your mother?"

He nodded, didn't know what else to do. In part it was true. He was finding it difficult, her difficult. He loved her, more than anything else in the world, but he needed some help. He worried about her all day, sometimes closing the store for a half hour when she didn't answer the phone and running the quarter mile back to his house. And he wasn't good at running: his body jiggled too much, his chest hurt and he felt dizzy. So he couldn't do that every day. If something bad happened, he wouldn't be able to get there in time.

"Does the medication help?"

"A little."

She took steroids, lots of them. They were supposed to ease the pressure on her brain, slow the swelling down and reduce the pain. Sometimes they seemed to help, other times they did nothing at all. She screamed. Some nights she screamed for hours on end. He'd try to calm her, to stroke her hair and rub her feet, but it was like she couldn't see him. So he'd get back into his bed, and he'd bury his head beneath the pillow, and he'd cry. And he felt so bad when he cried, so utterly useless, that he'd wish the tumor was in his brain instead.

Lisa held his chubby hand in hers. She stroked the back of it. It was a gesture, a gesture that made him realize how stupid he was to think that she could ever like him back. Her hand looked so small in his.

He took his hand away. She smiled, then stepped back.

"If you need to talk to someone, I'm here."

He nodded.

She settled on to the stool.

"Is Max here? I said I'd meet him for lunch."

"He's sick."

"Oh. He sounded fine yesterday. Is it bad?"

"No. I mean, I don't know."

"Hangover?"

"I'm not . . ."

"You don't have to cover for him, Jerry. I'm well aware of what he's like. I'm just hoping he'll settle down once we get married."

Jerry nodded.

"Have you thought any more about the competition?"

"A little."

"And?"

"I don't think I'm going to do it. I mean, there's all the forms," he said.

He wasn't good at spelling. His handwriting was awful. He'd struggled since junior high. He'd asked his mother for help, but she'd just baked him blueberry muffins.

"I'll print them out, fill them in. All you have to do is sign your name. Oh, and take the winning shot."

He shook his head, started to protest but she cut him off.

"I'll print them anyway, even if you don't use them."

Furat liked watching her mother make *bamia*. She had done since she was a little girl. She'd sit on the counter while her mother talked her through each step. She'd never remember them though.

Her mother chopped the beef, from Berlinsky's, into chunks and then placed it into a large pan with some onions and garlic, then seasoned with her own mix of spices before covering it in water.

"What's in the spices?" asked Furat.

"I've told you a hundred times."

"Can't you just write it down?"

"No. You have to commit to memory, just like I did. Your grandmother used to test me."

Furat laughed, then reached forward and pressed the button for the extractor fan.

Her mother turned to her and smiled. "I'm sorry. We don't want your clothes smelling, do we?"

Though Furat smiled, it was a smile tinged with guilt. The same guilt that she'd felt when she was younger and she used to lie about where she was from. She'd always come up with somewhere less controversial. Somewhere that didn't invoke such hostility in people—hostility and suspicion, especially in Americans. Though she had no accent, no hijab and certainly no loyalty to her place of birth, she couldn't help but feel that people judged her when they knew where she was from. And that sullied her, made her feel unworthy or something. Not dirty, just not clean either, like she were somehow inferior, someone to be polite to but not invite round for dinner. After all, what would they cook for her? Would it need to be Halal? Then there were the boys. She was pretty enough, she knew that, but found that often the boys in her class would deem her off-limits. Perhaps destined for an arranged marriage in some faraway makeshift mosque, trying to keep her simple peasant dress free from the sand that whipped about while her fifteen uncles, all wearing scarves pulled up over their mouths, looked on, machine guns in hand. She wouldn't mind if they just asked her, asked her what she believed in and whether she was just a regular kid like them, or bound to live a life governed by some old book that she had never even picked up. But they never did. It was far easier just to ignore her, not get too close; there were plenty of other pretty girls in class after all; girls that definitely ate normal food and had normal parents.

In part that was why she liked Manny so much. He had taken the stereotypes, the ones that she thought about herself and her family, and rammed them down her throat with such severity that to think them anything other than ridiculous was completely ridiculous.

"So you've chosen your dress now? Was it the red or the silver?" her mother asked, as she stirred in two tins of chopped tomatoes.

"The silver. With the sparkly shoes."

"And Manny, will he be dressing as Al Capone?"

Furat laughed. "No. Regular dinner suit."

"I imagine he'll look quite handsome, if his head heals in time."

"It should do. I've banned him from wearing his fedora from now until prom."

"Will he be going off to college after summer? You'll miss him. It's nice to have a friend right next door."

Furat watched her drop a large handful of okra into the pan and stir, placing the lid on it.

"He's not. I don't think they can afford it, not this year. His father took off. I think he covers the bills but he emptied their savings account when he left. Manny said that his mother calls and writes his father all the time but he never replies."

"It must be difficult for them."

"Manny says that he doesn't want to go to college anyway. I think he worries about leaving his mother and Thalia."

"He's a good boy. Terrible mouth on him though. I had the window open when he was building that fort; I looked out and saw him fire a nail through his shirt."

"Maybe we could invite the family round for dinner one night?"

Her mother smiled and kissed her head. "Ask them. It will be nice to make some new friends. And it will be a good chance for your father to get to know his daughter's suitor."

"I think it's best we tell Dad that he's just a friend."

"Your father's not that bad."

"Tell that to Noora."

"I do."

"You speak to her?"

Her mother smiled. "Of course. She's my daughter too."

"But Dad said . . ."

"Your father can be stubborn. He loves you though, both of you. You have to remember that we were raised very differently from you; it's hard, adjusting to life here. I know we've lived here all your life but we had a very different life back in Iraq. We followed rules; rules that were instilled for generations."

"Yeah, but things are different here. That's why you came to America, to escape."

"In part that's true. But I still miss Iraq—it's still home. For your father too."

Furat turned the gas down when the lid started to rattle. "So what will happen?"

"You leave your father to me. He misses her too—he just doesn't show it as much."

Furat grinned. "I can't believe you speak to Noora. I thought you were scared of Dad."

Her mother smiled. "I have to. She's carrying my grandson after all."

"It's going to be a boy?" Furat asked, excitedly.

Her mother nodded, holding out her arms.

Furat stepped into them, hugging her tightly, and smiling.

"Hung-Fu. What's up?" Manny said, walking into the pharmacy.

"Oh, no. Are you here for your money?" Hung said.

Manny laughed, then doffed his hat to Lisa.

"So, you've heard then?"

Lisa frowned. "Stan was really shaken. He came in here trying to buy Xanax."

"Yeah, well, you don't need to worry. I've already decided to give you a break, because you look after me."

"Thank God for that," Hung said, his smile barely in check. He'd known the family since they'd first moved to Tall Oaks.

"How is it?" Lisa said, glancing up at Manny's head.

"A little better."

"You should really stop wearing the hat, Manny. At least until it heals."

"I appreciate the concern, but this three-piece needs the hat to make it work."

"Otherwise you'd just look stupid?"

"Exactly."

"Oh."

"Hey, Luli," Manny said to Hung's wife.

"Hello," Luli said.

"How are the English lessons going?"

"Good."

"What are you doing? Counting and alphabet shit?"

"No," she laughed. "I learned about irony last night."

"When you saw Hung take his pants off?"

Hung laughed.

Lisa reached for the pack of bandages and handed it to Manny.

Manny took his wallet out but Hung waved him away.

"We can't have the other businesses seeing you pay. Imagine what that will do to your image."

"Good thinking," Manny said. Then he winked at Luli and strolled back out into the sunshine.

"Is there something wrong with him?" Luli asked.

15

At Home in the Dark

Jim looked up from his desk as Adam appeared in the doorway.

"Got a second, boss?"

"Sure."

Adam pulled out a chair and sat down opposite him.

"I got a complaint from the manager of Pizza Hut—a bit of a strange one. He said a kid called M was trying to shake him down for a few bucks, like protection money or something. He got the plates. I found out the kid's name is Manny Romero."

Jim sighed. "Call the manager back. Tell him we're on it. Leave the report on my desk, I know the kid's mother. She's had a tough time. I'll handle it."

Adam went to stand, and then sat back down again.

"Anything on Jared Martin?"

Jim reached for his pen and picked it up. "Not much."

"You don't think he's our guy?"

"Not really. It's strange though."

"What?"

"He shows up in Tall Oaks about five months ago. He gets a job selling cars, doesn't do it long and then quits."

"So he's left town?"

"Not yet, working his notice period, wants the reference. Got a couple of weeks left I think. He worked construction before, same deal. Six months maybe."

"Maybe he likes to travel."

"Maybe."

"Have you seen Jess lately?"

"Yeah."

"Is she okay?"

"What's up, Adam?"

"My uncle lives in Despair. I saw him the other night for the first time in a while, and he said Jess was in that shitty bar, The Squirrel. You know the one?"

"Yeah."

"He said Jess was drinking with a guy named Billy Brooks. He owns a sawmill next to the Sierra. So she was drinking and then some of Billy's friends come over and they're all buying her shots of vodka and getting her real oiled-up, you know. About a quarter to midnight, the owner, a guy named Guns if you can believe that, says he's closing up, which is strange since he never closes the place, just waits for the last drinker to pass out cold and then dumps them out front and locks the door. Could be three in the morning before that happens. So he kicks my uncle and a few of the others out, but when he locks the door Jess is still in there, with Billy and his friends. Now, I'm not saying anything bad happened, but my uncle said Billy is a real piece of shit with a nasty temper. So maybe you should tell Jess to steer clear of that place for a while, keep some better company."

Jim nodded as Adam stood and left his office.

He remembered the fresh bruising on her face, the swelling on her lip. He felt the familiar anger start to build. The anger that had been his friend during high school, when he got into scraps with the older kids, but had soon turned out to be his worst enemy when he got into the real world. It saw him follow the stepfather home one night, the stepfather with his shit-eating grin and his team of soulless lawyers—the real reason he'd left Boston and come back home where he was safe from himself. He didn't regret what he'd done to the guy, some people had it coming to them. He could control it now, but in that instant when his mind ran to Jess—Jess with a bulls-eye on her chest that told drunken assholes like Billy Brooks that she was vulnerable and wouldn't put up much of a fight—he felt the anger start to warm his blood and pump around his body, gradually getting hotter and hotter until he was walking to his car with one aim in his mind. And then he was driving out of Tall Oaks, and joining the East Ridge Road toward Despair.

"Are you sure you're going to be okay? I can always call Hen and tell her I can't make it."

Jess hated these conversations, where her mother implored her for reassurance. Reassurance that she'd be okay. She'd done it her whole life: whether it was reassurance that Jess wouldn't fuck up at school anymore, or reassurance that Harry was eating his vegetables, she'd always needed it. Jess wondered if it would absolve Alison of guilt if she came home one evening and found her slumped over the table with an empty bottle of Vicodin by her head. If she'd say to the doctors, "She told me to go. She said she was okay."

Maybe it would. But getting the words to come out of her mouth was a struggle.

"You go, Alison. Tell Aunt Hen sorry I couldn't make it."

She said it, even managed a smile. She wanted to tell her to get in the fucking car and leave now, so that she could breathe again, so that she didn't have to act. Alison watched her—all day, all night. She watched what she ate, when she used the bathroom, how long she stayed in bed for. Always watching, always worrying.

"Why don't you come, Jess? I hate leaving you here by yourself."

Jess felt the tingle in her fingers. She needed to run, or drink, or meet a guy—needed to do it now. She just needed to see Alison leave first, so that she wouldn't come back and she wouldn't worry. She could do that.

"You go, have a night off. Get out of here. I'm going to go for a run."

She knew that Alison liked it when she ran—it was a healthy pastime, like chess or reading. Not like drinking, or fucking strangers.

"You call me if you need anything."

Alison gripped her face in her hands and tried to meet her eye, but Jess was determined to look past her.

"Doesn't matter what time, call me and I'll come home. I won't be far away."

She knew every word that was about to come out of her mother's mouth. Every single one of them. The practiced routine. She was starting to bounce on her feet now, her heart racing, her body begging for some kind of release. She clenched her teeth, tried to smile again but it nearly broke her.

Alison got in the car just as the first tear rolled down Jess's cheek.

Jim watched the bar from the parking lot. He'd seen Billy Brooks arrive an hour earlier. He drove a pick-up with Brooks Sawmill scrawled across the hood.

He was exactly as Jim had pictured—hard face, broad shoulders, and barrel chest. The kind of man that had so many scars on his hands he didn't even notice when he got a new one. He looked tough, but that was okay. Jim wasn't looking to prove himself against the guy. He just wanted to hurt him.

He reached into the glove compartment and took out a stack of photos. He flipped through them until he came to the one of Jess and Harry.

He held it up to the moonlight. She looked so happy, a hand on his shoulder, her smile wide. He wondered what would happen to her if Harry was dead. She wouldn't smile again, he knew that much.

Jim glanced up as another pick-up pulled into the lot. He sank low in his seat.

He watched them get out—a couple of guys who looked a lot like Billy. As they opened the door to the bar he heard music spill from inside. The door closed behind them.

He turned back to the photograph.

"He would have been twenty-five today," Henrietta said.

"I know." Alison sipped her wine. "Does Roger ever speak of him?"

Henrietta shook her head, staring across the yard as the sprinklers rose from the ground and began to hiss. "No. He did, of course, back then. But he's moved on now . . . it's been so long."

"I went to visit his grave a while back. It's nice, him being buried beside Dad," Alison said.

"Roger wanted him to be buried in England. But I knew we'd come back here. Tall Oaks is home."

Alison stood and topped up her drink. She thought of Jess, out running somewhere, coming back to an empty house. A house so vast that it always felt empty.

"How's Jess?" Henrietta asked, reading her mind.

"Same," Alison replied, noticing that Hen had barely touched her wine. "Am I drinking too quickly?"

"You need it more than I do."

Alison smiled.

"I wish that Jess would talk to us . . . to you. I wish she'd let us help. Roger asks after her all the time," Hen said.

"There's nothing we can do. I feel so guilty coming here, leaving her, talking to you and drinking wine like life is normal. I asked her to come . . . but you know her. She stays out all night sometimes, I don't know where she goes. I hate to think about it."

"Reminds me of when she was younger. You can't judge her now, with all that she's going through. My heart breaks for her, but she can be difficult. She's always been headstrong, like her mother."

"I wasn't that bad, surely?"

"No. Not that bad. But Dad had his hands full."

"Now I wonder why I kicked so hard, when we had so much. I don't remember anymore—maybe I choose not to."

Alison watched a firefly zip across the pool. She followed it until it became a speck in the distance.

"She settled with Michael, though," Hen said. "I liked him when I first met him. He was charming, like you said, and maybe a little arrogant. But they always are when they're that handsome."

"He had me fooled too. Then once they were married he began to control her. He didn't want her to see me, didn't want me to come over and help with Harry. He wanted her to himself, but he wanted others too. Typical man."

"I saw him a month back," Henrietta said.

"Michael?"

"Yes. I didn't tell Jess. She needs to forget him."

"Did you speak to him?"

"No. He looked awful, not the man you remember. His hair is longer, his eyes were bloodshot. He was staggering down Main Street. He looked drunk. I wanted to grab him, to yell at him."

"What would you have said? What's left to say?"

"I'd tell him what the whole town is saying behind his back. That he should be there for his wife. That he should take care of her, because she needs him."

Billy Brooks left The Squirrel early. He was drunk, far too drunk to drive yet still he found himself wandering toward his truck. It was only two miles to his house, two miles of winding track roads and then he'd be home and dry, no chance of getting pulled over. No one bothered them in Despair. That's why he loved the place. The name alone kept most away. It was so dark, so hopeless.

Billy liked the dark. People like him were at home in the dark—people that were capable of doing dark deeds.

The only people that came to Despair were those that sought out the dark, for whatever reason, like that crazy girl had, the one that had flirted all night—thinking that she was at home in the dark with them. But she was just visiting.

Just visiting, like the guy that stood in front of Billy now.

The visitor stood still, blocking his path, his feet shoulder width apart. He looked jacked up, ready. He had something in his hand—it looked like a can.

Billy started to smile, but checked it when the visitor raised the can and sprayed something into his eyes. The pain was instant, and fierce.

Despite the burning, he swung, but it was a sloppy swing.

His momentum carried him forward. He fell, the gravel rough against his face. He felt his boot come off, but that was the least of his problems. Whatever was in his eyes was burning his throat now. He struggled to breathe.

And then the visitor was on him.

Through the blows that landed heavy on his face, Billy caught a blurry glimpse into the visitor's eyes and saw something that scared him.

Maybe he wasn't a visitor after all.

Maybe he was at home in the dark too.

The movie was bad, though the date wasn't. Jared seemed more relaxed, and that made Elena feel more relaxed.

"I love it when Cage tries to do an accent," Jared whispered, leaning close.

She laughed, drawing an angry glance from the man sitting in front of her.

"Let's get out of here," she whispered to Jared.

He nodded, and took her hand in his as they walked out. He might have just been helping her because it was dark, but when they found the door and squinted their way into the foyer he didn't let go. And she didn't want him to.

The run had been Jess's longest yet. Six miles at a frightening pace. But it was only as she panted her way back up Alison's driveway that she finally felt the tension leave her shoulders, the anxiety leave her mind to be replaced by a heavy, welcome cloud of exhaustion.

She climbed the stairs and ran the faucet, filling the bathtub. She pulled off her shorts and peeled the T-shirt from her back. She stood naked and looked into the mirror. The bruising on her thigh was the worst; an angry mix of yellow and purple, where Duane or Bobby had clamped his meaty hand on her and forced her legs apart. There was a bite mark on her shoulder, but that was already beginning to fade. She'd hoped that she'd been drunk enough to fog the memory, but found it troublingly clear, though she took some comfort in the fact that it gave her something else to think about when she tried to get to sleep at night.

She stepped into the bath slowly, her body trying to adjust to the temperature.

She lay down, her skin red, the water hot and cleansing.

It was as she closed her eyes that she heard it. A bang.

A loud bang.

And it came from downstairs.

She climbed out of the bath quickly, her heart racing. She beat back the fear by moving fast, pulling on her gown and taking the stairs two at a time.

She saw him outside.

Sitting with his back to the door and staring off into the distance.

She opened the door and he stood, turning to face her, his eyes dark.

"What are you doing here?" she asked.

She looked down at his hands, at the swelling, at the blood sprayed up his shirt.

"I went to Despair."

She lunged at him, mashing her lips against his so hard that she could taste blood.

He kissed her back just as hard, months of longing dissolving under the moonlight, the feeling that replaced it just as hard to deal with.

16

An Easy Target

Jess watched him sleep. He looked beautiful when he slept, like a child: untroubled, at peace. She wondered if she looked that way, but felt certain that she didn't.

He hadn't left afterwards, like she thought he might. After she had kissed him, tasted his blood and wanted more. He had kissed her back, but he didn't have much of a choice. She drew him into her, consumed him and took away the darkness in his eyes, took it away because in her he saw only light. He saw the good, the innocence that she longed to see in herself again. It was one of the reasons she liked to be around him, to keep him close by.

She knew that he'd fallen for her. To her it was obvious. And now that he'd crossed the line their relationship was no longer strictly business, though she thought it funny to think of his work as business, a job. It clearly meant much more to him than that. When she'd led him up to the bedroom, she felt it pouring from him. The desire. And not just to fuck her, though that was there too. Despite what was going on around them, he wanted to save her, to bring Harry home and save her. Maybe save himself too; save himself from whatever it was that he was hiding from, the part of him that he hated and thought that she could take away. Or Harry could take away. Make himself worthy again . . . whatever. Except she was the wrong person to do that. Where he saw light, she saw only dark. Where he saw warmth, she saw the bitter cold.

She wondered if he'd want more now, not that it made a difference. She belonged to somebody else. And even if she didn't, it could never work between them. They shared something that two people shouldn't, not two people who wanted to be together. They'd lived the nightmare side by side, like those couples you read about in the newspapers. The couples that had lost a child in some awful way. They never stayed together, because that's all they would ever see in one another. That pain. They needed someone new, someone that couldn't see what they had seen. Someone that wouldn't wonder how they could laugh at a funny movie, or enjoy a summer's day and escape into a book; wonder how they could do that after what they had seen, like they didn't care anymore. Because how could they laugh if they did care? How could they ever smile again if they remembered?

"You watching me sleep?" he said, his back to her.

"No."

He rolled over and smiled at her.

She didn't smile back.

He sat up, reaching for his pants.

"I got somewhere I need to be," he said, checking his watch.

It wasn't awkward. She'd long since stopped feeling awkward afterwards.

"You okay?" he said.

She nodded.

She watched him glance at the floor, at the posters of Harry. She saw the guilt bite him then.

"You going to knock on doors again?" he said.

"Yeah."

He nodded.

"The guy in the PhotoMax looks at me funny."

"Jerry? He looks at everyone funny."

"I knocked on his door, but he wouldn't answer."

"He's a good guy. Has a tough time with his mother," Jim said, buttoning his shirt.

Jess shrugged. "It's just funny, the way he looks at me."

"You seem chirpy today. What's up?" Elena said.

"Nothing," French John replied.

He crouched by the cake, carefully removing the last of the hand-carved flowers from the bottom tier. Though a painstaking job, he still couldn't keep the smile from his face.

"Seriously, what is it? Or rather, *who* is it?"

"I wish I had something more exciting to tell you, but alas, I fear I may never meet the man of my dreams. Not in this town anyway."

He placed the flower onto a tray, then started on another.

"So why the smile then?"

"No reason in particular. Can't a boy just smile without a reason anymore?"

"If I didn't know any better I'd think that you were seeing Richard again."

"Richard who built the closet then lived inside of it?"

Elena laughed. "Yes, manly Richard with the big tool . . . belt."

"Why did I finish with him again?"

"I remember."

"I thought you might."

"You said that never again would you date a man that wasn't proud to have you on his arm. You said that living in the closet was for teenage boys in Bible-Belt towns or 1920s gays."

"That doesn't sound like something that I'd say."

"You said that he flinched when you tried to hold his hand on an empty street so imagine what he'd do if you put a hand on his ass or, and I quote, 'put a hand on his cock.' "

"Ah yes, I remember now. He was nice looking, and he had his own building company. Shame. How was the movie by the way?"

"He held my hand," she said, smiling.

"Wow, he held your hand. Does that mean that the two of you are going steady?"

"Stop it," she laughed. "I think it's sweet."

"I wonder what will happen on your next date. If it all goes well then I think you should seriously consider letting him kiss you on the cheek."

She threw a glacé cherry at him, one which he expertly caught in his mouth.

"Very impressive. Quite skilled with your mouth, aren't you."

"So will you see him again, this hand-holding dreamboat?"

"He's already asked me to go out for dinner again."

"You still don't sound too convinced."

He carefully removed the last of the flowers and the cake was bare again, ready for a redress, if only he could think of a way to give Louise McDermott *more*; a way that didn't involve a handgun and a lengthy spell in prison.

She set down the tray she was holding. "I don't know what it is really. He's perfectly nice, more than nice. He's funny and charming and good-looking."

"But?"

"But I always feel like he's holding something back. Like he's so worried about dropping his guard that he can't relax, and that makes me feel tense. And there's no reason that he should have his guard up. He's never been married, so no cruel ex-wife to worry about, and no children to ask him who Daddy's new friend is."

"Maybe he's been hurt before."

She waved him off. "I like my men tough. I don't want some sissy crying on my shoulder and making me promise to be gentle with him."

"Maybe he's gay."

"Maybe he is. Then why bother going after me?"

"Because you look like a man?"

This time the cherry hit him square in the forehead.

Jerry was nervous. He had ironed his best pants, the pair with the pleat down the front and the American eagle badge on the back pocket. The man in the store had said that, for his size, they were the closest he could get to fashionable. Jerry liked the eagle. It looked proud and noble, not like the birds on his bed covers. They were back again, the scary birds. This time, when he got into bed, he could smell something funny on his sheets, and then his legs were burning and his skin bright red. His mother had said that she'd been trying to clean them. He'd found the empty bottle of bleach in the linen closet. She was getting worse. But it wasn't his mother that was making Jerry nervous. It was the evening ahead.

Jerry had never been to a bachelor party before. And he felt sick too, as well as nervous. His mother had made lasagna, lasagna with crunchy layers. She'd sat opposite him, watching him eat every mouthful and asking him how it was. She'd asked him twenty-six times. And he'd replied, "nice," twenty-six times, even though it wasn't. He'd needed to eat though—he didn't know if Max would be providing food.

He'd been to a party once before. For Donald's tenth birthday. Donald had been in his special class. He was small, remained so even as everyone else got bigger. Donald hadn't even invited him to the party, his mom had. When Jerry had arrived, with a cake that his mother had baked, iced with the words To DONALD, LOVE FROM JERRY, some of the other kids had laughed at him. They'd laughed even harder as Donald threw the cake onto the floor. Jerry had cried; cried because he felt bad for his mother, because she had spent so long baking it. And once he started crying, he found that he hadn't been able to stop. So Donald's mom had phoned his mother, and just as they were laying out the sausage rolls and the sandwiches, the kind that were cut into small triangles that stuck to the roof of your mouth, his mother had come to collect him. But then she'd seen her cake splattered on the floor, and that made her cry too. And she'd cried so much that Jerry's dad had to come and collect both of them.

"What's that in the oven, Mom?" he called out.

His mother didn't answer. He'd learned that silence was rarely a good thing where she was concerned.

Jerry ran down the stairs, the wood groaning under the strain, and into the kitchen where he saw his mother, bent over and peering into the oven.

She was naked again.

The linoleum floor felt spongy beneath his bare feet, which reminded him, he'd have to iron his new socks too. His mother used to iron for him. He wasn't very good at it. Max had told him that he needed to smarten up, because his shirt was so creased.

"It's a cake. I'm baking it for Max."

Jerry gently draped her housecoat around her.

"I don't think they have cakes at bachelor parties."

"Sure they do. It's not a party without a cake."

Mom turned to look at him. "You're not going like that are you?"

"Why?"

"You look so big in that shirt."

She poked his stomach with her finger. He took a step back.

"I'll change," he said.

"No point really. All your shirts make you look big. What time will you be in? I'll wait out front."

"No, don't do that, Mom."

"You'll need to run my bath. Tonight is Sicilian lime and avocado. It helps. The doctor said relaxation helps. He also said that you should be doing more for me. Looking after me."

"I'm not sure what time I'll be back. Max said that there might not be enough room for me in the limo, and if that happens then I might have to come home early."

"Because you're so fat."

She had that look in her eye again, the vacancy. He shouldn't leave her, he knew that. But he'd told Max he'd go, and Max was someone he found it very difficult to say no to. Though younger than him by six years, Max had a quality that Jerry had always been without. He wasn't sure what the quality was called, but Max had it in abundance; the ability to get people to do what he said. It wasn't just that he was physically imposing, which he was, it was the way he talked down to people. He did it to Jerry, which Jerry was more than used to, but Jerry had seen him do it to others too, people he shouldn't talk down to. Like Lisa. *Treat them mean, keep them keen*, that's what Max had told him; told him that right after he'd reduced Lisa to tears over a supposed slight so trivial that Jerry had trouble recalling it. Jerry guessed that was why he saw all the other girls, because that was a mean thing to do to Lisa. Max always made Lisa smile again, usually by buying her a nice gift. Max had lots of money. Jerry couldn't imagine being mean to Lisa, to anyone really. Lisa once told him that good things happened to good people. Though Jerry had yet to see any concrete evidence of this, he liked to believe it. He liked to believe that the world was a good place, that people were innately good, which was why he struggled so much with what he had done, and with what he needed to do to make things right. There was no easy fix, no resolution without far-reaching consequences for him, and for his mother. It was an accident. He hadn't meant to do it. He hadn't meant for any of it to happen. He wondered if that were a valid argument. He doubted it.

"Will there be women at this party?"

Jerry shook his head, though he wasn't certain.

"You wear a condom if you fuck someone."

He looked down. He guessed it was the tumor making her this way. He'd done more research online. It was in a part of the brain called the frontal lobe.

"You probably won't. You'll cum too quick," she laughed. Her stomach shook, the skin that hung from her arms rippled.

"She'll get pregnant. I need you here, Jerry. I need you here." She began to cry.

He stared down at his feet; puddles of flesh that spread out so wide he had trouble finding shoes that fit.

"What have you got in your hair?" she said, between sobs.

"It's wax. Dad's old wax. I found it in the bathroom."

"It looks all greasy. Like sweat. Big and fat and sweaty. You won't get laid."

He wriggled his toes.

"Look at me, CUNT," she said, spit flying.

She brought a hand to her mouth when she saw the man standing in the doorway. She tried to fix her hair, then pulled her coat tight around her waist.

Jerry turned, his face red.

"I'm sorry to disturb you. I knocked, the front door was open."

"Jerry never remembers to lock it."

Jerry met Jim's eyes, then looked back down at his feet.

Jim had known Jerry since school. He stopped by the PhotoMax sometimes, always tried saying hello but rarely got past that. He knew his mother. She called them often, when Jerry was at work. For all kinds of shit—from thinking someone was in the house, to telling them that Jerry hadn't come home in weeks. He knew she was sick, just not exactly what was wrong with her. She'd always been sick. Jerry used to come to school wearing the same clothes for weeks at a time, used to smell bad. He'd eat his lunch alone, not wanting anyone to see the junk his mother packed in his lunchbox. Mountains of it. He was an easy target; the other kids had been ruthless.

"You okay, Jerry?"

Jerry nodded.

Jim glanced at Jerry's mother. She was staring at him.

"Is there somewhere we can talk?" Jim said.

Jerry led him out of the kitchen and into the living room.

Jim looked around, tried not to wrinkle his nose at the smell. Damp, maybe. Could've been shit too. He saw stains on the carpet. The pile was deep in places, bare in others. The couches were mismatched: greens and grays, a yellow one too.

Jerry sat down on the yellow chair. He sank deep.

He'd been big in school. Jim wondered what he weighed now.

"I saw Jessica Monroe earlier. She said she stopped by the PhotoMax."

Jerry nodded.

"I just wanted to say thank you, for helping her out with the posters."

"Max did most of it."

Jim looked past Jerry, at the television in the corner of the room. It was wood-paneled, a vase balanced on top. The flowers were dead.

"You sure you're okay, Jerry?"

Jerry nodded.

"I know it's tough, with your mother. If you need anything . . ."

"Thank you," Jerry said, quietly.

Jim sat for a while longer, listening to the tick of the grand-father clock.

He stood.

"Have you found him yet?"

Jim shook his head.

"But you're still looking?"

Jim nodded slowly.

Jerry rubbed his eyes.

"You okay? You look like you want to tell me something?"

Jerry looked at the door, saw his mother staring back at him.

"Jerry?"

"I hope you find him soon."

17

First Kiss

With little money to spare, Jerry walked the two miles to Max's house. He'd left his mother sleeping on the couch. She had taken a pill, one that calmed her down and allowed her to float away. He'd already decided that he wouldn't stay long at the party. He'd try and make it back before she woke, as there was no telling which of his mothers she'd be when she did. He tried to think back to a time when things had been easier, not just for him, but for them as a family. He kept a photograph on his nightstand, taken at SeaWorld when he was eleven. They'd been on every ride. They'd sat on the blue seats during one of the shows and got soaked to the bone. His father had brought his mother's wheelchair so they didn't have to queue. People had stared, because they knew she was only in it because she was fat, but it had still been one of the best days of his life.

By the time he got to Max's house he was breathing hard. Carrying the cake had started to make his arms ache too. He was reluctant to take it in. He'd stopped by three trash cans on the way, each time wanting to drop the cake in, but found he couldn't bring himself to do it.

He heard music. A heavy bass line that thumped and vibrated straight through his stomach. He swallowed hard, trying to force his nerves back down. There was an inflatable woman on the doorstep. He tried not to stare because she didn't have any clothes on.

With a shaking hand he knocked on the door.

He waited and waited, looking around nervously as he did. He'd put his T-shirt on after he'd left home, because he didn't want his mother to see it.

I FUCK ON THE FIRST DATE

Max said that everyone had to wear the T-shirt. He'd kept his jacket done up as he'd walked. The sweat was pooling at the base of his spine.

He took a few steps backward. He could see people inside, but they didn't look up.

He glanced at his Death Watch. His mother had made him update his weight. He'd lost three months.

He knocked again, this time a little harder. And then, finally, someone came to the door.

"Holy shit." The man had long hair and pierced ears. "What the fuck have we got here?"

Jerry tried to smile, didn't know what else to do.

He noticed that the man wasn't wearing a T-shirt like his. He was wearing a T-shirt, though his had a picture of Max on it. He wished that the man would invite him inside, or say something else, anything else, just stop staring at him.

"I'm Jerry, from the PhotoMax."

The man laughed, tilted his head to the side and laughed again.

"Max," the man shouted, and then walked back inside, leaving Jerry and the inflatable woman alone again.

Jerry had never felt so pleased to see Max when he appeared at the door.

"What's up, Jerry? Glad you could make it. Come inside."

Jerry smiled and tried to give Max the cake, but he had already disappeared into the house.

There were lots of people inside, and they all laughed when Jerry came in and slipped off his jacket. But they were laughing at his T-shirt so that was okay. And when he caught Max's eye, Max winked at him and that made him feel a little better.

The music was even louder inside. The smoke in the air made Jerry cough.

The man with long hair handed Jerry a drink, and though he didn't particularly like the taste, he didn't want to appear rude so he drank it anyway.

He followed Max into the kitchen and took the cake out of the box.

"My mom made this. For the party."

Max nodded and looked embarrassed, but before Jerry could hand the cake to him the long-haired man grabbed it and took a big bite.

Then he spat it into the sink.

"What the fuck, man. It tastes like chemicals or some shit."

Max laughed, and then the long-haired man laughed too.

Jerry looked down at floor. "I'm sorry. She's not well."

Max and the long-haired man were laughing so much that they weren't even listening to him.

"What the fuck is up with your voice? It's like you've been sucking down helium."

Jerry looked at Max, but Max avoided his eye.

Jerry saw another man walk into the kitchen, and then Max handed him the cake. He took a bite, then spat it out too.

They all laughed again. So Jerry laughed too, but then he thought of his mother, and felt the tears start to weigh on his eyes, so he turned away from them and looked out of the kitchen window.

As the first tear fell he felt a hand on his shoulder, and it was the long-haired man, and he said that he was only fucking with him, and to have another drink.

So Jerry did, and then he started to feel better. And the more he drank, the better he felt.

Manny sat back, watching the sun begin to set, turning the sky a deep shade of purple. His mother was out with the squint-eyed bastard again so he was stuck home on a Saturday night. Not that he minded. He was with Furat.

"Where's Thalia?" Furat asked.

"In the kitchen. She said she wanted to play with the stove."

He stretched and yawned, finding the long summer days quite exhausting.

"Isn't that dangerous?"

"She knows what she's doing. She's sick of playing with that toy shit that doesn't even heat up, just makes noises like it's sizzling or something, but ten seconds later it cuts off. How the fuck are you supposed to prepare a meal like that?"

"But she's three."

He nodded, interlinking his fingers behind his head and praying that his deodorant was winning its battle for control under his armpits, a battle that was hard enough without the addition of a three-piece working for the opposition.

"Three, right. And my mother acts like she's a baby. Would a baby be in there now trying to get the stove hot enough to make popcorn? No, it fucking wouldn't. But that's the beauty of children: the shit that adults forget once they get past thirty. Children are thirsty for knowledge, you know, and the only way to quench that thirst is to let them explore the world around them. And how can they do that if they're always being told no? That's why I never say no to her, even when she asked to use the nail gun."

Furat stared at him.

Manny laughed. "It's too easy to fuck with you. Should've seen your face. Brilliant."

She punched his arm.

"She's watching that show she loves, the one with that girl that used to be cute and then turned into a whore bag piece of shit after she found the key to unlock her Disney handcuffs."

She laughed.

"You looking forward to prom?" he asked.

"Yeah."

"You're lucky you get to go. They pushed it back twice because of Harry Monroe."

"What do you think happened to him?"

"I don't know . . . nothing good," he said, quietly.

"You know sometimes when I walk around town it seems so safe, almost like we're in a bubble. But then I think about what happened, and I can't believe it. It's so sad. Wherever he is, I hope he's okay, because I see his mom sometimes, and she looks broken. Like there's something broken inside of her."

They settled into silence. It wasn't an awkward silence, both already more than comfortable in each other's company.

"Have you heard any more about your sister?"

She shook her head, brushed a bug from her knee. "She's okay. My mom said she's okay, that everything is going well with the pregnancy."

"What's the guy like?"

"He's nice enough. I didn't get to see him much. They're in love. They've got a place together. So that's something. I know she's young, but that should count for something, right?"

"Sure."

"My father doesn't see it that way."

"How come you're not religious, yet he is?"

"My mother. She worried about us fitting in. She said we could make up our own minds once we were old enough."

"And he was okay with that?"

"My mother wouldn't come to America unless he agreed."

"Then it's not really fair of him to judge your sister like that."

"I know. I think he thought we'd convert."

"What will he think of me?"

She laughed, laughed so much that she held her stomach.

"He'll probably like me. Most do. Anyway, I've come up with a way to charm him."

"Oh God."

"When I meet him, I'm going to say *kiziniz sicak*."

"That's Turkish."

"For *your daughter is hot*."

"He speaks English, Manny."

"Yeah but if I come at him in his mother tongue he'll be seriously impressed. Probably offer me a sweet dowry. I've got my eye on the Porsche."

"His mother tongue is Arabic."

"I know, but that language is fucked-up. It's just lines and dots . . . some kind of code, probably terrorist shit."

She laughed.

"Have you tried to talk to him about it, about your sister? Told him how you feel?"

"He sees what he wants to, and nothing else."

"It's easier that way."

"How do you mean?"

"It's much easier if things are black and white. My father was the same. He had this vision of what a son should be. Black and white. You fall outside and he can't see you."

She turned to him and smiled. "Is that why you do it? The gangster thing, the boxing, the cursing?"

He shrugged.

She smiled again.

He looked down. "Sometimes, when you smile at me, I forget about trying to be someone that deep down I know I'm not. And it's not just the cursing, which comes natural to me by the way, a habit I couldn't shake even if I wanted to. It's the constant need to be somebody else. Anybody else. Somebody whose father gives a shit about them, or somebody so tough that they don't care whether their father gives a shit about them."

She put a hand on his shoulder.

"I forget that I heard him say to my mother that he was tired of being around me, that he couldn't understand how someone like him could have a son like me; a son that he's embarrassed to talk to his friends about. And I forget that he said he hates my mother, and when he looks at me all he sees is her, and that makes him hate me too."

"That's awful, Manny."

"He wanted me to grow up tough like he did, have that hunger that he had because he grew up with nothing. But when he looked at me, he saw I was soft. And it wasn't because I didn't have to look over my shoulder when I walked down the street, like he did, or because I got bought everything I ever asked for, which wasn't much at all really. It was because of my mother. That's why I was such a wimp. He said that. Said I was a wimp. Because of my mother, because she wouldn't push me to do shit that made me miserable but made him happy; because it was her job to raise me while he was at work, and she fucked it up." He swallowed. "That's why I do it. Because how bad must the real me be if my own father hates me?"

He turned to look at her. "So that's why I like it when you smile at me. But not just because it makes me forget, but because it's far and away the most beautiful smile I've ever seen in my life."

As the sky turned from purple to black, the sun to the moon, and the clouds to the stars, Furat leaned forward, took his face in her hands and shared her very first kiss with him.

And if he was honest, if he was sure that no one was listening and it wouldn't come back to bite him on the ass, he would acknowledge the fact that it was his very first kiss too.

Lisa sat on the front step and looked through the forms. She'd knocked on the door a couple of times, then remembered that Max had invited Jerry to his bachelor party. She hadn't thought that he'd go.

She could see a light on in the house. She knew that his mother was in there, but with her being so sick she knew she probably wouldn't come to the door. She'd met his mother a couple of times. She was a bitch. She'd seen her belittle Jerry, every compliment masking an insult. Jerry didn't seem to notice, or maybe he did, but he didn't show it. He took it all. That was Jerry. Someone that took everything thrown at him, and did it with a grace that belied his size. She'd seen Max do it too. They'd argued about it, but Max had never been one to back down. On occasion he'd apologize, but was hardly contrite when he did. He held an arrogance that she had once found attractive, but now hoped might fade as the years passed. He could be cold, detached, like her father was in many ways. Her mother didn't like him. Her friends didn't like him. They'd dated since high school. He'd been a football star, destined for great things until an awkward hit by a 300-pound linebacker shattered his knee. She'd stuck by him through the subsequent dark days. She couldn't very well walk away. His insurance payout meant he wouldn't have to work all that hard for the rest of his life. He had a nice place, and his own business. She reasoned to her mother that she could do worse. They'd been engaged for seven years; it had taken an ultimatum to finally see him set a date.

She turned as she heard the door open, then stood when she saw Jerry's mother standing behind it.

"Lisa."

Lisa smiled. "Hi. I just had some stuff to drop off for Jerry."

Jerry's mother beckoned her in and then closed the door.

Lisa followed her into the living room. She'd never been inside before. She noticed the smell first—it was strong. She knew it well. Jerry's clothes often smelled musty. She couldn't help but stare at his mother. She was big. She had big hands and feet, like a man. She wore toweling sweatpants. Lisa could have fitted into one leg. She walked with a stick, the floor creaking with every step she took.

"Sit."

"I don't want to impose."

Jerry's mother waved her off. "I'll be glad of the company. Jerry's normally home, so I get lonely when he's not. We watch *The X-Files* most nights, and then a movie. Jerry knows all about movies. He reads the reviews."

Lisa smiled.

"He likes the ones with sex scenes. He gets an erection. Thinks I don't notice. He's a man. He has needs."

Lisa looked down at the carpet.

"What have you got there?"

Lisa clutched the papers tightly. "Just some work stuff. Max asked me to drop it off."

"You're getting married soon."

"Three weeks."

Lisa watched her shift in her seat, searching for a comfort that must prove elusive when you're that big. She wheezed, each breath more labored than the last.

"Do you know what time the party finishes?"

"Late. Knowing Max it'll probably go on all night. They're going to a strip club."

"Jerry won't stay late. He knows he has responsibilities. And he won't like the strippers. He blushes when he helps me into the tub. I see him looking though, sneaking a peek whenever he can. He has needs."

Lisa fought the urge to get up and run. She couldn't imagine growing up in a house like this, with a mother like that. She glanced over at the gas fire, at the photograph on top.

"That's Jerry when he was sixteen. He was always big. Fat. Do you want a drink? We have soda, all different kinds. Me and Jerry like Dr. Pepper. We could drink gallons of the stuff. Jerry said it's bad for our teeth but it's just so tasty. We pour it into wine glasses sometimes, pretend we're on a date. He likes to practice. He needs to. He's never been on a date before. Can you believe that, Lisa? A virgin at his age. I think it's sweet really. He wants somebody like me, that knows how to look after him. But girls nowadays, they can't cook. Can you cook, Lisa?"

"A little."

The tick of the clock was loud.

"Max is making him pay for that camera. I hear him crying, at night. He's too old to cry, too big."

"What?" Lisa said.

"He's not good with his money. He spends it all on his photographs. He's always buying paper, and memory cards. After my medication there's barely anything left for groceries. And he likes to eat. His father wasn't good with money either. I had to hide it all. All our savings. Behind the bed. There's a false wall, you know, behind the bed. You push on the bottom right-hand corner, where the baseboard is, and the wood panel pops off."

Jerry's mother smiled then, a vacant smile.

"But don't tell anyone, Lisa," she said, the vacancy quickly replaced by fear. "They'll break in and steal it. They'll tie me up. That's what they do. And Jerry can't protect me. He's big, but he's soft. A big fucking pussy boy. He shouldn't leave me alone. He'll regret it when I'm gone. He'll get his punishment. 'For the wrongdoer will be paid back for the wrong he has done, and there is no partiality.' Colossians 3:25. I haven't got long, Lisa. I know that. I'll be with God soon."

Lisa stood quickly, no longer caring if she was being rude. "I better get going now. Where should I leave these?"

Jerry's mother looked up, smiling again. "In Jerry's office. He likes to call it his dark room. But it's all digital now, right?"

Lisa nodded.

"Second door on the left."

Lisa opened the door, switched on the light. It was bright, the bare bulb hanging low. It was neat inside. A small desk sat against the far wall, beside a file cabinet. There were photographs on the walls, maybe fifty. They were all landscape shots, all of Tall Oaks. Though the quality was poor, he was clearly talented.

She looked at his desk, spotless and polished. His camera lay on it, it was an old model. She picked it up. It felt light, cheap. She placed it back down again.

"Leave it in his file cabinet. In the top drawer. On top of his photographs. He thinks I don't know. He has needs."

Lisa kneeled down and turned the key, opening the drawer.

The photographs were on top. At first she didn't want to look, embarrassed for Jerry, because the lady was naked. But then she saw someone else in them.

A man.

Max.

Her car was old. She floored the gas pedal. Jerry's mother had watched her leave, watched her leave with a big fucking grin on her fat face.

Lisa was mad. She could feel the anger, her heart racing and her fingers white as she gripped the wheel tightly.

She watched the needle climb as she drove out of Tall Oaks, the trees hurtling by as she kept her foot to the floor. The roads were empty. She didn't know where the club was exactly, but Crandall was a small town. A shitty town, with a shitty strip club in it. *The Eager Beaver*. Max had loved that name. He didn't try and hide the fact that he was going there, because she'd been cool about it. It was his bachelor party. They were strippers, not hookers. She'd trusted him.

She saw a sign for Crandall and turned off, passing through Despair. She wanted to kill him. Fucking pervert. Taking photographs and giving them to Jerry. She wondered why Jerry had kept them, though she didn't blame him. His family was so fucked-up there was no doubt he would be too.

She thought of her mother, of her wedding dress and the church they had booked. And then the tears came.

She cried hard, her eyes blurring, the unlit roads blurring too. She came to a bridge, the Half-Chance Bridge.

She tried to wipe her eyes.

She kept her foot on the gas.

She didn't notice she had veered until she saw the lights coming toward her.

And then she screamed.

The last thing that Max would see—would ever see—as he stood up and stuck his head out of the sunroof, was the sight of the car coming toward them.

And that was followed by the sight of the limousine passing through the flimsy, wooden barrier.

And, finally, the sight of the ravine rushing up toward him.

18

The Suburban Coffin

Jim hated Sundays. He wasn't sure why exactly, but he hated them. It wasn't the religious connotations, though he was a non-believer—the things he had seen making it hard to believe there was any higher power than a crazy person aiming a gun at you—it was just the feel of the day. Maybe that changed if you had kids, or had someone to spend the day in bed with, someone to help you forget the fact that tomorrow was Monday and you'd have to face another week all over again.

He thought he'd be happier, after what had happened with Jess. He thought he'd feel less like every day was a Sunday, like he was biding his time waiting for something to happen. And he had thought that something was Jess. If he couldn't find Harry then it had to be Jess. He wondered what the future held for them. He guessed that he wanted more than she did, and then felt stupid for thinking she wanted anything more than for him to bring her boy home. It was a conversation for another time, maybe even another life. He took a deep breath. He had fucked her. And he had fucked himself. Fucked himself when he drove to Despair and beat that hick half to death. He already felt the weight of what he had done clouding his mind, taking away his energy and refocusing it somewhere it didn't need to be. He needed clarity, he needed single-mindedness. He needed to find Harry when no one else could.

The pressure was about to ratchet up again. After the accident, the circus was coming back into town. They'd focus on Max, but they'd run pieces on Harry too. Jim supposed it was a good thing, that it would get people talking about the case again, but he also knew their rabid gaze would shift to him as well. They'd see he'd gotten nowhere, made no progress. The small-town sheriff way out of his depth. They'd be right about that. What they wouldn't know was that he had managed to fuck the mother of the missing child too. The mother who was anybody's. And that made him as bad as all the others that had used her grief for their own selfish reasons.

It was quite the accomplishment. He should be given a Service Cross, or a Medal of Valor. Yeah, he liked that, a Medal of Valor for not finding the kid and for fucking his mother. If that wasn't courageous—that complete disregard for ethics and for the damage he might do to the case—then he didn't know what was.

He walked along State Street, past the mansions set so far back from the sidewalk that the owners would break a sweat reaching their own mailboxes. Then he turned into Harrison, where the houses were still impressive, just not embarrassingly so.

This was where the bankers and the lawyers lived. Lines of BMWs and Mercedes sat in front of the houses, the odd Prius too. The front yards were all neat, beautifully colored. The fences were painted, the windows gleamed.

When he reached the end of Harrison, he turned right into Roanoke Avenue. And this was where he found Manny, sitting on the curb and squinting up at the clear, blue sky.

"What's up Gambino, or is it Gotti, or maybe Balboa? I can't remember anymore."

Manny turned and looked at him, smiling. "Oh shit, the feds."

Jim laughed, and sat down beside him on the curb.

They sat in silence for a while, enjoying the morning rays before they turned angry.

"Where's your suit? It's only going to be eighty-nine degrees today. Thought you might have teamed it with an overcoat—you know, hide your pump-action inside."

"Nah, I'm thinking of turning my hand to something new. Can't fucking move in this town for cops. It's no place for a gangster. And what's with all these big name stores? How am I supposed to shake down Pizza Hut if I've gotta meet with the regional manager to do it, and then put it in writing before he passes it to someone else to approve? It's ridiculous. I bet Giancana didn't have to put up with this shit."

Jim lit a cigarette and sucked the smoke down deep.

"The manager of Pizza Hut called us, made a complaint. You're lucky you've finished school. I could've shown up there and hauled you away."

Manny looked at Jim, his eyes wide. "That would have been awesome. I could've screamed some shit at you like: 'You ain't got nothing on me. Fuck all this bullshit.' And then I'd wink at Skinny, tell him to call my lawyer. Fucking gangster."

Jim laughed.

"Seriously, Manny, you going to cut this shit out now? Your mother's been through enough."

Manny looked down at the street, watched an ant struggle with something three times its size. "Yeah, I'll cut it out. Too hot for that three-piece anyway."

"You thought about what you want to do with your life yet? There's a whole world out there. You're young enough to do whatever you want. It's a gift you know. Don't throw it away."

"Says the man that came back."

"Yeah, says the man that came back."

"You heard from my father lately?"

"I saw him a couple a months back."

"Where?"

"In Tall Oaks. He was going to see his accountant, needed to collect some papers."

"He ask about us?"

"No," Jim said.

Jim felt bad for the kid, but there was little point lying to him. Danny Romero was a piece of shit, everybody knew it. He was another Michael Monroe. Still hadn't grown up since high school. It was easy to see why Elena had fallen for him; teenage girls liked that whole bad-boy thing he'd been working on. He'd got lucky, that's how he first made his money. He worked in the family restaurant in Brooklyn, inheriting it when his father died. A few months later he got a letter from a developer saying they wanted to buy him out, wanted to bulldoze the restaurant and build a high rise. They owned the rest of the street and his was the last piece of the puzzle for them. Danny hired a lawyer, the smartest move he ever made, and the lawyer nailed the developer's balls to the wall: took them for two million when they wanted to pay a half. All of sudden Danny Romero and his young family were rich. Not too rich—not by New York standards—but rich enough to start over in a nice town with nice schools and nice friends for Manny. He reinvested his money in real estate just as the boom began, making even more in the process. But Danny wasn't cut out for small-town life; he missed the hustle too much. So it was no surprise when he took off. If anything Jim was surprised it took him so long. Thalia was the final nail in his suburban coffin. Danny kicked against the lid and broke free. No way he was coming back now. Last Jim heard he was shacked up with some dumb blonde, eager to spend Manny's college fund on weekends in Vegas and surgical enhancements.

"I've seen some more stuff online about Harry. Said there's no leads, that the operation is being scaled back since the media lost interest," Manny said.

"Lot of bullshit on the Internet."

"Don't suppose you're any closer are you?"

Manny looked at Jim and saw something in his eyes. Could've been pain, could've been fear, Manny didn't know. He thought back to that day. The day something shifted in the town, some kind of energy or something. It wasn't like Tall Oaks was some "Leave it to Beaver" town, where people walked around in a cocoon, but it wasn't the kind of place where kids got taken. People had been wary since. They saw a strange car, they took notice, they made extra sure the windows were locked at night and their kids didn't leave the yard. He hadn't slept for weeks after—him, a teenager, because he was listening out for Thalia, making sure she was safe, his mother too. Safe from what he didn't know—no one did—but there was some sick fuck out there that had taken Harry.

He often Googled the name, Harry Monroe, lots of kids at school did too. He had lined up with Abe to help search. It felt like the whole town did. And the whole town felt it when they'd turned up nothing. They held their collective breath a few weeks later when Jim called a meeting with the press, and then exhaled a sigh of relief mixed with frustration when he told them they still hadn't located Harry. And the frustration grew and grew over the subsequent weeks, along with the weight on Jim's shoulders. And then it began to level off, and as the story slipped from the front pages, as the reporters stopped calling and kids found other things to Google and talk about, the panic and stress was slowly turning into a memory. Because you couldn't maintain it or else it would swallow you whole, and you'd never breathe clear air again. And when he looked at Jim, and when he saw Jessica Monroe, he knew that's what was happening to them. And he felt bad for them, but there was nothing anybody could do about it.

"It's strange," Manny said.

"What is?"

"I see Jess. I see you. I'm worried about prom, and school, and other shit. And you're worried about finding a missing child. It's like we don't belong together . . . in the same town . . . like we're not connected in any way."

"Everyone has their own shit to deal with."

"Yeah."

"Yeah."

"We're all connected, Manny. We're all people. You know what else?"

"What?"

"We're all fucked-up, in one way or another."

Manny smiled. "But how do you do it? You go from looking for Harry, to talking to me about some stupid shit I've done."

"Sometimes it's a relief, you know. You can't stand in the dark all the time, because then you forget that there's daylight out there. And you can't forget that. It's nice to remember the other side of life."

Jim stood, flicked his cigarette toward the storm drain.

He followed Manny's gaze to the pretty young girl coming out of the house next door.

"I'll leave you to it."

"Jim?"

Jim looked back.

"Thanks for not telling my mom."

Jim smiled, then headed back toward Main Street—back toward his shitty Sunday—the weight of his mistakes clouding the clear sky above him.

"I think we should call Doctor Reid. You've been vomiting for days now and I don't think it's getting any better," Roger said.

Henrietta waved him off. "It's just a bug. I'm feeling a little better today. I may come and join you by the pool later on, though I think you might be getting too much sun—maybe put the umbrella up today."

Roger looked down at his bare chest.

"You don't like my color?"

He looked over at her, the sunlight streaming through the windows causing him to squint.

"Why are you looking at me like that?"

"Like what?"

"I'm not sure. If I didn't know you better I'd think you were making your bedroom eyes at me," she said, thinking back to the first time she had seen his bedroom eyes. They had been out for dinner at Mon Plaisir, along the river, and then he had walked her back to her room and kissed her goodnight. Only he hadn't walked away. He had stood there, one eyebrow raised and both eyes kind of flickering, like he was trying to flutter his lashes at her. For a moment she had thought that he might be having some kind of seizure, but then she'd felt his hand on her ass and she quickly closed her eyes as he kissed her again, desperate to block out the image that she now used to help keep her size-four figure. Every time she wanted to eat something calorie-laden, like one of the double-chocolate fudge cakes in the Tearoom, she forced herself to picture Roger's bedroom eyes and felt nauseated enough to never eat again.

"Don't be absurd."

"So why were you looking at me like that?"

He cleared his throat, the way he did before he said something that might embarrass him, the way that she used to find charming but now just found irritating.

"I was thinking that you looked quite beautiful, despite the sickness."

She smiled at him, and then felt the tears welling in her eyes. She was a mess. A kind word from her husband and she was in pieces.

He sat on the bed and took her hand in his. "What's the matter, Hen? I know it's more than just feeling a bit under the weather. Whatever it is, whatever is upsetting you, just tell me and you'll feel better."

For a moment, for one fleeting moment, she wished that she could love him, really love him like he was the man for her. She wished that she didn't find him so annoying, that she didn't feel happier when they were apart, and that she didn't long to go back in time and politely decline him when he'd first asked her out for dinner.

"It's just everything . . . Harry."

He squeezed her hand.

"I want to help her—Jess—but I don't know how to. I can't give her Harry back. And I think that's all that will help her."

Roger let go of her hand. "I think it's best if you just leave her alone. She knows you're here for her. Don't push."

She stared out of the window.

"Seriously, Hen. Just leave her alone."

She thought about what she needed to do. She thought about how she was going to do it. And then she vomited again.

Jared picked up the telephone and dialed, not needing to look up the number. It was the last Sunday of the month, and it was midday. And that meant he had to call her. She would be waiting, and even though they rarely had anything to say to each other, she lived for his call.

"Hello."

"Hi, Mom, it's me."

"Hi, Jay. You sound so different that sometimes I have to think for a minute who's calling me. And then I think, who else would call me Mom?"

She laughed; a sound that brought a lump to his throat.

"So how are you? How's the weather there? I looked it up on the Internet. Can you believe that? Your old mother climbing the web?"

He laughed. "Surfing, Mom. You *surf* the web."

"Well that doesn't make any sense at all."

He brought a hand to his mouth and touched the corners of his smile. Then he reached for the knife. His father's. He hadn't given it to him, Jared had taken it. He cleaned it every week, sharpening the blade and polishing the handle. They used to use it when they fished the Red Deer River.

"Okay, *surfing* the web. I'll have to remember that. So I looked up where you are and every day has a little sunny face next to it. Is that right? Surely it can't be hot every day."

"It is, Mom. It's hot every day."

He walked over to the window and looked down at the street below, then at the park opposite. He could see the statue, Artemis, the Goddess of the moon. She stood tall. The kids liked to run up to her and wrap their arms around her legs. He watched them do this often, sometimes for hours at a time. He liked the little boys, how they were so fearless, how they tried to climb up and grasp her stone hand.

"Hot every day. I can't imagine that. Our summer here only lasts a few weeks and it never gets too hot."

"I remember, Mom."

"Of course you do. It hasn't been that long after all."

He closed his eyes, trying to picture her face. It *had* been that long. Eight years, three months and nineteen days since he had left their small town in Canada. He could probably tell her the hours and minutes too.

"How's Dad?"

He could feel her bristle on the other end, feel her eyes dart around and look to see where her husband was. He touched the tip of the knife, then brought it up to his bare chest.

"You know your father," she said, her voice noticeably quieter.

"I don't suppose he wants to say hello."

She sighed, a long deep sigh. "Jay . . ."

"Forget it."

He traced the knife along his skin, just below his nipple. He could see the scars all over—a lifetime of pain, a lifetime of hurting himself.

"Sometimes I think that he just needs more time."

"More time for what?" he asked, sitting down on the brown suede dining chair and then getting straight up again.

"To forgive you. For what you've done."

He walked through to the hallway and looked in the mirror. He pressed the knife until it pierced his skin. He wanted to cry out, to beg for help . . . but only for a moment.

He watched the trail of blood run down to his navel. He could see what he had done, the damage, it was impossible not to, though he saw it mostly in his eyes—they were different somehow. Darker, maybe. He had caused so much pain, it was hard to see anything else. He walked back to the window, stared out at the kids again. He watched them run, saw their carefree smiles as he dragged the knife along his skin, tearing it open. He didn't feel the pain anymore, not the physical pain. He felt the blood seep from him. He relaxed. He breathed and relaxed.

"Don't worry, Mom. It's not your fault—it's mine. Just tell him that I'm sorry, that I wish I could make things right again." Same every time.

He heard her clear her throat, could imagine her shaking her head. He knew that a subject change was coming.

"So tell me about your job. How's it going?"

He set the knife down, walked through to the kitchen and grabbed a fistful of paper towels. He pressed them against his chest, watched them turn pink, then dark red.

"Not much to tell really. I sell cars, Mom."

"What kind of cars? I wanted to tell your Aunt Mary the other day but couldn't remember."

"Fords."

"Oh."

He laughed.

"I thought you'd work construction again, like at the last place. You seemed to like it there."

"Yeah, well. It didn't work out after all. I like it in Tall Oaks now. I didn't at first, I didn't think I'd stay. Everyone seems so different. But now I've made friends. It's expensive though. There're houses for sale here for five million dollars."

It would have been easier to disappear in a big city, though he felt more at home in a small town.

"Five million dollars? I don't believe it. Must be as big as palaces. Wait until I tell your Aunt Mary. She won't believe it either. My Jay, rubbing shoulders with millionaires."

He laughed again. He wondered if it was his real laugh, his old laugh. He didn't know anymore, he'd been acting for so long. He wondered if his mother could tell. He wouldn't ask, he *couldn't* ask. He wanted to tell her about Elena—he wasn't sure why—but he knew that would lead to too many other questions; questions he wasn't prepared to answer yet.

"How much is your rent? Are you managing okay?"

"I have all that money Uncle Frank left me, so I'm doing okay. I'm thinking of buying somewhere with it, once I know for sure where I want to settle."

He breathed deeply, waiting for the bleeding to stop.

"Mom, are you still there?"

"I wasn't going to say anything, but your father doesn't think you should keep that money."

"Oh. Why didn't he say something at the time?"

"You know how he is. Bottles things up and then it all comes out."

Another long silence.

He could hear her breathing.

"Jay?"

"Uncle Frank left it for me. I would have come home for the funeral but you said not to." He walked into the kitchen and stared at the small chicken defrosting in the sink. That was the worst thing about being alone—he hated cooking a meal, and sitting down to eat alone. Sundays growing up had been the day when his cousins would come round and they'd all play ball, even though his mother used to worry about him getting hurt, seeing as he'd been so much smaller than the others. And then they'd go in and wash up and he would help his mother lay the table and then watch his father carve the meat. Then they'd sit down and say grace, and he'd open his eyes and peek at his father, who'd be peeking back, pulling faces and trying to get him to laugh. But now Sundays were days spent alone. He still cooked a big meal, but he sat down in his shiny kitchen, on his brown suede chair, at his solid oak table, and he ate alone. And he practiced his act— the way he ate, the way he drank. He practiced and practiced.

"Your father said if Uncle Frank had known what you did then he wouldn't have wanted to give you all that money."

"And what do you think?"

She sighed again. "I don't know, Jay. You know Uncle Frank. Even though he didn't have any kids of his own he doted on you, thought the sun shined out of your keester. But he would have been disappointed in you. Maybe not as angry as your father was, but still. Anyway, I don't know. Legally it's yours to keep so you do what you feel is right. I should probably go now, I've got a chicken to cook and your cousins are coming over to watch the game. I'll speak to you soon."

He stood up again, suddenly feeling tired. He looked at the chicken and felt a sadness wash over him. He bit his bottom lip and swallowed down a cry, trying desperately not to let it escape.

"I'm sorry, Mom," he whispered. "I'm so sorry."

But she was already gone.

He picked up the knife, and walked back to the mirror.

19

A Ruthless Summer

"I thought it was good," Furat said.

Manny wiped the tears from his eyes and shook his head. "My biceps are good. My mother's enchiladas are good. *Rocky II* is a fucking masterpiece."

The weekly movie, always of Manny's choosing, had become something of a ritual for French John since he'd moved to Tall Oaks. He yawned—a long, exaggerated, stretched-out yawn.

Manny looked over, then pointed a finger at him. "You got something to say?"

"I fell asleep halfway through, missed the end. Did the black guy win? He looked in much better shape."

Manny scowled. "You closed your eyes 'cause you were starting to get hard during the training montage. Didn't want to scare us with it. And you know that Balboa won in the end. I've shown you this film four times now. I've seen you well up too—same part I do—where Adrienne says, 'Win, Rocky, win.' "

"I really don't think I did well up. Maybe you were hoping that I did, so you wouldn't be the only person crying in the room."

"You'd have to be dead inside not to cry at that. She nearly fucking died. And they got a new kid just been born all small and pink, and she's petrified he's going to get hurt in the ring and then she'll be a single mother, and nobody in their right mind wants to be a single mother. It's so fucking lonely and you get all desperate and shit."

"Thanks, Manny," Elena called, from the kitchen.

"But as much as she's scared, and even though she's still all groggy from the coma, she sees it in his eyes—the need to win, because he's a fucking winner. And she knows that he needs her support to win, because they're a team. And that scene is why *Rocky II* might just be the greatest movie ever made."

"But it didn't win an Oscar," French John said, pulling a cushion close to his chest, for protection.

"Fucking *Rocky I* won an Oscar. They don't give you that shit twice. Stallone should have been given one just for his fucking abs alone. Not to mention his guns, and his traps. I'd like to see Jack Nicholson get ripped like that."

"He's too busy acting," French John said, the cushion now joined by another.

Manny rubbed his temples and closed his eyes. "Stallone's portrayal of Rocky Balboa proves that he's one of the greatest actors of his generation. And he still found the time to get ripped up in the process. So, fuck Jack Nicholson, and fuck you too."

"Manny," Elena shouted.

"It's okay, Elena, we've touched on a nerve in here."

"Why?" she called back.

"We're discussing *Rocky*."

"I don't know what your problem is anyway. Two young men in the peak of physical fitness, all sweaty and shit. Should be like porn to you guys."

Elena appeared in the doorway. "I told you about that, French. Last time you two discussed *Rocky IV,* Manny didn't sleep all night. He was pacing around his room and making notes on why the end fight scene wasn't too long, and why Rocky's natural training methods beat the Russian's steroid-based approach. He was muttering to himself too—kept Thalia awake for hours."

"You're right. I'm sorry."

"And?" Manny said.

French John stood and threw a cushion at Manny. "And *Rocky II* is a good movie. I enjoyed it."

Manny nodded, smiling as French John followed Elena back to the kitchen.

"Well, I *liked* it. I think Stallone was cute back then, before he got all funny looking, like someone filled a creased-up old sack with air."

Manny laughed. "I knew you'd like it. Better than *Rocky I?*"

"Yeah, better," Furat said.

"I hope I get one of those moments," he said, quietly.

She turned to him, grabbing the television remote and muting the sound.

"What moments?"

"You know. The 'Win, Rocky, win' moment. When someone believes in you that much, sees the potential in you and just says fuck the consequences, go for it. I think it's more heartfelt than saying I love you."

"There are lots of people that see potential in you, Manny. You just need to figure out what it is that you want from life."

"Who the fuck knows at our age? I'm supposed to know now what I want to do out in the real world, even though I've spent all my time at school. How do I know what it's like to be a lawyer or a doctor?"

She shrugged.

"And yet I'm supposed to commit the next four years of my life, and get into a shit load of debt, to end up doing something that actually isn't as much fun as it sounded in those dumb career books they give us at school. The book that tells you a lawyer starts his day at nine and has time for an hour's lunch break before leaving the office at five to have dinner with his wife and kids. Except we know that's all bullshit. I've read Grisham. I know they work you like a prisoner of war, and, when you do get home, you find out your wife's banging the gardener, because he's got the time to listen to her moan all day, and your kids are away at boarding school; the one perk of earning all that money. It's all lies."

She laughed, curling her feet under her and leaning back in the couch. "What about the career days, when they get someone in to speak? They're better than the books."

"We had an astronaut come in one day. Except when I started grilling him it turned out he worked in the accounts department at NASA. Nearest he had got to space was when his wife walked out and took the kids."

She laughed.

"Seriously, he was a mess by the time he left. I asked him a few simple questions and then the teacher stepped in to save him, but by that time the astronaut was near to tears—fucking fraudster. He even gave out his business card at the start, had the NASA logo on it. I kept calling him at work and asking what it was like up in space, what it was like to feel weightless and look back on earth from that far away. He changed his number in the end. Teach him to lie to a bunch of kids though."

"I thought about becoming a teacher once—maybe kindergarten," she said.

"I think you'd make a good teacher. I think the kids would like you. Thal does. She keeps asking if we're going to get married."

Furat smiled. "What do you tell her?"

"That you're not marriage material."

She punched his arm.

Then his lips found hers.

They broke away quickly when they heard French John coming back to the living room.

He sat down and looked at Manny.

Manny smiled back, his heart beating a little faster.

"*Rocky III?* Watch Mr. T get his ass kicked?" Manny asked.

"As long as you promise not to cry when Mickey dies."

Manny shook his head. "I'm not promising shit."

Jerry opened his eyes. His head hurt and his tongue felt furry. He had a horrible taste in his mouth and his stomach was churning, the contents swishing about even though he was lying still. He was in his bed, though he didn't remember how he'd gotten there.

He remembered the limousine coming, and then he remembered Max telling him that there wasn't enough room, because he took up two seats. He remembered the others laughing. Then Max had given him a bottle of something for the walk home.

He'd drunk it all, because he was thirsty, because the walk had taken him so long. And then nothing. A void.

He sat up. His head thumped, his eyes felt sore. He licked his lips. They felt dry.

He made his way into the bathroom and ran the faucet, splashing cold water on his face. He reached for the mouthwash and swirled it around his mouth. He felt a little better.

And then he heard the bell ring.

He walked across the hallway, each step making his head throb.

His mother sat up in bed, glaring at him.

"Look what the cat threw up."

He swallowed.

"You look awful."

"My head hurts."

"You came in late. You dropped a glass in the kitchen. It scared me."

"I'm sorry."

She coughed, reached for her water and took a long sip.

She banged the glass back down.

"I didn't get to take my bath. So I couldn't relax. I've been awake half the night."

"I'm sorry."

She pulled the sheet up to her chin and coughed again.

"Why don't you love me, Jerry? Do you want them to take me away? Then you can go out every night. Is that what you want? To see your own mother taken into a home? They beat you in there; they leave you sitting in your own shit. I read about it in the newspaper. They left an old lady lying in her own shit for three days. Her skin rotted away, and then the shit got into her bloodstream and killed her."

She was crying now, but he could still see the venom in her eyes.

She picked up the glass again and hurled it at him.

It sailed past his head and shattered against the wall behind him.

"Nice place," Jim said, looking at the high ceilings, the expensive furnishings, the stone fireplace.

"Just a rental," Jared said.

Jim sat on the leather couch.

"Can I get you a drink?"

"Water, thanks."

Jared walked calmly into the kitchen, then closed the door behind him. He ran a hand through his hair and began to pace. Up and down, up and down. He closed his eyes and tried to focus. There was a cop in his house.

He eyed the knife, his father's knife. He needed it now—the release. He'd never been good with stress, had always folded under the lightest of pressure. He hated that about himself. He hated lots of things about himself. But at that very moment, if he could have changed anything, he would have turned into the kind of man who keeps cool, who tries to remember that the cop didn't really know anything about him. He couldn't. He'd been careful.

He reached for a glass, filled it with water from the refrigerator. He tried to stop his hand from shaking. The cop would see that. He'd think there was something wrong. He glanced at the knife again.

"How much is the rent in a place like this?" Jim asked, as Jared walked back into the room.

"Quite a bit."

"I can imagine."

"It's an expensive town to live in."

"For a car salesman," Jim said, smiling.

"I have family money."

"Everybody does around here."

Jim sipped his water slowly.

The apartment was large, the whole top floor. The McDermotts owned it, along with the rest of the building.

Jared watched him look at the walls, at the paintings—all expensive, all tasteful. Jared tried to read him, to see if he'd noticed there were no photographs anywhere, no personal touches.

"You like it here?"

"It's nice. Everyone's friendly."

"But you're leaving?"

Jared paused for a moment, searching his mind, certain he hadn't told anyone he was leaving.

Jim smiled.

They sat in silence. Jared jammed his shaking hands deep into his pockets.

"John's an old friend. He said he'll be sorry to see you go, said you've shifted a lot of cars. He was surprised. Said you hadn't been there long."

Jared breathed again.

"Yeah. I guess I just like to keep moving."

Jim nodded. Nodded and smiled. He picked his drink up again, took another sip then set it down.

Jared heard sounds floating in through the window. He glanced over, then cleared his throat.

"I'm sorry, Jared. I'm just knocking on some doors as part of the Harry Monroe case."

"Right. How's that going?"

"I feel like I'm getting closer. I don't even know why . . . just a feeling—like I'm going to find him."

"That's good. I can't imagine what his parents are going through."

Jared rubbed his chin, the stubble felt rough against his finger. He liked that feeling.

"You know where you're headed next?"

"Not yet. I might stick around for a while longer. I haven't decided. I get restless."

Jim shifted, crossed his legs.

"You're dating Elena Romero."

Jared looked up.

Jim laughed. "Small town."

"Right."

Jim continued to stare at him.

"She's nice. But we've only been out a couple of times. It's not serious."

"You met Manny?"

Jared nodded.

"He's a good kid really. He keeps me entertained. He's been dressing as a gangster. He tried to extort money from Pizza

Hut . . . it's funnier than it sounds. The manager called us, real nervous guy. Adam, one of our officers, he took the guy's statement. He's trying to keep a straight face, but this guy tells him how Manny said his car was nicknamed 'the rolling bomb,' and Adam just bursts out laughing. Said he couldn't hold it in."

Jared glanced out the window, at the boys running up to Artemis.

He felt Jim follow his eye.

"Okay then," Jim said, standing.

Jared followed him to the door.

Jim opened it, then turned. "Shit, I forgot to ask. You didn't hear anything that night? I know it was a while back, but you didn't see anything, did you?"

"No."

"Give me a call if you remember anything," Jim said, as he walked away.

Jared closed the door, leaned on it and exhaled heavily. Then he walked back through his apartment, took his case out of the closet, and began to pack.

"Jess."

Jess span around.

"I'm sorry, I didn't mean to startle you," Roger said, panting.

He bent down, placing his hands on his knees, his running vest clinging to him. He wore a headband, and sweatbands on each wrist. Articles of clothing she hadn't seen since the late eighties.

"How are you?" he asked. "Sorry, stupid question really."

"I didn't know you went running," she said.

He smiled. "I see you sometimes. Thought I'd give it a try."

She tucked her hair behind her ear.

He stood in the grass.

She looked down at his running shoes; they were new, too new. They glowed.

She shifted her weight, leaning on one leg.

"Have you heard anything?" he said.

Another stupid question.

She glanced up the street, saw a mother walking toward them pushing a small boy on a trike. The pedals were turning, but the boy was just a passenger.

He looked up, met her eye, then looked away quickly.

"I'm not going to say anything, Roger. If that's what you're worried about, then don't. I've got no interest in breaking up a marriage."

"That's not what I meant. I just . . ."

She turned and walked away, leaving him standing in the grass.

Jess walked for miles, to the very edge of town. She saw Harry's face on every streetlight she passed. She slowed for each of them, sometimes smiling back at him, sometimes just staring, and trying not to cry. She liked the town at night, when the heat of the day began to subside, when drapes were closed and televisions flickered from between them. She used to take Harry for a walk in his stroller, every night after they'd eaten dinner. He was quiet. He'd take everything in through his big, blue eyes. She'd talk to him, tell him who lived in which house, and how she knew them. He had a comforter, a small piece of red cloth. He called it Ralph. She and Michael had laughed about it when he'd come up with the name all by himself. He'd grasp Ralph tightly in his small hands as they walked and walked. He didn't ask for much. He wasn't one of those kids that you had to cross the street with to avoid passing by the toy store window. Alison spoiled him. Whenever she stopped by she'd bring another toy. Harry worshipped her. He used to beg her to stay for dinner, sometimes even for the night, crying as she waved goodbye and walked out the door. Alison would tell him not to be silly, though Jess could tell she was inwardly thrilled. Harry used to shake hands with people. He'd see the mailman and stick out his hand. He was beautiful. She could say that with some surety. Max kept his photograph on the wall in the studio, said he was nearly as beautiful as his mother.

She walked up to the old clapboard house and rapped on the door, dislodging some paint chips as she did.

The house was located on the southern edge of town, far away from the white picket fences and manicured lawns. It sat on the border of Tall Oaks and the much smaller, much less desirable town of Marsh Creek.

Something about the place made her shiver. It wasn't because the house stood alone, the neighboring houses hidden by a dense copse. It was because, in all the times that she had knocked, and it was fast approaching double digits, no one had ever answered. Even the time she'd heard movement inside.

She needed to speak to the owner; she needed to be thorough, to cover every house.

She'd once caught her mother on the Internet, trawling for stories about missing children—the ones that were found safe and well. Jess had sat beside her. They were hard to find, the stories, especially after more than a few days had passed, and the Internet was a vast place. Still, it happened. Her mother said miracles sometimes happened.

She banged the door again, this time hard enough to feel pain in her knuckles.

She walked along the veranda, past the fallen swing seat; its chains long since pulled free of the roof, and then peered through the window.

The glass was dirty, caked in the haze of a ruthless summer. With night closing in she could see little but her own face reflected murkily back at her. She tried to rub away the dirt, but it was thick beneath her hand. She picked at it with her nail and managed to chip away a small circle in the grime, just big enough for her eye.

When she leaned forward and stared through, the air was sucked from her lungs.

She felt the tingling in her fingers, the twitch in her legs and the heat rise to her face. She tried to make sense of what she was seeing.

There was somebody in there, lying on the floor.

Facedown.

And it looked like a child.

20

The Burn

The funeral was arranged quickly. It was surprising how many people turned up at the church. People that didn't even know him; people that felt compelled to come for their own private reasons, and those that came simply because it gave them a break from mundanity.

Jim was there, of course, and so were the other members of the Tall Oaks Police Department. Though they weren't there in any official capacity, they ended up having to run crowd control when the church burst its banks and the mourners started to spill outside, blocking the street.

He looked different in the photograph. They always did when they're gone, Father Andrew thought. As if you could tell, just by looking at a snapshot, that they were no longer with us. Father Andrew had been worried about the ceremony. Not because he knew him, which he did, or because so many people had turned up, which he expected, but rather because the circus was in town. He didn't like them, the noise they brought with them, the attention. But he understood why—it was big news. He knew of some of the other priests that would have made the service about something else: a chance to show their stuff, to work the room. Perhaps make the odd joke, just to show the new faces that they were normal after all, even if they based a life on nothing more than blind faith. They'd project, their voices booming and echoing around the arched roof. They'd want to say something about him being with God now, about how God, in his infinite wisdom, wanted him there by His side. That was supposed to make the parents feel better, as if his life were never in their hands. But it rarely did. The pain was too raw, too sudden—they'd just want it to be over with as quickly as possible. Then they could head over to the church hall and stand at the back of the room, wondering how people could feel hungry when his death still hung so fresh in the air, darkening the flowers and dulling the music. They'd see people quickly form a queue when the Saran wrap was taken off of the aluminum foil trays, and then wonder if it was okay to take two sandwiches and two chicken legs. They'd watch people deep in conversation, conversations that had nothing to do with him and his life; conversations that often ended with smiles and laughter, like they had place in the room. They'd make eye contact with the odd person, and that person would smile at them and try their best not to make it a happy smile. All of this, when all they wanted to do was let the grief wash over them and drown them for a few months . . . or years. Until such time that the raw feeling tempered and they could look forward again. And Father Andrew knew all of this, because he had lived through it when his own son had passed. So he kept the service brief. He spoke of his short life, he asked a few of those closest to him to read something. And then he dismissed everybody, back outside to where the cameras were waiting to capture their grief, then email it to their copy editor who'd polish it and slap it on the evening edition for all to enjoy.

Jerry stood at the back of the hall. He tried to blend in, though rarely could. His mother had told him about Lisa, about how Lisa had left the forms in his file cabinet. He'd run straight into his dark room and frantically opened the drawer, then seen the photographs of Max and the naked girl, splayed out on top.

He hadn't seen her since then. He hadn't slept, and he hadn't eaten either.

He could see her now though, in the corner, standing beside Max's parents. Her arm was in a cast. She'd been lucky—that's what it said in the newspapers. He looked at her face, at the sadness. She didn't look lucky.

She glanced up then. She met his eye and the busy hall around fell silent to his ears. He held his breath. His collar felt tighter, the paisley tie choking him.

And then she smiled.

And he breathed again.

She nodded toward the door.

He found her outside, standing beside the gravestones.

He walked over. The grass he waded through was long.

"I'm sorry," he said.

She cried. Then stepped toward him and leaned into his chest. He patted her back lightly, looking around as he did. The church stood tall behind her, leaning on them, pressing them down into the earth. He didn't understand religion—he wondered how anyone could. His mother did, that's why he'd joined the choir. He hadn't liked wearing the white robe.

"I've thrown the photographs away."

She stepped back, wiped her eyes. Dark lines streaked her face.

"Max gave them to me, for my birthday. I didn't ask him to. I should've given them back. I shouldn't have kept them."

"It's okay," she said, quietly.

She looked thin, gaunt.

Jerry had read all about the accident in the newspaper. He wondered who wrote the stories, if they had even known Max. They made him sound so different from the Max that he knew. They showed photographs of him at school, wearing his football jersey.

The others had survived. A miracle, apparently. But then Max had been hanging out of the roof.

"Will you be okay?" he asked.

"Yes," she said.

He wondered if she would.

He followed her over to a bench in the center of the small cemetery.

She sat. He sat beside her, careful not to touch her leg with his.

"I can't sleep, Jerry. I just keep seeing it. I crawled out my car. I looked over the edge. I heard screams. I still hear them."

He swallowed.

Jerry heard the church bell sound behind them. He turned to look up at it.

He heard voices, then saw a man with a camera emerge from the side of the building. Lisa stood quickly, then walked back inside. Jerry waited a moment, then followed her.

"Can you feel the burn? Come on, Roger. Can you feel that burn?"

Roger was breathless, his hair damp with perspiration. But he felt good.

"I can feel the burn, Aleks. And I like it."

The barbell was light, the dumbbells coated in neon foam. Lady weights.

"If you can feel it then own it. Own it, pansy. OWN IT."

So terrifying was Aleks that had Roger any inkling what the big man wanted him to own he would have purchased it in a second.

He lifted the barbell up and then lowered it quickly, while Aleks loomed over him.

Roger marveled at what $100 an hour could buy you. He had never seen a man as large as Aleks. Muscles bulged from every part of him, veins threatened to explode. His hair was military short, his manner terse.

Roger stood. Aleks handed him a bottle of water.

They walked together over to the mirrored wall of the gymnasium.

"Flex," Aleks said.

Roger flexed, pleased with what he saw. Gone was his pot belly and sagging breasts, breasts that had taken on a kind of teardrop shape over the years. And if all it took was a little degradation by a mentally unstable Russian then so be it.

"Looking good," Aleks said.

Roger nodded.

"For your wife?"

"No."

"Younger woman?"

Roger shook his head, tried not to smile.

Aleks caught the smile and laughed.

"What next?" Roger said.

"Next we turn the chrysalis into a butterfly."

"I beg your pardon."

"Squat, my pansy. SQUAT."

Jared was sitting out front in the sun when he saw Elena turn into the lot in the canary-yellow Fiesta. She pulled into the drop-off bay and made her away over to him.

He thought her quite beautiful in her simple, white summer dress and sandals. Her skin was tan and smooth and Jared couldn't help but notice that one of her shoulder straps had fallen and he could see the lace of her bra beneath.

She smiled at him. It was a smile that warmed him.

And then he thought about the cop. Jim. He hadn't been able to stop thinking about him. It was probably nothing, but it didn't feel like nothing. He was ready to leave now, packed up and ready to go again. He wasn't sure which way. Maybe south. He was getting used to the warm weather. He'd paid his rent up front, settled all his bills and closed his bank account. His cell phone was prepay—he'd dump it. He always did. He'd call his mother when he got settled somewhere else, feeding her a romantic notion of him traveling, seeing the world.

He looked up at Elena, and smiled back. And it was in that moment that he knew he was in real trouble, because she made him not want to leave. She made him not want to run anymore.

"I can't believe this weather," she said, taking off her sunglasses and fixing her gaze on him.

He stood and kissed her cheek, softly. He could smell her perfume, and that, coupled with the feel of her skin, made him dizzy. She was something special, something to be admired from a distance, and, if by some small miracle, you were allowed close to her, to make her smile and kiss her lips, you'd do all you could to stay there. And yet here he was trying to think of a way to move back into the shadows again.

"I know. I have to wear sunscreen to work every day."

He swallowed. Sunscreen made him sound like one of those metrosexual guys. He felt his face redden. He tried to slow his breathing down and relax.

It was exhausting, the act, and it was getting harder and harder to maintain when it should have been getting easier.

"Yeah, I try and get Manny to wear it but he says his Latino skin is a friend to the sun so why would he fight it. He's an idiot."

Jared laughed, relaxing a little.

"I try and spend as much of my day as I can out here. I sit in the shade but it's just so nice to be outside."

"We used to live in New York and I could never cope with the winters, and all that pollution too. But the thing that used to get me most was the noise. It was so constant that when we first arrived in Tall Oaks I couldn't get used to the silence. It was like someone had flipped a switch and suddenly there was peace again. And I love it, I really love the peace and quiet, especially at night, when I read a book and I don't have to shake off the sounds of the city. It's heaven."

He smiled, thinking back to his home town. He knew what she meant about the peace. And he had loved it too. Loved it until he'd shattered it.

"I've never lived in a big city. I can't imagine I'd like it. Even when I go to the mall I don't like the crowds. I feel like I can't breathe, and then I relax again when I jump back into my car and put some miles between me and all the madness."

She fiddled with her sunglasses, opening and closing the arms again and again.

She wouldn't look up at him.

He knew that he had said something wrong. He tried to remember what—something about not liking the crowds. No, it couldn't have been that. It was the breathing thing. Just because he went to a busy shopping mall it shouldn't mean that he had trouble breathing. He sounded like a freak; a big, ugly freak with a nasty secret. He started to scratch his head, his eyes darting from her to the car lot and then up at the sky. He was about to turn and walk away, make an excuse, run to the bathroom and splash some water on his face. But then, finally, when he was nearing the edge, she looked up at him and smiled.

"Listen, Jared. I've been invited to a wedding. I helped make the cake, with French John. And Louise—that's the bride—Louise McDermott. You might have heard of her family—they own the big house at the top of Cedar Hill. It's hidden but you can just make out the pool house when they get the birch trees cut. I went there with French John to discuss the cake with Louise a few months ago; the place was as big as a hotel. They had a water fountain in the middle of the carriage driveway." She was rambling. "So my invitation says plus guest, and I was just going to go with French John, but I think he's been seeing his old beau Richard, but Richard's shy, so I don't think he'll show up. But anyway, even if he doesn't, even if French John goes on his own, I'd still like to ask you."

He smiled. "Ask me what?"

She bit her bottom lip and took a breath.

"I'd like you to be my date for the wedding, if you want to. And I know that sometimes men think it's a big deal, being a date to a wedding—like you're trying to announce that it's serious to all of your friends—but I don't want you to worry. I'm happy with the way things are going between us. You're exactly what I need, you know, after Danny. You're a cool guy. I don't feel any pressure when I'm with you. So that's why I want you to be my date."

"Because I'm a cool guy?"

She put a hand over her eyes. "I'm sorry, I thought I was a cool girl, but now I'm painfully aware that I'm actually an embarrassing single mom."

He laughed, then reached up and took her hand away from her face. Her beautiful brown eyes stared back at him. He knew what he should say. That he thought they should just be friends; that he didn't want to get into anything serious.

He knew that he should walk away, ignore the way she made him feel.

"I would love to."

Though he felt sure that it was reckless, and stupid, and completely unfair, he leaned forward, held her face in his hands and kissed her.

And in that moment, the past forgotten and the future, for once, worth striving for, he knew that he was falling in love with her. And he hoped to God that she didn't feel the same way about him.

Jess lay on the grass and stared up at the tall oak trees that loomed above her. She had set off in the direction of the forest and its acres of trails. She'd passed Burford Street, passed all of the pretty cottages that the rich downsized to after their brood left home. The cottages had stone plaques with engraved names; *Summer Cottage. Meadow View Cottage.* Names that made her imagine the life she and Michael might have had.

It was her fault he'd left. She'd been the one that changed.

Her mother had said that she was too good for him, that she was better off without him. It was all carefully contrived bullshit. Things that Alison thought she wanted to hear when she would have been better off had her mother just told her the truth: that he was too good for her; too handsome; too smart; too charming. And Jess was just pretty. That was all. She used to be fun, but lots of girls were fun. That's why she should've moved on when he walked out. She should've just accepted it. It was a fact of life. As they grew older his eye would wander, because he would get better looking, more successful, and she would just get older. Nothing more. Just older.

The kind of love she felt for Michael consumed her in a way that would have been just about bearable had he felt the same way about her. But she knew that he didn't. Even on their wedding day she'd felt it deep in the pit of her stomach. That he would one day leave her, and she wouldn't be able to recover from it. So she'd worked hard at being a good wife, at being a good mother, to delay the inevitable.

Harry had been her link to him. A constant link to a man that would've otherwise disappeared from her life completely. Wherever Michael went, whoever he ended up with, he would always see her when he looked at Harry. And that thought had kept her from going mad in those early days when he first left. Those first few weeks when she hadn't slept, not even for an hour. She just lay awake thinking of him. And it did funny things to her mind, the lack of sleep. It convinced her that he was seeing somebody else, which she now knew to be true. And it convinced her that he would never come back. A thought which drove her to reach for the handgun that he kept locked away in his desk drawer and place the barrel in her mouth.

The metal had been cooler than she had thought, the gun heavier.

Had Harry not appeared in the doorway she might have pulled the trigger. Might have. She had it in her. She knew that.

The tight coil of tension that knotted her muscles, and her mind, always eased when she lay beneath the tall oak trees. Here, she came as close to a relaxed state as she could anywhere else. The Clown left her mind. The horrible things she had done, once alive and vivid, turned gray in her mind and raced further and further from the forefront. She could breathe.

That's why she had come here on that day. After she had called Jim and said that she could see Harry through the window of the old clapboard house. She had broken the glass with her bare hands, slicing them to pieces, not noticing the blood dripping as she climbed through the window. The stress had been almost unbearable as she turned him over.

It wasn't Harry.

It wasn't even a boy. It was a man. A very old man. Long since dead, his face drained but his eyes frozen wide.

She walked back to the clearing, checking her phone until she could get a signal. Then she called him.

"It's your birthday today. You don't need me to tell you that. I got you a gift. I'll keep hold of it until you're ready to see me again. When will that be? I was thinking about your last birthday. Harry was sick but you still wanted to go out. I got my mother to come over and look after him. Remember that? He was burning up. I put you first. I'm not doing well. I'm not coping. I need you, Michael. I need you."

21

Carnival

Jerry had watched them setting up all day through the window of the PhotoMax. They came every year, for one night only: one night full of noise, and color, and candy floss. And he loved it. He loved the rides, the ones that he wasn't too big to go on. And he loved the games, even though he could never manage to throw the horseshoe and land it on the post, despite the man that ran the game saying he was a natural.

Though excited, he was also exhausted. Lisa had told him that Max's parents wanted him to run the PhotoMax until they decided what to do with it. So he hadn't had a lunch break, because there was nobody to cover for him. He still wasn't sleeping either. His mother had told him, in a roundabout way, that it was his fault that Max had died, because he was disgusting, because he had kept the photographs. So that was why he couldn't sleep. Because he knew she was right. Though Lisa had forgiven him, and though she didn't cry as much when he saw her, she looked so desperately sad that he wondered if she'd ever really smile again.

He turned the key and opened the door.

"Mom, I'm home."

He walked into the living room.

"Mom, do you want to come to the carnival with me?"

He walked into the kitchen.

"Mom?"

He climbed the stairs slowly, gripping the rail tightly. He glanced at the photographs on the wall. He'd taken them—one of a deer, one of a red squirrel. He reached out and ran his finger along the glass frame. It was thick with dust. He blew it, coughing lightly.

He passed his mom's bedroom—the drapes were closed. It was dark inside. He pulled the door to, not wanting to wake her. He was starting to enjoy the moments when she was asleep. He felt guilty about that. He felt guilty about lots of things. He thought it a funny thing, guilt. He supposed it was what made us human. It could torture the mind, stop you living a life. It had been eating away at him for months now. He'd thought it might ease—"Time is a great healer," his father used to say—but it hadn't. And now the guilt was mounting up. He felt it in his shoulders, in his stomach and even in his toes.

If we confess our sins, he is faithful and just to forgive us our sins, and to cleanse us from all unrighteousness.

His mother had told him that when he was a boy. She'd also told him about heaven and hell. Life was easier when you had clarity of thought. He'd had that as a child. That was why he'd never lied to her. He wondered if withholding the truth was the same as telling an outright lie. He guessed that it was. Otherwise you could hold onto any number of sins and never confess them so long as nobody asked.

He stopped in his dark room before he left the house. He opened his file cabinet and took out the forms, and the envelope, and finally the photograph. The bird was beautiful, every bit as beautiful as Lisa's father had said it was. He was looking at it more and more now; worrying more and more too. He placed it all into the envelope, then back into the drawer.

He'd do the right thing eventually. He'd decided that. Because he couldn't cope with the guilt much longer. He just needed to make sure his mother was okay, that she wouldn't be alone, and then he'd do the right thing. He just needed a little more time.

Main Street had been transformed. There were stalls in the street, rides that took over the grassy sidewalks and the heavy bass line of a hundred different songs all competing for attention.

"I'll take that pink bunny. The big one at the back. For my girl here."

Manny put his arm around Furat and pulled her close. She looked up and smiled at him.

"You can't have a prize. You didn't hit the target," the greasy man said.

Manny glared at the greasy man, at his helmet-strap beard and his sleeveless denim jacket. He wondered where you could buy a sleeveless denim jacket, if there were some kind of carnival clothing store. Maybe he just took a perfectly nice denim jacket and cut the sleeves off.

"Well, what the fuck made that pinging sound then?"

The greasy man sighed. "I didn't hear nothing."

"The fucking target dropped down too."

"Yeah, but then it popped back up again. You gotta hit the thing with force, kid."

"It's your fucking gun. I can only point and pull the trigger."

The greasy man looked past him, trying to catch the eye of the group of high-school girls standing by the Haunted House.

"You must have been standing too far back."

"There's a fucking white line on the ground. You drew the fucking thing. I had my foot on it. You said not to step any closer."

The greasy man waved him off, smiling at one of the girls when she glanced over.

"Listen to me, you greasy piece of shit. I shot the fucking target, and the fucking target pinged. Now give me the pink bunny."

The greasy man stared at Manny.

Manny stared back.

"You got some mouth on you, kid."

"Yeah, I got some fucking fists on me too. You try and fuck me, in front of my girl no less, and you expect me to bend over and take it. Not going to happen, my greasy friend. Not tonight. Now give me the bunny, or step outside of your box and we'll dance."

Manny raised his fists, hoping and praying that the greasy man would back down.

The greasy man looked up. Manny followed his eye and saw Jim heading toward them. Though it appeared to pain him greatly, the greasy man turned and grabbed the pink bunny from the shelf, then shoved it at Manny.

Jim kept his head down, much too tired for all this shit. The carnival came to town every year and lit up the sky like it was

July 4th only to disappear in a puff of hamburger wrappers and cigarette ends come morning.

The rides tore thick holes in the grass by the sidewalk, and every year some asshole's truck-cum-bedroom left a deposit of slick, black oil on the street. But then maybe he just had too much flying about in his head to enjoy anything.

When he'd phoned Brycewood Memorial Hospital that morning he had expected to be told that Billy Brooks was out of danger, or at worst there was no change. So when the nurse told him that Mr. Brooks had taken a turn for the worse, and that even if he did wake up there would be limited brain activity, Jim had to get her to repeat herself.

After he'd put the receiver down he'd walked to the bathroom and locked the door, then stood there, staring into the mirror. He might have felt guilty, but then he'd thought of Jess. He'd done it for Jess.

As he walked around, and saw all the smiling faces, and listened to the screams and the laughter, he wondered what people saw when they looked at him.

He'd get away with it. No doubt about that. He was tough. Tough enough to not fall apart, tough enough to ride out this storm and come out on the other side, even if Billy Brooks died.

Jerry walked through the crowds of people carefully, not wanting to bump into anyone. He'd won a goldfish, though the game had been so easy that everyone won a goldfish. His father had loved fish. He'd bought Jerry an aquarium for his tenth birthday, then set it up in his office and rarely let Jerry venture inside. "You'll kill them," he'd said.

Jerry breathed deeply, savoring the smell of candy floss and toffee apples, mixed with the thick, blue smoke that pumped from the rides.

He passed a group of boys, the same boys that threw eggs at him. He heard Dylan say something, and they all laughed. Sometimes he dreamed about hurting Dylan. He'd pick him up by the throat, then squeeze and squeeze until Dylan's eyes bulged and his feet shook. He woke up happy after those dreams; happy, but frightened too, because he wondered where his breaking point was, and what might happen if he reached it.

He felt something hit his shoulder, glanced down and saw a toffee apple on the grass. He heard more laughter. He walked away quickly, his goldfish sloshing about in its bag. He passed between the Flying Scooters and the Pendulum, glancing back over his shoulder, then bumped into the man that ran them.

"You're too big, pal. The thing won't get off the ground," the man said.

Jerry heard more laughter.

"Looking sharp, Abe," Manny said.

Abe was wearing a white polo with khaki shorts; shorts that mercifully covered a fair amount of leg. He'd dropped the brogues too, relieved when Manny told him that the heat from the feds was making it impossible for a gangster to operate in Tall Oaks.

"I'm going to ask her to prom," Abe said.

"Who?"

Abe nodded in the direction of the Waltzer. "Jane Berg."

Manny stifled a grimace. "Are you sure, Abe?"

"Yeah, I'm sure. Why?"

"No reason. I just always see her with Dylan McDermott. I thought they had a thing."

Abe glanced over at Jane Berg.

She was beautiful. And she stood in a small group of other, almost equally beautiful, girls.

Abe turned to Furat, looking for assurance. "She sits next to me in math," he said. "I think she's single. We used to play together at the Jewish preschool on the corner of Ingalls Street. Our parents are friends."

"Well, if she chose to sit next to you that must count for something, right?" Manny said.

"What should I say? I've never done this before."

Furat was about to speak when Manny cut her off.

"Stick your chest out and strut over there."

"I'm not sure how to strut."

"Remember Travolta, in *Saturday Night Fever?* When he used to be all money with that luscious black hair? He didn't walk the streets, he strutted. And the ladies could tell, just by his strut, that he was a fucking champion in the sack. That's how you need to walk over there. Can you lose the glasses?"

Abe took them off, suddenly appearing strange; a turtle without its shell.

He squinted at Manny, his eyes reduced to tiny beads.

Manny shook his head. "Put them back on. You can always take them off again when you're banging her after prom."

"I'm shitting myself," Abe said, pacing the street.

"Calm down," Manny said, grabbing Abe's face in both his hands and holding his cheeks tightly.

"Look at me. Look me in the eye, Abel."

Abe reluctantly met his eye.

"You can do this. You're a sweet kid with a big heart and Jane would be lucky to have you on her arm. We're at the carnival now, the home of romance, so there's no better time. She's having fun with her friends, kicking back before the serious business of college begins. She's probably a little nervous too, because no one's had the stones to ask her to senior prom yet, and she can't bear the thought of going stag. Sure, she's thought about Dylan McDermott asking her, or one of the other jocks, and that's who her friends expect her to go with. But if I know anything about women . . ."

"I don't think you . . ."

Manny held up a hand to silence Furat.

"And I'm sure that I do, then deep down she just wants to please her father. And what could make him happier than his little princess going to prom with a fucking sexy, six foot four, Jewish prince, with a voice so deep he's bound to have a set of balls big enough to give the man the ten grandchildren he's always wanted."

Manny pulled Abe's face down and kissed his forehead.

"Now go make magic happen."

As Abe turned to walk away, Manny slapped his ass and winked at him.

"What do you think she'll say?" Furat asked.

"It's in the lap of the gods now."

"I'm worried he's picked someone a bit too . . . popular."

"Yeah, well, the problem is that when we were growing up Abe used to hang around with her a lot. Back when she had an external brace and her mother tried to cut her hair and fucked it up so bad the hairdresser had to give her a buzz cut."

"A buzz cut?"

Manny nodded. "We all thought she was sick, possibly dying. He might have had a better shot back then. But they drifted apart."

"Why?"

"Puberty hit. She got a nice set of tits and a firm ass, and Abe grew tall enough for the janitor to come get him every time a seventh grader threw their football onto the roof of the cafeteria. And then his balls dropped so low that James Earl Jones worried that his voice-over work would dry up. Couple that with her perfect smile, and his lack of muscle, and they became chalk and cheese."

Abe walked back toward them, his head low and the eyes of the most popular girls in school searing a hole in the back of his head.

He shook his head and Manny pulled him in for a tight hug.

"She said thanks for asking but no."

"Could be lesbian?"

"No. She's going with Dylan McDermott."

Jess walked into the police station and steeled herself as the memories flooded her mind. They always did, every time she came in. It had been busy that day—people jostling and phones ringing, cameras outside and news vans blocking the street. Jim had held her tightly, leading her through to the back room where she'd given her statement. A few days later she'd had to stand beside her mother and appeal for Harry's safe return. She didn't know who she was appealing to, but she had been thoroughly coached beforehand. Not that it helped—as soon as she felt the eyes burning into her, the camera lenses, the flashes, she'd fallen apart. She'd dropped to her knees and sobbed. Jim had quickly picked her up and led her away. Her grief had been so raw, so unflinching that it turned out to be far more powerful than any heartfelt plea might have been. The outpouring of sympathy that followed had been overwhelming. Letters came addressed to her from all over the country. She'd read some of them, though taken little comfort from being in the prayers of strangers.

She'd been back to the station every week since. She'd watched it slowly empty as the months passed. Now it stood quiet, day and night. The pace slowed, the bustle a memory.

She knew State Police were still involved, that sightings were still being followed up and that Jim was in regular contact with the FBI. She drew no comfort from any of it.

She saw a picture of Harry on the notice board; it had been there since day one. He'd loved the police station. He'd always wanted to go in, to look at the cars and get a glimpse of the bad guys.

She walked up to the reception desk and rang the bell, then stood, waiting. She looked at the envelope in her hand—more photographs of Harry, ones she'd found hidden away in Alison's house.

She rang the bell again, shifting her weight from one foot to the other. She drummed her fingers on the desk.

She walked through to the back, then opened the door to Jim's office. It was dark inside so she switched the light on. She took out the photographs and set them out on his desk. He hadn't asked for them—he had more than enough.

She turned, and then she saw the file, left out, left open.

HARRY MONROE.

It was thick. She turned each page slowly. There were hundreds. She passed the forensic reports, then the interview transcripts. She skimmed her own, remembering each word spoken. Then she came to her mother's, her aunt Henrietta's. There was nothing in them, nothing of note. Jim had spoken to everyone that knew them, and not many people really did.

She came to Michael's. She thought it would be difficult reading: the questions Jim asked; the answers Michael gave. But she was numb to it. She knew he'd cheated. She'd known about Cindy Collins from his office. She'd known there'd been others too.

She looked at a photograph of the single green hair. There were numbers written next to it. She didn't understand them. She turned the page again. She saw another interview transcript, this time with Dr. Stone. She saw her name mentioned. She wasn't surprised. It wasn't a long interview.

She turned the page again. She saw Jim's neat handwriting. There were notes—pages and pages of notes. And there were photographs. A series of photographs of a man she'd never seen before. She stared at his face. Then at his name. Then she stared at the words written below. Person of Interest. She stood, and taking one of the photographs, she walked out of the door. She clutched it tightly as she walked back toward town, back toward the heat and noise of the carnival.

"You can see for miles," Elena said, as the Ferris wheel turned slowly and their car swayed gently.

"I'm shit scared," Thalia said, from between them.

Jared put his arm around her and pulled her close. She smiled up at him as he stroked her back.

"There's a Ferris wheel in Las Vegas that's twice the size of this one. It goes so high that you can barely see the ground," Jared said.

Thalia leaned forward and looked down. "I can see Manny. He's holding hands with Furat."

Elena looked down and smiled.

"Do you like Furat?" Thalia said.

"I do."

"Does Furat's mommy like Manny?"

"I very much doubt it," Elena said, and then turned to Jared. "Thanks for coming with us."

Jared smiled at her. He'd been sitting in the dark when she'd called, his mind sinking to the darkest of places that told him to push the knife a little deeper.

He turned away quickly, sucking down great mouthfuls of air. It crept up on him, the darkness, and then it hit him hard. He wanted to get off, to get away from them, from everyone.

"Are you okay?" Elena said.

He wanted to say no. To scream at her to look at him, to see what he saw, what his parents and everyone that really knew him saw.

He nodded, though kept his eyes pinned on the twinkling lights. "I'm fine."

He calmed as the car began to move, as the wheel brought them back down from the sky. He felt his mind lighten as he stroked Thalia's back. He found they calmed him down, kids. That's why he liked to watch them from his window. They were so pure, so unaffected. He looked at them, especially the little boys, and he felt jealous, because he missed being a child. He wanted to go back, to try it all again.

He stepped out of the car and was about to turn and help Elena and Thalia when he was knocked off his feet. The first blow caught him above the eye, the second square in the nose. His eyes blurred. Her screams mixed with the music. He brought his hand up to his face and tried to defend himself. He heard Elena shouting, and Thalia crying. And then he saw the cop dragging the woman off of him. He pulled himself up and got to his feet.

"WHERE IS HE?" she screamed.

Over and over.

A crowd gathered quickly.

He felt Elena's arm round him as she led him away.

22

A Good Wife

Lisa tried to smile at Jerry. She'd just told him that Max's parents were going to sell the PhotoMax. He'd nodded as she told him, as though he expected it. But Jerry was difficult to read. He rarely met her eye; he blushed whenever she smiled at him. He was painfully awkward around her, from the way he stood with his arms folded across his chest, to the way he kept his head dipped low, as though his chin were glued down. He did all he could to appear smaller.

"Are you okay?" she said.

He nodded.

She tried to smile again but it was difficult. Her life had taken a turn she was struggling to cope with. She rented a small apartment above the pharmacy but had moved back in with her mother, just until she got herself together. She wondered when that might be. Max's mother blamed her. She hadn't come right out and said it, but she now regarded Lisa with an icy detachment far at odds from the warmth she was used to. Lisa didn't miss him. As bad as that sounded, she didn't miss him. She might, one day, when the feeling came back, when the numbness faded. She did feel the guilt though. She felt it so deep in her bones that she knew it would be with her forever.

She'd felt her share of pain over the years.

She thought of Max. She thought of her father. She found that she was crying. That happened often now. Her mother would pass her a tissue, then she'd notice that her cheeks felt wet.

"Are you thinking about Max?"

"My father, actually."

"What was he like?"

"He had dementia, at a young age. He'd go days without saying a word, to me, to my mother. On good days he'd talk to me. He'd call me Lisa and spend time with me. On bad days I was a stranger." She spoke quietly, without emotion.

"Oh."

"He loved birds," she said. "I'm not sure why. He used to feed them and they'd shit all over the yard."

Jerry smiled.

"I still miss him. When he died I didn't think I'd ever get over it. I stayed in bed for a whole summer."

"And then you felt better?"

"And then my mother gave me his old photograph album. It was as I flipped through the pages that I began to feel better, because I could feel him in every shot. Does that sound stupid?"

"No," he said, quietly.

"I recognized the ones we had taken together, in the forest, while we had been searching for the red-billed cuckoo. He didn't like me tagging along, said I made too much noise. I wondered if it even existed. My mother said that he probably hadn't seen it. She said that he claimed to have seen lots of things that never were, because his mind left him so often."

"Oh."

"He spent his whole life looking for it. I don't know why it was so important to him."

"Maybe because it's so pretty?"

"Maybe, but I think it was probably more than that. My mother told him he was wasting his time. It became an obsession. And then one day he came in and he was crying. He couldn't speak. I'd never seen him cry before. He wasn't that kind of man."

"Because he had seen it?"

"Yeah. But he didn't take a photograph. He said he hadn't been able to move—he'd just sat there, watching it. He was so happy, Jerry. I'd never seen him so happy. He took me back with him that night. And we sat together on the ground, among the damp leaves, and he described it to me. And he made it sound magical. He said it was beautiful, but not as beautiful as me. And then he told me that he loved me. It was the only time he ever said it. In my whole life it was the only time he ever said it. But I can't be sure that he meant it, because I don't know who he saw when he looked at me. I don't know if that was a good day or a bad day. If the bird wasn't there, if it wasn't ever really there, in Tall Oaks, then he can't of meant it, can he?"

"This is beautiful, Al, really top notch. What is it again?" Manny asked.

"It's called *burek*. It used to be Furat's favorite when she was a little girl," Mrs. Al-Basri replied.

"It's still my favorite," Furat said.

"It can't be. I've seen how quickly you eat a Big Mac."

Everybody laughed.

"So how are you settling in to Tall Oaks?" Elena asked, while she pulled Thalia's bib tight around her neck. Thalia was wearing her new, yellow dress, and seemed intent on destroying it.

"Jesus, Ma, I can't fucking breathe," Thalia said.

Elena held her head in her hands.

Manny glanced at Furat, both tried not to laugh.

"I'm so sorry, Mrs. Al-Basri. You see, Manny has Tourette's, at least I hope he does, otherwise he's just a foul-mouthed idiot, and Thalia picks up on all the cursing."

"Don't worry about it, Elena, Furat has already explained. And please, call me Aarfah."

"Can I call you Art?" Manny asked.

Furat laughed. Elena shook her head.

"No, why don't you just stick with Al," Aarfah said, rolling her eyes. "Anyway, you asked how we were settling in. Very well actually. My husband sends his apologies for not being here by the way. He's flown to New York to visit some friends from Iraq."

Manny raised an eyebrow. Furat shot him a look.

"I love it too. It's a lovely place to bring up children. The schools are excellent."

"Yes, we did a lot of research on the Internet before we moved. And with Doctor Livingstone retiring it seemed a perfect fit. A ready-made practice to take over. And it's such a pretty town, with one of the lowest crime rates in the whole country, although if you search for Tall Oaks now then the first pages that come up are stories about Harry Monroe. Every time I think about it I can't believe it all happened here, and not long before we moved in."

Manny nodded. "I think about him all the time, especially when I go to pick Thalia up from preschool. They used to play together."

"Do you still see his mother? I mean, aside from what happened at the carnival? Furat told me—it must have been awful."

"It was, especially for Jared, poor guy. I worry about Jess. We used to get together with the kids. When her husband Michael—a real asshole by the way—walked out on them, she kind of went to pieces. I chased her for months, trying to get her to come out of the house but she used to make her excuses. I went round there a couple of times and she looked awful. I don't think she had slept for days. She loved Michael so much. When we first got together for a meal, back when Danny was still around, Jess asked me not to wear anything too revealing, in case Michael stared at me. Strange right?"

Furat nodded. "Some women are like that though. They have low self-esteem. It's sad."

"And then ... Harry. He was her whole world. You should have seen the way she looked at him. I mean, I love Thalia, and Manny's okay once you get to know him."

"Thanks, Ma," Manny said.

"But with Harry, she worshipped the ground he walked on. We'd have play dates in the park, Harry loved the statue, Artemis. All the kids do. He'd want to climb it but she would never let him. She used to freak out about him getting hurt. She wouldn't even let him play on the slide. I used to ask her about it and she just said that she was scared; scared that something bad might happen to him. And, as much as she loved Michael, I used to get the feeling that she was scared of him too."

"How do you mean?"

"Well, one time I was round at her house and Michael was due back that evening. He'd been away somewhere on business. She was cleaning the place, and not just dusting and vacuuming—she had all the food out of the cupboards and she was wiping it down. The cans, she was wiping the cans. I think Michael was some kind of control freak."

Manny helped himself to another piece of *burek*. Furat smiled at him and he winked back at her. She was amazed that he hadn't cursed yet, though they were still only on the first course. He looked handsome in his light blue shirt and dark pants. Now that his head had healed, and he'd had his hair cut for prom, he looked really good.

"I tried to be there for her. I tried everything. I used to go to her mother's house to see her, but she would never come down from her bedroom. The few times I've seen her in town she just smiles and rushes off before I can speak to her. I just wish we could help her, but without Harry, or Michael, I don't think she can be helped. It's just so sad."

Jared stood in front of the mirror and practiced his smile. The dinner suit was Armani. The jacket felt snug on his shoulders, fitted, to the untrained eye. The shirt was Yves Saint Laurent—a nice bright, white that complemented the Armani perfectly. And the bow tie was Tom Ford, a sparkling champagne color that added a touch of style to what could have otherwise been a rather bland look. There were still two days until the wedding so he would have time to go over everything in his head, think up some good conversation starters and perfect his dance moves. There was a video on the Internet that showed him the basics—waltz, tango and fox-trot. He should have really known the steps by now, but being a small-town boy meant black-tie events were not something he was accustomed to. And he'd have the best looking lady in the room on his arm so had better not fuck anything up.

This would be his last date with Elena. He knew that now. And then he would move on. He always knew that there would come a time when he'd have to stop running, stop hiding too. And that time was nearly upon him. There were things he couldn't undo; things that he'd have to live with. He was tired now. He was still shaken from the attack. He had a small bruise on his head and dark lines beneath each eye. He wouldn't press charges against Jessica Monroe. That would be a stupid thing to do. The cop had been grateful about that when he'd stopped by to check he was okay. Hopefully grateful enough to leave him alone for a few days, so he could say goodbye.

He'd make things right again. He'd start to move toward home, but he'd have to make a stop along the way. And then, when he made it back, he'd beg forgiveness. Say that he'd lost his way but now he had found God again. They'd like that.

He could fix everything, he hoped—there was still time.

It wasn't too late for him.

"Fits like a glove," Roger said as he looked into the mirror.

"A latex glove," Henrietta replied.

"What do you mean?"

"It's a little tight, darling, especially across the shoulders. It looks as though you're wearing a straitjacket."

Roger flexed his biceps and heard an awful sound. Stitches snapping.

"I think I should be commended for getting into it in the first place. There's not many men that could still fit into their graduation suit."

"There's not many men that would want to."

"Meaning?"

"Meaning that styles have changed over the last thirty years."

"Yes, but class never goes out of fashion. And a Gieves & Hawkes suit is pure class. It would have been fine, but in case you haven't noticed I've gotten a little bigger in the muscle department."

She peered over her glasses at him. "You do look a little bit bigger. What on earth have you been doing at that gym? You've only been going a few weeks."

"Ah, well, I have a Russian."

"A Russian?"

"Yes. And he works me hard this Russian. Really knows how to get inside of me and stoke the old fire."

"I'm not even going to touch that one."

Roger laughed, and she began to laugh. But then it caught in her throat and turned into a cry. Just like that. Abrupt, without warning.

And then the tears were streaming, and she was struggling. Because the time had come, she felt it. It wouldn't get any easier.

He sat down on the bed beside her and took her hand in his.

"Hen, what's the matter? It can't go on, all of this crying."

She took a breath, composing herself. "It's nothing. I've just been a bit under the weather that's all. I'll be better soon. Forget about it. Anyway, you have enough to worry about. You have to get a new suit now, and there're only two days until the wedding."

He nodded, wiping her tears away.

"How do we know the McDermotts again?"

"Family friends. They're very wealthy, and flashy with it too, so it should be quite an event. I called in to see French John, in the patisserie, and he said the cake would be the death of him. Apparently she's quite a demanding bride. Roger? Are you listening to me?"

He looked up at her and she could see something in his eyes. She wondered if he knew.

"Have you read about this?" Elena said, pointing at the newspaper.

"What is it?" French asked, glancing over.

"This guy in Despair. Sounds like he might die."

"Yeah, I saw it. It's on all the front pages."

"It says here he's been convicted of battery seven times, twice against a woman."

"Sounds like a peach. I'm sure he'll be missed."

"They're all like that over there."

"Snobby," he said, laughing.

"Seriously. I mean, who'd want to live in a town called Despair?"

"It's actually quite beautiful in parts."

"I forgot to ask—how was it with Louise? Was it awful?" Elena said.

"No, actually she was quite pleased. I think, were it not for all the Botox, that she might have been trying to smile."

"Wow. High praise indeed. Did she notice that you've changed the shade of the flowers?"

He crouched by the cake. "I'm not sure she's intelligent enough to tell the time, let alone notice a subtle change to the shade of icing on her own wedding cake."

"But she was happy anyway?"

"She said it was exactly the kind of *more* that she had wanted the first time round."

"I hope you made her pay for it."

"I added a thousand dollars to her father's bill. That ought to teach her a lesson."

"I don't think they'll even notice."

"Why is he so rich anyway? I mean, it's not like Tall Oaks is Beverly Hills. Billionaires stand out around here."

"I don't really know. Something to do with real estate I think. I've met the son a few times. He's in Manny's class."

He stepped away from the cake. It was magnificent, the finest work he had ever created.

"Is the son as brain dead as the daughter?"

"Maybe more so. Dylan McDermott has that air about him, you know, like he's been spoiled to the point of ruin. There's no backbone in kids like that. No appreciation for anything. If it all comes that easy then why would there be? When I met him he looked down on me, if that's possible for a kid to do. I could have slapped his pretty face, seen if there was any fight in him. Give me Manny any day of the week, cursing and all."

"So, you're bringing Jared with you? How is he? I heard about Jess."

"He was shaken. Hard not to be. But he was nice about it too. We all know what she's going through. She needs help though. She can't go on like this."

"Well I'm glad he's okay."

"I'm looking forward to seeing him again. It's nice to spend time with him."

"Are you thinking that Saturday night might be *the* night?"

She shrugged. "Who knows. It's been long enough though. And what about you? Is Richard going to grace us with his presence?"

He shook his head. "I never even said I was seeing him. You just assumed . . ."

"Trouble in paradise?" she said, putting an arm around his shoulder. "Let's close up for an hour, get some lunch. You can tell me all about it."

"Okay. But there's really nothing to tell."

"Tearoom? You can get those scones you love."

"How about Bel Canto?"

"Wow, French. You feeling flush?"

"I've got the McDermotts' money to spend now."

"Champagne all round."

He laughed.

Jerry stood by the bed. The plate was where he'd left it, untouched. The drapes were still drawn. The air was thick. He wanted to open a window but worried about waking her. She needed to sleep. He'd done more research. She'd sleep for longer at this stage.

He stood above her, trying to see her face but it was so dark in the room he could barely make her out.

He walked over to the chair by her dressing table and sat down.

He was going to be out of a job. The PhotoMax was closing and he'd be out of a job. His eyes felt heavy, his muscles ached. He hadn't eaten for days. He thought about Lisa, about her father. He'd liked it when she said he was odd, because his family was odd too. And that made him wonder if everybody was odd in their own way.

He left the bedroom and walked down the stairs slowly. They creaked loudly under his weight. He passed the living room, the tick of the clock louder than it had ever been, and then he walked into his dark room.

Mom was dying. She wouldn't have long left. Then he'd be on his own.

The fan spun slowly. Jim stared up at it. He didn't bother switching the lights on in his apartment. He kept the blinds open. The moonlight bounced off the walls.

"You're asking the wrong questions, Jim."

Michael's voice was smooth on the tape, lulling.

Jim turned up the volume, though not too loud. It was late and the neighbor had a kid.

"What should I be asking?"

Jim sipped his beer, wondered where Jess was. Somewhere, with someone.

He could hear the whispered voice of Michael's lawyer telling him to shut the fuck up.

"My lawyer's telling me to shut the fuck up."

"They always say that."

He heard Michael laugh.

"Why aren't you worried?"

"I am."

"You don't sound worried. You called your lawyer. You waited for him before you spoke to us. You didn't rush back from Houston."

"I couldn't get a flight."

"You seem calm."

"It's just how I am."

"Your son is missing. Every second counts. We need to find him fast. He's out there, Michael. Someone's taken him."

They broke then. Michael's lawyer went to get coffee, Michael went to take a piss.

Jim grabbed another beer from the fridge, opened it and sipped the froth from the top. He could still see the bruising on his knuckles, thought he might have broken a bone. It would heal. He looked in the freezer for something to eat, a meal he could put straight in the microwave. It was empty. He sipped his beer again as he walked back into the living room.

"Tell me about Jess."

"What about her?"

"Why did you leave?"

"She's needy."

"That's it?"

"What do you want me to say?"

"Is she a good mother?"

"She loves Harry. So yeah . . . but not a good wife."

"What's a good wife?"

"A dead one."

He heard Michael laugh, his lawyer whisper something again.

"He thinks you don't know that I'm joking. I have to make it clear that was a joke."

He skipped forward.

"Business."

"What kind of business?"

"Hedge fund."

"You've had a tough couple of years."

"Like everybody else."

"Tell me about Aurora Springs."

"What about it?"

"You put a lot of money in. Your clients did too. What went wrong?"

"The economy. People can't afford the luxury of a second home. Construction costs were higher than we thought too. Everybody's got their hand out."

"You went there often."

"So?"

"With Cindy Collins."

"She's my assistant. It's business."

Jim laughed. "So you've shut the site down now?"

"Temporarily."

"You ran out of money. A lot of clients pulled funds out."

"Why ask questions if you already know the answers, Jim?"

"Jess kept you afloat."

"Not really."

"*So you didn't ask her to invest?*"

"*No.*"

"*So she just decided to? She's savvy like that?*"

"*Her family's got so much they don't know where to put it.*"

He skipped forward again.

"*Domestic abuse. Jess called us herself.*"

"*She retracted her statement in full, didn't press charges. You guys let me go, remember, Jim?*"

"*Why'd you hit her?*"

Michael sighed. "*No comment.*"

"*You ever hit Harry?*"

"*No.*"

"*But you hit your wife.*"

"*You're fishing, Jim. It's not going to get you anywhere.*"

"*YOU'RE WASTING MY TIME.*"

"*I CAN'T TELL YOU WHAT YOU NEED TO KNOW.*"

"*That's enough.*" *A new voice; Michael's lawyer.*

Jim stopped the tape. He'd lost his temper, it was hard not to. Michael answered the questions he wanted to, no-commented his way through the ones he didn't. It was frustrating. They should've been on the same side, finding Harry their only concern.

He took the tape out and put it back in the case.

23

No Rough Stuff

"I'm worried about you," Jim said, quietly.

He turned to look at her, knew she didn't have the energy to tell him that she was fine. It was too big of a lie, like telling him the sky was green and the grass was blue. He'd stopped by because he hadn't seen her for a couple of days. He found that she hadn't left her bed. Her mother was worried, gave him a call because there was nobody else.

She shifted in the bed, rubbed her eyes.

"You're lucky Jared isn't pressing charges."

"Who is he?"

He walked to the window and opened the shutters. Sunlight poured in. It was hot out. He couldn't remember a summer this hot. There would be a storm soon enough though, just to take the edge off. There always was.

"Nobody."

"You can't tell me, is that what you're saying? He's my fucking son, Jim. My son," she said, squinting up at him, sunlight falling over her.

He turned. "You shouldn't have looked at the file, Jess. You shouldn't have confronted Jared."

She sat up, anger flaring in her eyes. "I'm the only person doing something. I'm the only person on the street every day. Where's the fucking urgency gone, Jim? I see you, taking your time. I see Adam, and all the other officers. I see them in town, stopping for coffee and catching up with people. And I want to scream at them. I want to fucking scream at them to do something—to get up and keep searching, keep people thinking about him. At least act like they're busy, like they give a shit."

He looked down at the grass and saw the gardener. He was working hard, pulling at a weed that had managed to grow between two slabs of stone. He was trying to pull it at the root, where it was strongest. He'd give up in a minute—just chop it as low as he could, deal with it another day.

"Jim, are you even listening?"

He turned around. He wanted to wait, for her to calm down. There wasn't much he could say that she didn't already know. She was right. The urgency had died, but that was inevitable. It couldn't be sustained when there was so little to go on. The reporters had moved on to other stories. They'd call him for updates, see if there were any angles they could work but he had nothing to give them.

"I'm doing all I can, believe me. I'm meeting Dr. Stone again in half an hour."

"Another waste of time."

"He called. I don't have much else at the moment, Jess."

She was sitting up in the bed, her thin top doing little to cover her breasts. He felt bad for noticing, and then worse when she leaned forward and grabbed his belt, pulling him toward her. Worse, because he didn't stop her.

Henrietta sat with him all day. She hadn't left the room, she hadn't wanted to leave his side. She pressed her face into his hair and breathed him in. Occasionally she glanced out of the window, at the shimmering pool, and then at the trees in the distance, as they swayed beneath moonlight that fell onto his face and drained the life from it.

She rocked him slowly. The chair glided back and forth, silently. She'd heard Roger come and go, then come and go again. She wondered what he did each day, how he passed the time. He played golf often, and badly. He played with other members of the club, all former masters of the universe. She'd been out for dinner with them a number of times, quickly realizing that the only common ground they shared was money. They spoke of it as if it wasn't a crass thing to do, not even reining in their boasts when the waiter delivered their drinks and pretended not to be listening. Boats and cars, houses and stocks.

She brought his head up to her shoulder and nestled it there.

"I suppose I should say goodbye now," she choked out the words.

She hugged him tightly. Tears fell onto his blanket.

"But I don't want to. I don't want to say goodbye. You need to know that. You can't be replaced. Not ever. I'm so sad that you're gone, and I always will be."

When she could cry no more, when her chest ached and his hair was wet through, she once again lay him in his bed and covered him.

Then she walked out of his bedroom, along the hallway and down the stairs.

She stepped into the backyard and unlocked the garage.

The shovel felt heavy. She walked far across the grass, until she came to the willow tree she sometimes sat beneath.

Its branches hung low, streaking her face as she swept through them.

There was no breeze, just stillness.

She sank the shovel into the ground and began to dig.

Jim entered the house silently. There was no alarm.

He stood in the hallway, cream carpets, badly stained. He stared at the marks: looked like mud. They'd all worn shoe covers at first. Forensics had worn coveralls, their eyes peeking out over the tops of their masks, their hoods pulled tight and their purple-gloved hands sifting through Harry's belongings carefully. They had photographed every inch of the house. He knew it better than his own.

He flipped the lights on—spotlights; too many—and felt the heat on the top of his head. There was a bathroom to the left, never used. Jess stored Harry's toys in the shower stall. He opened the door. There was a smell, maybe the drains. The floor was tiled, white, unblemished. He caught his reflection in the mirror.

Next to the bathroom was a closet, for coats and shoes, and anything else Jess could fit inside. He moved past it, then descended slowly into Harry's bedroom.

A single bulb hung above, uncovered. They'd removed the shade. It hung low; they thought it might have been knocked.

The road-map rug was gone. There were drawings on the wall—scribbles of greens and reds—Picassos to Jess. She hadn't been back since it happened. He didn't blame her. Her mother had collected what she needed, once Jim had said it was okay.

He tried to imagine it, seeing a clown in the corner of the room, watching him, whispering to Jess.

He took the stairs, passed the kitchen and the living room, then went straight up to the top floor. To Jess's bedroom. The master bath was next to it.

The bed was big. Jess must have been lost in it when Michael left. Jim walked over and glanced out of the window. There was nothing much to see, just more houses. More people inside, preoccupied with nothing much at all. He took a step back. He could see the neighbor's light on, the glow from her television. Mrs. Lewis.

He wasn't sure why he still came here. He'd stopped trying to see something that wasn't there.

He answered his cell phone on the first ring.

"Detective?"

The voice was gruff, slurry.

"Yeah. This is Jim. Who's calling?"

"It's Clifton."

Jim searched his mind, then it settled on Echo Bay. On the guy with the hacking cough.

"Right. What can I do for you?"

"You remember Arturo? Jared Martin dated his sister."

There was background noise, a bar.

"Sure."

He heard Clifton take a sip of something and smack his lips.

"So Arturo's moved to another site, another developer. He took all my guys with him. Really left me in the shit."

Jim glanced out the window again. "I'm sorry to hear that."

He heard Clifton cough, then spit. Then someone yell something.

"So his sister is back in town. The rack on her, big ass, not fat, shapely . . . curvature."

Jim sighed.

"Anyway, I don't think she's got papers. So maybe you could come haul her in. I tried to tell the sheriff, but he's sweet on her. Everyone's sweet on her. Can you put her in jail or something?"

"What's her name?"

"Mia. She lives on Coral Street. Number seven. They got a shitty place."

"That it?" Jim said.

"So if you come down now stop by The Saturn Bar. You can buy me a –"

Jim cut him off.

Roger dabbed the sweat from his forehead with his wristband. He leaned down as low as his back would allow and stretched. His muscles burned. He'd sprinted back.

He entered through the side gate and walked round to the pool.

He hadn't run far really, though he'd been gone for hours.

He wondered if Henrietta was still up. He glanced at the house, though he couldn't see any lights on. He'd stay outside until he cooled down. He'd shower in one of the guest bathrooms. He didn't want to wake her.

As he surveyed the garden he saw it: a lump in the grass beside the weeping willow tree that Henrietta loved so much.

He'd bought it for her as a gift. She was impatient; they'd delivered it on the back of an articulated lorry ready-grown. It had taken four men to place it. Instant character.

He walked over slowly, taking care not to tread on any of the fuchsias or purple coneflowers that Henrietta adored. The gardener tended to them daily; each bed fanned from a central pathway of striped lawn.

He walked up to the lump and leaned down, running his fingers through the pile of damp earth. Then he parted the willow's canopy and stepped through, falling straight into a deep hole.

He scrambled out quickly, his knees dark with mud as he crawled back out and onto the lawn.

It was then that he saw her, walking toward him, with a blanket in her arms and tears streaking her face.

"Hen," he said.

She looked up, startled.

She looked back at the house, and then down at his knees.

He stood, and then took a step toward her.

"What is it? What's going on?"

She clutched the blanket tightly.

He saw the shovel, discarded to the side.

"What have you got there?"

She shook her head.

He looked back at the hole again, then up at the blanket, at the shape beneath it.

He reached out.

She stepped back again.

"What is it, Hen? Give it to me."

She took another step back, then cried out as she toppled backward.

The blanket unraveled.

He looked down and gasped.

"It's a baby."

She sat up. Roger kneeled beside her, his face pale.

Then he gently picked it up. It was light.

"It's a doll," he said.

He brought it level with his face.

He recognized the face, the likeness incredible, the wisp of hair, the pink mottled cheeks. It was a face he still saw every day, when he closed his eyes. It was a face he would never forget.

"Oh, Hen," he said.

She fell into him, burying her face in his chest as sobs shook her body.

He held her tightly.

And then the sprinklers came on.

They didn't move.

They stayed there for a long time, not noticing as the spray soaked them with every pass.

Jim couldn't decide if the car was burned-out or just badly rusted. It was dark, with no streetlights burning, and no lights coming from any of the trailers.

The drive had taken him ninety minutes because he'd kept his foot to the floor. It was early, way too early to knock, so he'd decided to sit in his car until the sun came up.

But then he saw someone at the window, and a light come on as one of the doors opened.

He stepped out of the car, surprised by how cool the night air was.

She stood in the doorway, as if she had been expecting him.

He walked slowly, his hands by his side. He thought about reaching for his badge.

"You a friend of Arturo?" she said, quietly.

He stepped onto the creaking veranda. She was beautiful. Truly beautiful.

Her eyes were light, her cheekbones high. Her breasts strained at the robe, her legs were long and tan.

He nodded.

She walked back inside, her short robe barely covering her.

He followed her in.

A lamp burned above the stove. Wood paneling lined every inch of the walls and ceiling, chipped in places but polished to a hazy shine. The couch was covered in plastic, the dining bench too.

She sat at the small table, motioned for him to follow.

"Did he discuss how much?"

Jim shook his head.

"Fifty bucks for an hour, hundred for the night. You have to wear protection, but don't worry, I have some. No rough stuff."

"I'm Sergeant Jim Young, Tall Oaks PD," he said, finally offering her his badge.

She glanced at it, though remained composed.

"Tall Oaks. Harry Monroe," she said.

He nodded.

She looked away.

"You're Mia. I spoke to your brother a while back."

She nodded, pulling her robe tight.

He heard movement in one of the bedrooms.

"My mother."

She caught his surprise.

"We need the money."

Mia reached out and fixed the drape, then shuffled a stack of coasters.

"So guys just turn up here, no warning?"

"Sometimes. Arturo normally calls first."

"He's a good brother then," Jim said, immediately regretting it.

"Half-brother."

He watched her lips as she spoke—they were full, inviting.

"You're not here to bust me."

"No."

"But you show up at this time of night?" she said, glancing at the small clock tacked to the wall above her.

"I have trouble sleeping. I feel like I'm the only one up. Like the whole world is asleep."

She nodded.

He saw a photograph by the window—her with a young boy.

She followed his eye. "My son. Daniel."

She placed the coasters down.

"I wanted to ask you about Jared Martin."

She looked up. "Jared? What about him?"

"How well did you know him?"

She shrugged. "I saw him a couple of times. Maybe four. Why? Is he okay?"

"He's fine."

"So he's in Tall Oaks now, with the rich folk?"

He waited for more, but it didn't come.

"So what was he like?" he asked.

She paused.

"Different. Nice enough. Well spoken. Polite. Not much to tell really. Men like him, they don't pass through Echo Bay much. And they don't stick around for girls like me."

She spoke without a hint of self-pity.

He liked her.

"Do you know where he lived before?"

"No. Maybe he told me, I don't remember."

"Did you go to his place?"

She looked at him.

"I'm sorry; I'm just trying to find out more about him."

"No. I didn't go to his place. We went out, like people do, to the movies, to dinner. He was more like a friend. Nothing happened. He left town. He didn't tell me much about himself, and I didn't ask. He dressed well, he smelled nice. He was a perfect gentleman."

They heard movement again and she lowered her voice. "I'm sorry, Sergeant. But I think it was a wasted trip. I can't tell you much about him, because I don't know much about him."

He looked at the photograph again.

"How old is he?"

"Four."

"Nice looking kid."

She softened.

"Jared ever meet him?"

She frowned. "I don't think so."

"Where is he now?"

"With his father. He spends every other week with his father."

Jim nodded.

She followed him to the door.

He stepped out, then stood on the veranda, the sun rising behind him.

"Harry Monroe was three," Jim said.

"That's not why you're interested in Jared, surely?"

"If there's anything else you can tell me . . .? Anything at all?"

She met his eye. "He wouldn't fuck me. I wanted to. He came to pick me up, I wasn't wearing much. I don't usually get turned down. Not ever. He left me standing there. I was upset. I told Arturo that maybe he was gay or something. I think Arturo told the guys, and they gave him shit. I didn't see him again."

"Okay," Jim said, turning to leave.

"Will you tell him sorry? I was embarrassed. It was stupid."

"Yeah. I'll tell him."

Jerry sifted through the drawers, then pulled each one out and emptied the contents onto the floor. He knew it wasn't there.

He climbed the stairs, tried taking them two at a time but felt a pain in his chest. He'd even searched through the trash, in case she'd thrown it out. He could see pasta sauce on his hand, an old band-aid stuck to his knee. He smelled of garbage.

He walked into her room. It was hot inside, boiling hot.

Jerry shook her.

"Mom," he said.

He shook her again, this time harder.

"Where is it? The envelope. Did you take out the trash?"

He knew that she hadn't.

He knew that she'd sent it.

He walked over to the window and pressed his head against it.

24

The Wedding

"Is there something wrong with this car?" Henrietta said.

Roger shook his head, his mirrored Aviators slipping down his nose as he did.

"Nope, nothing wrong."

"Well, why are we moving so slowly?"

"I thought you'd enjoy a leisurely drive."

"Look over there." She pointed to the sidewalk. "Mr. Thompson is actually walking faster than we're driving."

He turned his head to look, taking his foot off of the gas as he did.

"Ah, see. He's power-walking. I thought about doing that."

"You already do, with your sticks."

"That's hiking."

"I fail to see the difference."

"Look at the wiggle in his hips, and his attire. I dare say I wear lycra far better, now I'm in shape."

She laughed.

"Anyway, my Russian said it's for old men. He said that a stallion like me needs to gallop. Imagine that, Hen. Me, a stallion."

"I always thought of you more as a pony."

He laughed. "Yes, quite. But no, apparently your old husband is a stallion."

"Well, do you think the stallion might put his foot down a bit? At this rate we'll miss the first dance."

He laughed again.

She smiled at him, for a moment feeling glad to have him by her side. They'd stayed up most of the night, lying beside each other and talking, mostly about Thomas, about the kind of man he might have been. Roger liked to believe he would have been a doctor—a man brimming with confidence, popular and funny. She'd been surprised by how much better she felt just by talking to her husband, and listening to him talk about their son. Roger had said he still visited the grave often. Every time he went running he would stop and kneel for a minute. The thought had made her want to cry. And it made her love him. Not in the way that she should, in the way that a wife should love her husband, but in a way that made her see him in a different light. He couldn't do it again. That's why they didn't try IVF. That's why they didn't adopt. He couldn't go through it all again. She understood.

The wedding was a lavish affair. So lavish that the McDermotts, worried about interlopers, had hired a group of ex-Secret-Service personnel to run security. They were so overly thorough that a queue of cars was starting to form from the main gates of the McDermotts' home halfway back down Cedar Hill.

"Is it really necessary, all of this security?" French John asked from the back of the car.

"You tell us? You're the one that's already been inside this morning."

Elena turned around in her seat to talk to him.

"Well, it is fabulous in there," he replied.

"You know, you've ruined that word for everyone."

"Who has?"

"The gays. Now straight guys can't ever say it without feeling self-conscious. Isn't that right, Jared?"

Jared turned to her. "Sorry, I wasn't listening. By the way, have I told you how fabulous you look today?"

Elena laughed.

"Well, I think you look fabulous too, don't you think so, French?"

"Actually, I do. For a straight guy you dress impeccably well, Jared."

"Thanks, French. And you haven't even seen the best part yet. When I take the dinner jacket off my shirt is sleeveless. Sleeveless shirt with a dickie bow. How cool is that?"

Elena poked him in the side, jolting him so much that he swerved the car. Thankfully they both laughed, and no one noticed the sweat that was starting to bead on his forehead.

Jared swallowed, and tried to concentrate on making his smile appear natural. He was doing well: charming and funny, and yet to say anything stupid. He just needed to get out of the car and breathe some fresh air.

And then he saw the unsmiling faces of the men at the gate.

"Right, boys, I have the invitations, and you just need to get your IDs out."

"We need identification to go to a wedding?" Jared said, bristling.

"Yeah, this isn't just any wedding. We had to supply guest names in advance, and not just for the place settings, rumor has it they ran background checks on everybody too. I just gave Jared Martin, right? No middle name?"

He opened the window. He checked the rearview mirror; there was another car right behind. He was trapped.

"Jared?"

He turned to her, his eyes wild. He blinked a couple of times, trying to remember what she had said.

"Sorry?"

"It's just Jared Martin? No middle name?"

He nodded. There was only one car standing between them and the checkpoint now. He could say he had left his wallet at home. That might work. He started to calm. And then he saw his wallet on the dashboard. His license was fake. A good fake. It had held up at the Ford dealership. They'd just made a copy and stuck it in his file. But now, on closer inspection . . .

He heard French John say something. And then he heard Elena laughing, so he smiled and tried to join in. But his laugh sounded all wrong, not how he'd practiced. They had to notice that. Then they'd start asking him questions, like why he was sweating so much, and why he didn't want his identification checked? Was he a fugitive? they'd ask. And then they'd laugh at that, because it was such a ridiculous thought. Imagine that, they'd say. Elena has been dating a wanted man. And then French John would make some joke about dangerous men being sexy, but he wouldn't mean it, he'd just say it because he wanted to make everyone laugh, especially him, because he looked so nervous.

The car in front drove through the large gates, and he had no choice but to inch forward.

"Good morning," the agent in the dark suit with the dark glasses said, though it was clear from his expression that he was having a far from good morning.

"Invitations and photo identification, please."

Jared steeled himself and passed his license to Elena. She placed it at the bottom of the pile and gave it to the agent.

He checked Elena's license carefully, gave it back to her and then started to check French John's.

Jared brought a hand to chest, could feel his heart racing. He stared straight ahead, watching a squirrel dart along the street and shoot up the high wall that surrounded the house. He turned his head and sank low in his seat when he saw the agent hand French John's license back to Elena. And then, just as the agent glanced down at his license, they heard the crunching of metal and the sound of car horns blasting behind them.

The agent looked up.

Jared jumped out of the car and stared back down the hill.

"What's happened?" French John called out.

"Looks like a red Ferrari has run into the back of a black Rolls," Jared said, a slight tremor in his voice.

He heard the agent curse, thrust his license back at him as he pushed past, and set off briskly down the hill.

Jess brought out two cups of coffee from the kitchen.

She handed one to Jim, and then sat down beside him on the edge of the terrace, her bare feet in the grass.

She turned to him and stared into his eyes—not smiling, just staring. She did that sometimes, without realizing.

He stared back, both content to sit in silence for a while.

He sipped his coffee slowly.

She bit her bottom lip and ran a hand through her hair.

"What are you thinking?" he asked.

"What am I always thinking? I need to be out there now, knocking doors and asking questions. I need to be seen, I need to be doing something, not sitting in the sun drinking coffee."

She stood, then sat back down, kneading the muscles in her shoulders. She looked over at him. He looked tired.

She looked down at her hands before placing them between her crossed legs to stop the shaking. She wondered if it would ever go away, even if they found him. She stood again, her feet sinking into the grass.

"Why are you here?"

He looked up at her.

"I mean now? Why did you come by? Why do you keep coming by when you've got nothing new to tell me?"

Her words sounded harsh. She didn't mean them to, or maybe she did.

"I . . ." he started to speak but she cut him off.

"Don't think that there's more to this, Jim. I still dream of Michael, of him coming back to me. And you can't compete with that dream. Nobody can."

"Still dreaming of Michael," he said, quietly.

She stiffened. "He's still my husband. Despite all the things I do, he's still mine."

"What about the things he did to you?"

"I know about the women."

"And when you called us, when he hit you?"

"That was . . ."

"A mistake?"

"Yes."

"He hit you by mistake."

"No. I mean, I don't know. We were drunk, got in a fight. We've been through this. It's a waste of fucking time."

He shook his head, looked away.

"What?" she said.

He turned back to her, got to his feet.

"You want to say something, Jim? Just fucking saying it."

"Michael doesn't give a shit about you, and he doesn't give a shit about Harry." He spoke quietly, evenly. "I saw it at the time, when he first came in: the difference. What I saw in your eyes, you were always searching him out, waiting for him to come and sit with you, help you when you needed him most, just like he should have. As you say, he's your husband, the father of your child. But you know what I saw when I interviewed him?"

She could feel his anger, though he didn't raise his voice. She wondered why he cared so much, why he wanted her.

"What?"

Jim took a moment, stared up at the sky.

"What did you see? Don't try and spare me now, Jim, now that we're really talking. Now that you've stopped trying to be my savior."

He looked down.

She walked over to him and stood close.

"How did you feel that night, when you fucked me? Was it as good as you thought it would be? I doubt it. It couldn't have been, because you must have felt it."

"Felt what?" he said, meeting her eye.

"Felt nothing. That there was nothing for you inside of me, because that part of me is dead to you; the part that you want to love you back; the part that belongs to Michael. It will always be dead to you. I could fake it. I could do that, Jim. But you'd know, deep down. You'd know."

He set his cup down on the table.

"For what it's worth, when I interviewed Michael, I saw nothing in him. That way you look at him, that way you talk about him . . . he doesn't feel the same way you do, Jess. He only cares about himself."

She watched him turn and walk away.

She breathed again.

He could have said more, she knew that. She'd read the file. He could have told her about the complaints Michael's lawyer had made, about her calls, her visits . . . but he didn't.

Always trying to protect her.

"Are you okay? You seem quiet. Is it because he didn't show?" Elena said.

French John smiled at her and shook his head. "It's nothing. I think I'm just tired, from all of my dealings with Her Majesty over there."

He glanced at the top table, though he could barely make it out from where they sat. The tables seemed to be arranged by order of importance, so that meant, by his calculation, that they were slightly more important than the lady who groomed the new Louise McDermott-Lodge's dogs, but not as important as the man that gave the groom tennis lessons.

He looked up at the domed roof of the marquee. It looked spectacular. There was thick carpeting underfoot, and large crystal chandeliers hanging above the thousand or so guests. The chairs were draped in silk, the cutlery sterling silver. An army of staff tended to them.

He had heard that there were some noteworthy names in attendance: former politicians; Republicans, of course.

He felt Elena watching him, worrying about him. She'd noticed how downcast he appeared, even given that his cake stood beside the top table, and drew such admiring glances that it was detracting from the speeches. Some of the guests had even had their photograph taken with it.

He surveyed the table quietly. He met Jared's eye, who smiled back at him.

"The cake looks great, French," Jared said.

On occasion he still shuddered when he heard that. *French John*. It was shortly after his arrival in Tall Oaks that he'd converted the top two floors of a handsome Georgian building into a wonderful living space, and then, once he had sold his apartment in The Castro, moved in and thrown the doors open for a lavish meet and greet with his new neighbors.

The first person to seek him out that fateful evening had been retired Army Colonel, Dick Stone. Dick had more than lived up to his name when, after Jean tried to teach him the correct pronunciation of *Jean*, greeted him with a silence so long, a silence so uncomfortable and unbearable that Jean, to his unending remorse, felt the need to fill it with the immortal line, "It's like John, only French."

And now here he was, sat at the same table as the man that had given him the awful moniker.

"A toast," boomed the Colonel, as everyone grimaced, "to the McDermotts."

They sipped their wine politely, most hoping that the Colonel's was laced with something poisonous.

The Colonel turned to Jared, who was the only male close enough to garner attention from him, aside from French John, who the Colonel was making every effort not to engage with.

"What do you do, James?" the Colonel asked, his voice resonating in a way that told everyone within earshot that they were in the presence of a military man.

"It's Jared. I sell cars."

Jared felt Elena squeeze his hand beneath the table. He glanced at her and smiled.

"Ah, a fellow car enthusiast."

"I have a Ferrari. A dented one," Roger said, somewhat dejectedly.

The Colonel turned to him. "The only good thing to ever come out of Italy is the food. Mark my words, that car will break down on you, probably when it's pouring with rain."

The Colonel's wife, Barbara, a woman who appeared to have applied her makeup in the dark, nodded in agreement.

"What about the clothes?" Jared asked.

"Don't poke the bear," Elena whispered.

The Colonel waved him off. "Every nationality has things they do well, and things they don't. Take the French . . ."

French John sighed.

"A toast," the Colonel bellowed, "to my new friend, Jarrett."

Jared had stopped trying to correct the Colonel after the fifth course was served.

Jared lifted his glass and drank. The Colonel had already worked his way through the extensive wine list, and then, after he had dragged Jared outside to stand with him while he smoked a seventy-dollar cigar, he had started to order shorts.

"Are you okay, Jared?" Elena said, patting his arm.

"Yeah," he replied, though he was starting to slur.

Mercifully, the waitress arrived and began to serve some much needed coffee.

"Are you not drinking, Hen?" Roger asked.

She shook her head. "Not in the mood."

He reached across and took her hand.

"Are you okay?" he whispered.

She nodded, then squeezed his hand. She felt closer to him. She wondered what the future held for them. She knew, in one way or another, that they'd both be okay. And it was a feeling that warmed her.

"I think I have some crab stuck in my tooth," he said.

"Ask for a pick. They probably have gilded ones."

He laughed.

"Are you tired?"

She nodded. She'd finally drifted off as the sun began to rise.

"But you feel better now?"

"Yes."

"I'm glad," he said, smiling.

It wasn't hard to find the realtor. There was only one in town, a guy named Burt Jackson. Jim had expected an old man, but Burt couldn't have been more than twenty.

He worked out of a rundown office on the highway that ran straight through the center of Echo Bay, carving it in half.

It was hot inside. No one seemed to have air-con.

Burt had a straggly beard. Jim guessed he thought it might add a couple of years to his baby face. Jim glanced around the deserted office, suspecting they didn't get many walk-ins, or much business of any kind. Burt seemed a little too keen, no doubt excited that a cop had showed up—something to tell his friends about.

"I know Jared Martin," Burt said, eagerly.

"He was a client?"

"He rents a big place over at Riverstone. They're nice the houses there—the nicest in town. Got a pool, air-conditioning too. Viking stove. Sub-Zero. I think we've got another available if you'd like to take a look?"

Jim leaned forward. "You mean he rented?"

Burt checked his computer.

"He still does. He paid a year up front. Haven't seen him much lately though. Not for a long while. I hope the house is okay. The developers pitched Echo Bay as the new Palm Springs, but the bank own it now. They'll be pissed if he's trashed the place. We're supposed to inspect it, but to be honest we never do, not when they pay cash up front and the deposit is two months. That'll cover the common stuff—cigarette burns and stains and stuff. But sometimes people mess up the . . ."

"Burt," Jim said.

"Yeah."

"I'm going to need the address, and a key."

"I'm not really supposed to, but seeing as you're a cop, and the bank aren't gonna say no to a cop, I could let you have one, as long as you bring it back, and don't make a copy. Otherwise I'll have to change the locks, and that'll cost, 'cause there's only one locksmith in town, and he's Irish, and a little . . ."

"You talk a lot, Burt," Jim said.

Burt laughed. "I'd take you over there myself but my dad said I'm not supposed to close the office until six. Technically, he still owns the business, but with his lungs being so . . ."

"I'm sure I can find it," Jim said. "Can you run me a copy of Jared's application?"

Burt nodded. "Sure. You looking for anything in particular, because it's not too detailed, especially seeing as he paid cash up front?"

"You got a previous address, or any kind of employment history?"

Burt stared at the screen, scratching his chin. "Says here that he worked in construction."

"Where?"

"Someplace called Aurora Springs."

"Waitress. My good friend and I would like to try the thirty-year-old single malt," the Colonel said, loudly enough for the team of McDermott accountants on the next table to flinch.

Before the waitress returned, a large gong sounded and a man in a red jacket announced that everyone should make their way onto the lawn for the fireworks display.

Elena held onto Jared, more to steady him than anything else. They walked out of the marquee and into the warm evening air.

"Are you sure you're okay, French? You seem a little down." Elena asked again.

French John nodded and smiled at her. "The fireworks should be good. Hung is running the show."

"Hung from the pharmacy?"

"How many Hungs do you know?"

"Just the one, sadly."

Jared laughed, loudly.

"You need somebody to run them? Don't you just light the fuse?" Elena said.

"It's a blend of fireworks and performance art."

"Put on by a pharmacist."

"Exactly."

"Do you ever think Tall Oaks is full of oddballs?" Elena said.

"I do," Jared slurred.

Hung bounced on the spot. His jumpsuit was white, covered with a thousand sequins, each hand-sewn by his wife, Luli, and unzipped to the navel, mainly because he couldn't get it over his stomach.

While the guests stood chatting to one another, Hung, who was standing a good 100 feet from them, raised his thumb and index finger high above his head and then pulled an imaginary trigger.

The explosion was loud, so loud that there were gasps from the crowd.

The floodlights cut out, and the lawn was plunged into darkness.

Hung pressed a button tucked into the waistband of his underpants and the jumpsuit lit up. And then the music started, and the crowd turned to face him.

Hung moved toward them slowly, savoring the attention.

He nodded to his right and six rockets lit up the sky in tandem.

He nodded to his left and another six went up.

And then his shoulder started to twitch in time with the heavy base line.

He fired his imaginary gun again and felt a tremor pass through his body when the explosion rocked the crowd.

Thirty minutes, and $200,000 later, Hung was lost in a world of smoke and color. The music came loud and fast and he gyrated and shook to every single note, winding down to the ground when the Aerial Shells exploded, thrusting his crotch back and forth in time with the Dragons Eggs.

Rockets were released with the twitch of his fingers, ice fountains erupted with the shake of his hips. His team, all twenty of them, were perfectly in tune with his every desire.

And then, just as the music reached its crescendo, and the rockets lit up the whole of Tall Oaks, just as the guests were about to applaud and cheer, Hung dropped to his knees and raised his hands toward the sky. A perfect circle of fountains surrounded him and he disappeared under their sparks.

And when the music finally stopped, and the fountains fell away in unison, the applause erupted, and Hung was nowhere to be seen.

All that remained in the center of the circle was a single red rose, and the rich smell of potassium nitrate that filled the air.

Henrietta, long since bored of the display, turned to see Roger applauding furiously, lost in the show, tears falling down his cheeks without a hint of embarrassment.

He turned to her and slowly shook his head.

There were no words needed.

It was magic. Pure magic.

"See, the Japs know how to put on a show," the Colonel said, when they made it back to their table.

"He's actually from China," French John said.

"You say potato."

"That's kind of racist."

He turned to look for Elena, but she had disappeared somewhere with Jared.

"It was a joke," the Colonel said.

Barbara laughed, her makeup cracking under the movement. "You guys are too sensitive."

"What do you mean by that?"

The Colonel downed the rest of his Scotch and signaled to the waitress to bring him another.

French John stared at him. On any other day, at any other time, he might have pressed him on it. He might have stood his ground, because he was quick with his words, and he would know exactly what to say to the Colonel to really cut him down. But not tonight. Not when he felt so low. So sad.

"I think you've had enough to drink now," Roger said, quietly.

The Colonel glared at him. "Excuse me?"

"I said you've had quite enough to drink, and you're being offensive."

The Colonel stood up.

Roger stood up.

They stared at one another.

The Colonel might have expected to see fear in the smaller man's eyes, might have expected him to apologize and sit back down, not say another word.

Instead, Roger continued to stare.

Guests from the tables either side looked on.

Hen tugged at Roger's hand, but he stood his ground.

Another gong sounded.

Barbara grasped the Colonel's hand and led him toward the bar. He glanced back over his shoulder as he walked away.

Roger breathed again.

"I was about to teach that pig a lesson," Roger said, a waver in his voice.

"I'm glad he walked away. He looked like he was going to hit you," Henrietta said.

"He could have tried."

"He's much bigger than you, darling."

"Yes, but I used to practice that martial art . . . origami."

"That's paper-folding."

"Oregano."

"That's a herb, Roger."

"Well, what were those classes I took with my mother, at the church hall, after she got diagnosed?"

"Tai chi."

"Are you sure you don't want me to get you some more coffee?" Elena said.

Jared shook his head.

Elena put her hand on his shoulder. They had quietly slipped away after the firework show, and now they found themselves sitting on a bench facing a large, man-made lake. There was a small island in the middle, and strategically placed lights hidden among the trees. The overall effect, much like everything else hidden behind the gates of the McDermott house, was breathtaking.

"I feel like such an idiot." He laughed as he said it.

"It's a wedding, people are supposed to get drunk. And you couldn't let the Colonel drink you under the table. You'd never live it down."

"You're right. I don't feel too hot right now though."

"Well, you still look hot, so don't worry about it too much."

He turned to look at her, his eyes glassy. "You're too good for me, much too good."

"Yeah, a single mom with a teenage son and a three year old too: every man's dream."

"No, I mean it. You're lovely, Elena, really lovely. When I look at you . . . . I see it."

"See what?"

"See how ugly I am by comparison. See that it's all bullshit, everything that I say and do. And it all looks so much worse when I stand next to you, because you're so honest—there's nothing hidden."

"I think we should go and get you some coffee."

He stared at her, through her. "You don't get it. Nobody gets it."

"Get what? What are you trying to say, Jared?"

He tried to laugh.

"Jared. Jared. Jared. I thought it sounded like a cool name. But now it just sounds wrong too."

"So Jared's not your real name?"

"No, it is my real name. At least I think it is. But I've spent so long running that I'm not even sure anymore. What's real, what's not, who knows?"

"You're not making any sense now. I think we should go back inside," she said, glancing back toward the marquee.

He reached out and took her hand in his.

"Will you just sit with me for a while? Just a little while, and then we'll go back."

"Of course, but will you tell me what the matter is? Why are you so . . ."

"I knew you could see it. With the others I had my doubts, but you, you could always see through me, see through my act, even though it's a good act. Well it ought to be, it's been a lifetime in the making. My parents could see through it too, my old act that is. They could see through it ever since I was a little kid, but they ignored it. They pretended they couldn't see anything at all, especially my father . . . he hates me. My father hates me. Can you believe that?"

"I'm sure that he doesn't hate you."

"How can you be sure? You don't know what I did to him; to my mother too. My mother still speaks to me though, because mothers have to. It's like they don't have a choice, no matter how bad their sons fuck things up, they always forgive."

She rubbed his hand. "I don't know what you've done, Jared, and you don't need to tell me, not now, but when I look into your eyes I see good in them—you're a good man. Everybody's done stuff they're not proud of, everybody makes mistakes. I know I have. But I don't look back too much, because then you might miss something that's right in front of you. Like us, sitting here now. This is happening now. Something you can control. But the stuff in your past, it's gone. And all the will in the world won't bring it back."

He kissed her then, and it took her by surprise, so she pulled away, just a little, but enough for him to notice.

And then he was on his feet.

She called after him.

But then he was running, and her voice grew softer as the lights grew brighter.

It was dark by the time Jim made it to Riverstone, a gated community on the edge of Echo Bay. There was a gatehouse at the end of the street, though it appeared unmanned and there were no barriers stopping him driving through. The street was wide, a line of palms dotted the sidewalk.

He drove slowly, looking for signs of life. The lots were well spaced, the houses stucco-fronted and painted in a variety of pastel shades.

Jared rented number nine.

Jim passed by once, then reached the end of the street and doubled back. He wondered how many were occupied, how many had got their fingers burned during the recession. Tall Oaks hadn't suffered—the prices hadn't fallen a cent.

He parked on the driveway, certain that no one was home.

He could see Burt's realtor signs hammered into the front yards on either side. He wondered who'd want to live here, so far away from everyone. Burt said they were heading out of the slump, enquiries were up and house-building starting up again. They had big plans for Echo Bay, a regeneration that would get people back into work and the market moving again. Jim had his doubts.

He stood on the driveway and stared up at the house. It was imposing, though most of the front was taken up by a garage door so it wasn't particularly attractive. The roof tiles were terracotta. Jim could spot a couple that had worked loose and were on the verge of sliding off.

He walked up the pathway and pressed the doorbell, hearing it chime.

He pressed his face to the glass, but could see nothing but darkness inside.

He unlocked the door, opened it, and stepped inside, switching the lights on.

The entrance hall was wide, smartly furnished but somewhat sanitary: an impersonation of a life; the model home.

He noticed the shattered mirror first. He looked down and saw shards on the polished wood floor.

He walked through slowly, taking everything in. It appeared untouched, much too neat, no sign that anyone had ever lived in it. He walked into the kitchen and ran a finger along the granite countertop. The dust was thick, a heavy covering dulling the shine. He noticed a fruit bowl, still with plastic fruit inside.

He tried to see signs of Jared—a magazine, a dish left in the basin, anything.

He opened a door to the bathroom and walked in. He heard crunching beneath his feet. He switched the light on, saw another broken mirror.

He climbed the stairs slowly, flipping the lights on as he went. There were paintings on the walls—stock stuff, landscapes and some modern splashes. The fixings were smart, the furnishings light and fresh, despite the dust.

He stepped into the master. It was a mess. Drawers hung open; clothes were strewn all over the floor. He opened the closets and saw a couple of shirts hanging inside. There was a lamp lying on the carpet, knocked from the nightstand. The sheets were balled at the foot of the bed.

He stood still, surveying it all carefully. It didn't fit. None of it fit.

It was then that he noticed the light creeping from beneath the bathroom door. He drew his gun, silently, and moved toward it.

"Jared," he said, calmly.

He raised his foot and gently pushed the door open, his gun trained in front of him.

He stepped inside, and then he gasped.

The blood was everywhere. Dry, dark.

It covered the tub, the walls and most of the floor.

A lot of blood.

He saw towels on the floor. Bloody towels.

And then he looked up and saw the mirror, the shattered glass.

He thought of Harry. He swallowed.

He reached for his cell phone and called Adam.

He told him to bring Jared Martin in.

25

The Long Day Is Over

Though he was drunk he had driven home. He was lucky he hadn't been stopped as he'd swerved all over the street and left his car parked halfway up the sidewalk.

He shrugged his jacket off and dropped it to the floor. He grabbed a beer from the fridge.

As he sat on the soft rug, in front of the open fireplace, he picked up the phone.

It was over now. His act was over. The drape had come down, the audience had long since departed. The reviews were in, and they didn't look good.

He put his beer down and rubbed his eyes.

He wasn't even mad at himself anymore. He was just tired, exhausted. There was nothing left to do but face up.

He held the knife in his hand, like he always did, but then he put it down when he heard the voice on the other end.

"Hello."

The voice was different, familiar but different. But that must have been because he hadn't heard it for so long. His father wouldn't have changed—it wasn't in his nature.

"Dad. It's me."

There was silence for a long time.

He could hear his father's breath, the ticking of the clock on their kitchen wall, the soft white noise of the television in the background.

"I'll get your mother."

"Dad, wait. I don't want to speak to her. I want to speak to you."

He heard his father close the door to the kitchen. His mother would be in bed by now, but his father sat up late watching sports network. He'd watch anything: tennis, football, soccer. It didn't matter, as long as it was competitive.

"Say what you need to."

He sounded hard, and he was hard: an outdoorsman, simple in his pleasures, unforgiving of those who were more complex.

"I transferred the money to you, from Uncle Frank, what's left of it. I'll pay you back the rest when I can. And what I owe you. Every dollar."

"You expect me to thank you?"

"No. I just . . . I wanted you to know that."

Silence again. Long and painful. Jared reached for his beer but didn't drink it.

"I barely recognize your voice."

Jared laughed, softly. "Yeah, it's been a long time."

"You keeping okay?"

"Yeah. I'm okay," Jared said, holding the receiver away from him as his voice broke.

"Well, if there's nothing else."

"I want to come home, Dad. Can I come home? I don't like it on my own anymore. I want to come home."

He tried to stop his voice from wavering.

"I could leave in the morning. I could sleep in my old room again."

"And who would be coming home?"

"Just me. Jared. Your son. I need you, Dad. I really need you."

He heard his father draw a breath. He heard the soft patter of his slippered feet as he walked around the kitchen, probably looking out of the window at the old swing set that he had once pushed him on.

Jared smiled at his reflection in the television set. It was going to be okay. Everything would be okay. He'd enjoy the long drive home. He'd need to make a stop first, in Echo Bay. He'd been putting it off. But that was okay. He could face it, because he was ready now, and because he needed them. He needed them to tell him that they still loved him, and that even though he had messed up it wasn't that bad. It was forgivable. And most of all because, even though he was thirty-five, he still needed his parents.

"I have no son."

The line went dead.

French John left with Elena. He'd seen the look on her face, the concern in her eyes. He hadn't wanted to stay anyway. So they had jumped into one of the waiting cars, a black Mercedes, with a driver under strict orders to keep his eyes on the road and his mouth shut.

"How do you know where he lives?"

"He told me, on our first date. We were talking about real-estate prices."

"Sounds like a fun first date."

She didn't laugh, didn't even smile—she was too worried.

French John held her hand tightly.

"He's probably fine, just needs to sleep it off."

"No. He was really upset, I think he was crying. He kept talking about his act and his parents."

"His act?"

She nodded.

"And he drove off in his car. He was way over the limit."

They pulled up in front of a smart mansion block on Palmwood Drive and Elena jumped out. French John followed her.

"He said he lived on the top floor."

They found the street door open, the mat caught under the hinge.

They took the elevator to the third floor and saw that there was only one door, the penthouse, and it was wide open.

"Jared," she called out, loudly. "It's Elena. I just wanted to check that you were okay."

They walked into the spacious hallway.

"Jared?"

"Maybe he's passed out cold?" French John said.

They walked into the large living room and saw a beer bottle sitting on the stone surround of the fireplace.

They walked into the kitchen, so clean it appeared unused.

"Jared?" French John called out, again.

They walked into the bedroom and saw clothes in a pile by the bathroom door. The light shone out from beneath.

Elena knocked.

"Jared, are you okay?"

"Jared, we're going to come in. I'll avert my eyes if you're naked . . . maybe," French John said, though he didn't smile.

She saw the knife first, on the tiled floor—its blade shiny. Had French John not pushed her aside and pulled Jared out of the red water, Elena would have screamed. Instead, she fell to the floor, Jared's head coming to rest on her lap. French John wrapped towels around his wrists and told Elena to keep the pressure on them. He ran back through to the living room to make the call.

Among all of the panic, and all of the blood and the hysteria, Elena couldn't help but look down at his naked body and notice what lay between his legs.

Or rather . . . what didn't.

26

Jaybird

Jerry stared out of the window. The trucks were back again. They'd come because of Max, but a couple of them were sticking around and running pieces about Harry Monroe again. He watched them with interest. The female reporters were pretty and wore lots of makeup. The cameramen sat around drinking coffee and looking bored.

He'd just finished spraying the glass and wiping it down with paper towels. The boys had thrown eggs again, though this time only a couple before one of the cameramen had shouted at them.

He thought about phoning his mother, but he didn't really want to wake her, especially as she seemed to be getting worse, not better. She was really pale now. And, when Jerry had wiped her head with a cloth, he had found that she was cold too. So he had put another blanket on her, even though her room was stifling with the windows closed and the drapes drawn. He needed to speak to her, to ask her what she had done with the envelope. But deep down he knew she had sent it. He could feel it in his stomach—fear—though as the hours passed, hours he spent looking out of the window, the fear had gradually been joined by a feeling of relief. It would all be over soon.

He turned and began to sort through the photographs. There was a backlog. He wasn't coping all that well as manager. He needed some help but there was no one to ask. And there had been lots more photographs to print after the wedding. The McDermotts had put disposable cameras on every table. He had liked looking at all of the photographs. He'd never been to a wedding.

As he was sorting them into the correct envelopes, he saw Jessica Monroe across the street. She was putting up posters again, even though there were already posters up everywhere. Sometimes he even saw her stick posters over posters.

He wandered over to the door and stepped out into the sunshine.

The news vans had their engines running, probably to keep the air-conditioning going. Jerry couldn't remember a summer this hot. He could even see the heat rising up in wavy lines from the street.

He saw Jessica look over as she noticed him. She didn't look away again. Just stood and stared. She wore a baseball cap and sunglasses. He stood still, staring back. Some of the cameramen noticed her and reached for their cameras. She ignored them, working slowly, smoothing each poster down with great care.

He turned, and walked back toward the PhotoMax. Just before he reached the door he tripped over a thick cable that was running into one of the news vans. He dropped the photographs all over the sidewalk.

He felt her eyes burning into him as he bent to pick them up.

Manny walked into the kitchen rubbing his leg. "One of those little fuckers kicked me. He's lucky he's a kid 'cause I felt all my training coming back to me."

"Save it for the next Somali that crosses your path," Furat said.

He kissed her.

She pulled away when she heard her mother call her. They walked back out into the yard.

"What's up, Al?" Manny said.

"I think Abe is stuck in the playhouse. He said he's fine but he's been in there a good hour now."

"I'm on it," Manny said, as he headed off to liberate his friend.

"Are you excited?" Aarfah asked her daughter.

"Yeah. A little nervous too."

"Well, don't be too nervous. You're going with Manny after all. I'm sure you'll have a lovely time."

Furat smiled.

"Is Elena okay? She looks awfully tired," Aarfah said.

"I think she has problems with that guy she was seeing. Manny keeps asking her about it but she won't say. We know that he's in the hospital though."

"Well, you tell her that if she needs anything, even if it's just someone to watch Thalia—or watch Manny—then we're here for her."

"I already have, though I don't think you could handle watching Manny."

They turned to see a group of children stood around Manny as he pulled Abe's legs free of the playhouse.

"VICTORY," he called out, and chased the squealing kids around the yard.

French John carried the cake out carefully and placed it in the center of the table.

Elena smiled at him and kissed his cheek.

"Thanks, for everything."

"How are you holding up?"

"I'm going to see him later. Would you mind sticking around for a bit after?"

"Of course."

"I keep seeing it. All the blood. It was horrible."

He nodded. "I do too. I can't believe the night ended like that. I mean, one minute we were watching Hung turn himself into a rose, the next we're at the hospital. I just hope he's going to be okay. I mean, it must be so hard for him. I still find it hard sometimes, and I'm only gay."

"I think we worked that one out, French," Manny said, as he appeared behind them and grabbed a fistful of potato chips. "Come on, the clown's about to do his shit."

They followed Manny over to where the children were sitting, cross-legged, looking up at the clown. All except for Thalia, who was in the kitchen, crying her eyes out.

"What's the matter, Thal?" Manny said, crouching down and pulling her close.

"It's the clown," she said, between sobs.

"You don't like him? Is it because you could smell booze on him? 'Cause I could. You want me to go and kick his ass?"

"Why don't you like him?" Furat asked, gently stroking her hair.

"Because my friend Harry used to love clowns, and I miss him."

Manny kissed her head. "Did he have a clown at his party too? Maybe it's the same clown. Maybe we can talk to him about Harry. Would you like that?"

She shook her head. "It's not the same clown."

"How do you know? It might be," Furat said.

Thalia looked up at her. "Because that's not Harry's daddy. And Harry only liked it when his daddy dressed up as a clown."

Jared opened his eyes, but the effort needed to smile proved too great.

Elena held his hand gently.

"You sure know how to show a girl a good time. What'll you do on our next date?"

He tried to laugh, though no sound came out.

He motioned for his water and she held the glass in front of him and put the straw to his lips.

He took a small sip.

"That's better," he said, his voice strained.

"You don't have to talk. I'm happy just to sit here for a while."

"I owe you an explanation. It's the least that I owe you."

She looked down at his bandaged wrists. He had lost a lot of blood. If they hadn't found him, if French John hadn't acted so fast, she didn't know what might have happened.

"I grew up as Jay. That was my name. Jay. My dad called me his Jaybird. I was a tomboy, of course. It could've been a boy's name, couldn't it? Could've been short for Jason or something."

He cleared his throat.

She gave him some more water.

"I lived as Jay for most of my life, but I knew—I always knew that I was born in the wrong body. And it just wasn't something I knew deep down. It was right there, always on the tip of my tongue, at the front of every thought. I was Jared, just in Jay's body."

She stroked his hand.

"I had lots of cousins, all boys, and my parents just thought I was a tomboy because I didn't have any female friends. And then they worried when I didn't bring home any boyfriends. That's what my childhood was. Worry; all the time, worry. Well, for me and my mother it was worry. My father was happy to hide behind a big wall of denial. He was happy to take me shooting and hunting, but not so happy when I wouldn't wear a dress to my uncle's wedding. They just thought I'd grow out of it. They thought that all the time I spent in my room was normal teenage angst."

"But it wasn't," Elena said, softly.

"No. I was so sad, Elena, so hopelessly sad. I grew to hate the skin I was in, hate it enough to try and cut it off. That got me sent to my first shrink. And it was actually the best thing that ever happened to me. Despite the two-hour train ride to visit her office, and the bills that arrived every month addressed to my father, she was amazing. She knew exactly what I was going through. She even offered to speak with my parents, who were horrified. That night after we got home my father was so mad I thought he was going to hit me."

"What are your parents like?"

Jared smiled. "They were great parents, if a little . . . *overactive* at the church, which made it all the more hard, especially when I started taking the hormones. The changes were gradual, over years and years."

"What did they say about the hormones?"

Jared laughed. "I didn't tell them."

Elena smiled.

"It was like a double lie. I started going to the gym, to explain my changing body. I kept my hair long, even though I hated it. And I wore so much makeup, to try and hide the hair growth that they thought I was finally happy being a woman. They still worried though, because my cousins were settling down, getting married and leaving home, and I was just stuck."

She shook her head in disbelief. "They must have known something was going on."

"My voice got deeper, but it was so gradual. If my mother said anything I told her I had a cold, and then, get this, I even started smoking to explain away the change. I worked lots of different jobs, never really fitting in."

"So you spent years like this, transitioning, and then you left home?"

He nodded, looking down. "I used their money to pay for the hormones. I took it without asking, and then I took much more to pay for my mastectomy."

She leaned forward and wiped the tears from his eyes with her thumb.

"It was all the money they had in the world, all of their savings. It was going to help with my father's retirement, but I took it, because I couldn't stand it anymore: to look in the mirror, to live the lie for another second. I said I was going away for a few days with some friends, even though I didn't have any. And when I got back I was so sore that I could barely move. It was obvious something had happened to me."

The words were coming faster now, the tears too.

"It was bad that night. My father ripped my shirt from me, and they saw what I had done. Their darling daughter, taken from them—that's all they saw. I had become the person that had stolen their little girl: a monster, covered in scars. And they hated me for it. I saw the pure hatred, especially in my father. He told me I was ugly, that I'd have big ugly scars for the rest of my life, and that I deserved them. I deserved to see them, so that they would remind me what I had done to my family. So I left. That night, I left town. I took the last of the money with me too, because fuck them. I thought. Fuck them."

Elena wiped her own tears away and kissed his hand.

"I moved from town to town, wherever there was work. Always some place different. I worked all kinds of jobs. I just . . . I just don't fit in anywhere. The last place was Echo Bay. I'd worked construction before. I liked it. I liked feeling like one of the guys. But then something happened there, with a lady. I fucked it all up. I went home and couldn't bear to see myself so I broke all of the mirrors—I shattered the last one with my hand and severed an artery. I nearly died."

"Oh, Jared."

"I'm sorry. I'm so sorry. It was all wrong, I handled it all wrong and I'm sorry. I just wish I could make my parents see that. And I'm not even happy now, because it's just an act. Without them I don't know who I am, or who I want to be. I don't know anything anymore, except that I'll never forget what I did to them. Like my father said—the scars. I don't let the scars heal, Elena, I don't let them heal. So that must prove that I'm sorry, right? That must prove that I haven't forgotten; that I'll never forget."

She held his face in her hands.

"You're a good man, Jared, and there are people that care about you. I'm one of them. You made a mistake, that's all, but you made it because you felt that you didn't have a choice."

He leaned back and closed his eyes.

Elena stood, and walked to the door. She nodded to the elderly couple sitting outside.

The man stood. He was tall, and proud, but she could see the fear in his eyes.

The lady was petite, and, if Elena looked hard enough, she could see Jared in her.

They walked into his room.

Elena turned in time to see them both lean over and take him into their arms.

27

The Sting

Henrietta found him at the end of the backyard, by the willow tree. The bench he sat on was new, the plaque glinted in the early evening sun.

"What does it say?"

Roger shuffled to the side, so she could see.

In memory of Thomas, our baby.

She smiled at him. She wouldn't cry anymore, she had too much to look forward to.

"I was going to put something in the ground but I didn't know if you'd like that. But the bench . . . I mean, I see you sitting out here sometimes on the grass, so I thought you might like it."

"It's perfect," she said, settling beside him.

"It's lovely out here."

"Yes, it is. Do you ever miss England?"

"Sometimes. But not today."

"The other day I was thinking, I never really asked if you wanted to move to Tall Oaks. I know we agreed to it, but that was a long time ago. Then I just went ahead with everything, arranging the move at breakneck speed. I was so desperate to get back . . . to get home again."

"I know. You mentioned it every day in London."

"It's not the same for men. You can settle wherever you lay your hat; women like to be close to family. But I never really asked if you were happy."

He shrugged, looking back at their beautiful home. "I suppose I am."

"Come on, Roger. We've been stuck in this dance for a long time now. The back and forth, neither of us saying how we really feel. I know that I can be difficult, stubborn."

"And I can be a bit of an ass at times."

She raised her eyebrows.

"Okay, most of the time."

"I would hate for us to hate each other, if that makes sense, if we carry on as we are. I would hate that, Roger, because you're a good person. Even if we don't see eye to eye on anything at all anymore, even if we drive each other mad by being so polite . . . I know that you're a good person."

He leaned across and took her hand.

"I know that you're pregnant, Hen."

"And I know that you're having an affair, Roger."

She smiled, a single tear falling down her cheek.

He tried to pull his hand away but she held it tight.

"It's okay."

"Is it?" he said, looking up at her, tears of his own forming.

"At first, I thought that you were having a mid-life crisis," she said.

"And I thought you were going through the change."

"How did you find out?"

"Because, contrary to popular opinion, I'm not a total idiot, just a partial one. Can I ask you the question that I don't really want to know the answer to?"

"Eddie, one of the builders."

He nodded, closing his eyes, taking a moment. If he was surprised then he tried not to show it. "Ah, Eddie: the body of a Greek god. Good choice, Hen. Good genes no doubt."

She looked at him and swallowed. "Are you crying, Roger? Please don't. Please don't do that."

He wiped his eyes with his monogrammed handkerchief. "No, it's not why you think. I'm happy for you."

"You are?"

"I am. I'm truly happy for you. You deserve it, Hen. If anybody does, you do. And you know why?"

"Why?"

"Because you'll be a fantastic mother, I have no doubt."

She smiled.

"What does Eddie think?"

She shook her head. "He doesn't want to be involved, and I don't want him to be. It was a stupid one-night thing, a little too much wine. He's a young man; I have no interest in having him in my life."

"Are you sure about that? It's a big decision."

She looked out across the bright, green grass, at their perfect house and their perfect swimming pool. It all looked so perfect.

"Yes, but it's my decision. It's my baby. I know this is strange, this whole situation, and we're probably not reacting the way we should, but I'd like us to stay close. I'd like you to be involved in the baby's life, in my life, in any capacity, even just as a good friend, because a baby needs a male role model. And above all else, I've always thought of you as a real man."

He sat back. "Really? Why?"

"Because you provide for me. I mean, I know we come from money, but you still worked hard for us, just like my father did. And that's what I think of when I think of a real man: a provider. Probably a bit old-fashioned, but who cares?"

"Is that why you could finally say goodbye . . . to Thomas?"

She nodded. "It wouldn't be fair on the new baby. I needed to let go."

He smiled.

"And what of you? Are you happy?" she asked.

"I am."

"Well, that's something."

"You don't seem surprised."

"I was . . . I am, but I think we've got to a point in our lives where we need to put our own needs first."

"I think I've always known that we weren't quite right for each other. Does that make me a horrible person, that I've always known and I didn't do anything about it? Didn't let you go?"

She shook her head, standing and placing a hand over her stomach. "No, Roger. I like to think that it makes you loyal. Well, up until now of course."

He smiled.

"How did you find out?"

"A mix up at PhotoMax."

She pulled a photograph from the envelope in her hand and handed it to him. Then she walked back to the house.

Roger looked down at the photograph and smiled at the memory. The memory of him and French John hiking through Despair, hand in hand, the sun setting behind them.

"I need to tell you something. I just hope that you're not going to be mad," Manny said.

Furat turned to him. "Okay. Go ahead."

He took a deep breath. "I said that Abe could come with us to prom, because he's been really down about the whole Jane Berg thing, and I've been friends with him for a long time, since we were little kids, and he said he wasn't going to come to prom. He said he couldn't face going alone." He kept his eyes down, not daring to look up at her. "So I said he should come with us. We'll still be able to dance and stuff, and there's other kids going stag, so when we get there he can go off with them—he just didn't want to walk in alone. I'm sorry."

When he finally did look up, she kissed him.

"It's fine. I'm glad you asked him."

He sighed. "Shit. I've been so scared to tell you."

She laughed.

"Oh yeah, one other thing, I kind of spent all my money hiring the dinner suit. And then your corsage cost more than I thought . . . so, the thing is . . ."

"Let me guess? You have to wear the wingtips, because you ran out of money?"

"No, much worse than that. You see, the limousine, it was like two hundred bucks. I think it would've been less but the fuckhead that owns it used to be sweet on my mother, and then she blew him out, and now he's getting revenge. So that's the thing. I couldn't afford the limousine, so we have to compromise."

He held up the keys to the duck-egg. "It'll be dark, and I haven't washed it so some of the shine has come off."

Elena came over and smiled at Furat.

"Thank God you talked him out of wearing the three-piece tonight."

"It wasn't easy."

"I can imagine. You know he wore it for his graduation ceremony? I'll have to ask Jerry if he can airbrush it out, the fedora at least."

Furat laughed.

"Is he still bitching about driving to prom?"

"Yep."

"It's a nice car, Manny. Most kids would be thankful to drive something nearly new," Elena said. "And you need to wash it before tonight. You can't pick up Furat in it when it's got bird poop on the hood."

He shook his head. "I've been praying that a bird would take a shit on it, dull the color a bit. And now, after I've spent two weeks leaving seed all around it, it finally happens and I have to clean it off. No fucking way."

"I sometimes wonder if you're really my son."

Furat laughed so much that Manny scowled at her.

"You're lucky to have a son like me. I'm the fucking man around this house. Who'd you call the other night when that spider was by your bed?"

"Yeah and I wish I hadn't now." Elena turned to Furat. "He came in with a baseball bat. There's a hole in the drywall now. And anyway, back to the point, Jared said to keep the body-work clean."

"He's not even here. How the fuck will he know?"

Furat smiled at Elena. "Is he any better?"

Elena was about to reply when Manny interjected.

"The thing about Jared is that she's a lesbian. That's what all this fuss has been about."

Elena glared at him. "I explained all of this to you, Manny."

"Yeah, I'm sorry, I got it." He turned to Furat. "I mean *he's* a lesbian, and he's a he. Except he hasn't got anything downstairs yet. Still smooth as an Action Man doll."

Elena slapped his arm.

"Jesus, Ma. I've gotta get my picture taken tonight. How are you going to explain the bruise to Child Services when I send them a copy?"

"So he's transgender?" Furat said.

"Yes, and he's been through a very tough time."

"Will he be okay? I'd never have been able to tell. I think he's really handsome," Furat said, holding a hand up to Manny before he could say anything.

"He is handsome, and nice too. And I think he'll be fine. He's going to go home for a while, to be with his parents. I think he needs that. We'll stay in touch. I may even go and visit him when he's feeling better."

Manny glanced over at Thalia, who was playing in her sandpit.

"Anyway. I'm going home to get ready now, so I'll see you later," Furat said.

"You've still got four hours. What the hell are you going to do for four hours? Bear in mind I like the natural look, not too much makeup. The complete opposite of my mother."

Elena went to hit him again, but this time he ducked.

"I've still got it. It never left me," he said, as he raised his fists and shadow-boxed around her.

"Somewhere out there, a Somali kid just pissed himself laughing," Elena said.

"You look like shit," Jess said.

Jim tried to smile. "Tough night. I've been at the hospital."

"Anything wrong?"

"No. Not really. Just something I was working on. Didn't pan out the way I thought it was going to, and I'm glad it didn't."

"You want to talk about it?"

He sighed, shook his head.

"I heard about that guy in Despair," Jess said.

"Yeah. It's in all the locals."

"You okay?"

"If I say yes does that make me a monster?"

"I don't think so, though it probably doesn't make you normal either."

He lit a cigarette, blowing the smoke up and watching it drift toward the tops of the tall oak trees. "Who wants to be normal?"

"Will he die?" Jess asked, her tone even.

"Maybe."

"Will anyone come looking for you?"

Her shoes crunched on the twigs under foot.

"No. It's a different jurisdiction but I know the cops out that way. And there was no one around that night. Even if there had been, it was dark. They've already chalked it up to a bar fight that got out of hand. He had no shortage of people that hated him."

She took the cigarette from his hand.

"I'm surprised you told me about it," she said, blowing the smoke away from him.

He looked across at her. "Why?"

She passed the cigarette back to him. "Because I could tell on you."

He smiled. She did too.

"I'm surprised because most people in my life think I'm so fragile that I can't take the truth; that I'll just crumble away if I see any more pain. But you don't."

He squinted when they made their way back into the clearing, the harsh sunlight too much for his tired eyes to take.

"I know how tough you are, Jess, just to keep going. To get out of bed and live each day, even if you do it from the bottom of a bottle or from the bed of a stranger."

"But you still like me?" She stopped walking and faced him.

"I never said I liked you."

She smiled. "I got your message. I got the flowers too. It was nice of you."

"I was angry, before," he said, quietly.

"Yeah, because you care. I don't have much left, Jim. I need you in my corner."

"I am in your corner. I always have been."

She kissed him.

She held on to him long after he tried to pull away.

She leaned into him, trying to stop the tingling that surged up her spine. She took a breath, tried to step back but now he held her.

And then she was crying.

Beating his chest and crying.

Letting everything out, the pain and the suffering, the things she had done and things she had let happen to her. She cried and she fell to her knees with him, and buried her face into his neck, biting him and scratching him.

He pinned her arms to her side and then, after she had nothing left in her body, no tears left to cry, she closed her eyes, exhausted, no fight left at all.

Because at that moment, by the tall oak trees, while in the arms of a man that really loved her, she felt it.

That he was gone.

And he wasn't coming back.

It had been a long day for Jerry. Longer still because he hadn't slept again, even though it was warm out, he liked to have a sheet to cover himself. But all of the sheets were on his mother now. Every single one of them. And the smell was stronger. So strong he could almost see it in the air, lying heavy, weighing down his lungs with every breath he took.

But he also couldn't sleep because he was worried about losing his job. And losing his job made him feel worthless and stupid, so perhaps his mother had been right all along. He was a little slower than the rest.

Some people had come into the PhotoMax to look at it: a mother and son. And, though the son was fat, like he was, he wasn't stupid and he didn't have a funny voice. He heard them tell the realtor that they wanted to turn it into a coffee house, even though there were lots of coffee houses in Tall Oaks, and only one PhotoMax. And then they had walked past him and gone into the office and dark room, even though they weren't really supposed to because only he and Max had been allowed back there. He should have stopped them, because he was the manager after all, even though he didn't feel like the manager, especially when the son had looked at his shorts, and his shirt and tie, and laughed at him.

Jim laid out the video tapes in front of him. Fifteen of them. He'd watched some of them before, not expecting to see much. They were news tapes: local and national; every piece ever run on the Harry Monroe story. Adam had helped collate them. Some of the segments were brief, others detailed. The reporters were a mix of male and female, all the right side of forty, all with perfect teeth. He noticed this because there wasn't much else to take note of.

He closed the blinds. He always did now, finding the sunlight harder and harder to take. He heard the phone ringing outside and cars passing by.

He rubbed his eyes, the exhaustion hooding them.

He put another tape in, watched another reporter standing in the lashing rain in the middle of Main Street the morning after Harry had been taken. The screen cut to a photograph of Harry as the reporter detailed what little they knew. Someone had leaked the Clown. Not one of his men. The reporter spoke animatedly about the sinister revelation, almost tripping over her words as she fought to get them out before her rivals.

The screen cut back to her. She stood beneath her umbrella. Behind her stood a thick crowd of a hundred, all lined up in their waterproofs, all waiting to be given instruction so they could start searching. All except for one. He was walking the opposite way, his shirt soaked through. Jim recognized the walk, the labored gait.

He froze the screen, zoomed in.

The picture was clear, despite the deluge.

Jerry looked nervous.

Jim leaned forward, calm, focused.

He saw marks on Jerry's face. Scratches.

He played the tape, then watched Jerry disappear into the pharmacy.

Jim grabbed his keys and left his office, then walked briskly up Main Street toward the pharmacy.

He found Hung inside, watching a small television behind the counter. He could see Luli out back, sorting prescriptions into bags.

"Jim. How are you?" Hung said.

"I came over to congratulate you."

Hung beamed. "You heard about the show?"

"It was hard not to. You lit up the whole of Tall Oaks. We got a call from Mrs. Lewis complaining about the noise, and she lives miles from the McDermotts."

Hung smiled, bashfully, then turned to Luli who grinned at him.

"One other thing. Can I take a look at your security tapes?"

"Sure, from when?"

"March 5th."

Hung stood. "The day Harry went missing."

They sat in the cramped back office, knees touching as Hung searched through the tapes.

He found the one he wanted and slotted it into the machine.

"Can you go to 12.30 p.m.?"

Hung forwarded the tape.

They watched in silence as Jerry walked into the store. Rain-water dripped from him. Jim could see his face clearly. The scratches looked raw—streaks of red against his pale skin.

Jerry kept glancing out of the window.

"Can you tell what he picked up?"

Hung shrugged. "What he always picks up: his mother's prescription."

"You don't remember the scratches on his face?"

"It was busy that day, with Harry."

Jim nodded.

"What's this about?" Hung said.

"Probably nothing," Jim said, his pulse quickening.

Jim stood up and walked to the door.

"Jim?"

Jim turned.

"Jerry didn't pick up his mother's prescription yesterday."

"Maybe he forgot?"

"She'll have run out by now, and he's never forgotten before."

Jerry kneeled beside his mother's bed. The smell was strong, her skin dull.

She looked so different.

Jerry reached out and held her hand.

It was cold.

He swallowed.

"I know that you're dead."

He heard the floor creak as he shifted his weight.

"I'm not ready to be on my own, Mom. I need you, just like you said."

He laid his head on his mother's chest and tried to pray. He longed to feel her push his cheek up and down, to feel the beat of her heart against his ear. He wanted Mom to ruffle his hair and ask him what he wanted for dinner, like she used to, when Jerry was small, before she found out he was special and started to treat him differently. He wanted his old mom back—before the tumor came along. Although, when he thought about it, he wondered if it had always been there. And while he was asking, seeing as God was already listening, he'd like his dad back too, and then they could be a family again. And that would make him happy, because nothing else could.

With his eyes closed he heard the sounds of Tall Oaks floating in through the open window. He heard children laughing and birds singing. They all sounded happy. And so he asked God to make him happy too, just this once, seeing as he had never asked him for anything before. He asked him to save the

PhotoMax, because he loved his job and he wanted to work there forever. But if God couldn't do that, if he couldn't do any of that because Jerry had asked for too many things at once, then could he please take him too? Take him to wherever Mom and Dad were? Because without them, and without his job, his place, he didn't belong anymore.

He rubbed his eyes but couldn't stop the tears.

He couldn't stop them when he heard the knock at the door. The knock he had been waiting for.

He couldn't even stop them when the bee flew into the room and landed on his hand, and especially not when the bee stung his hand.

He tried to stand, but he felt dizzy. And then his throat began to swell, and he had trouble breathing.

He fell backward into the wall, hearing the baseboard crack as the drywall crumbled.

He clutched his chest as he rolled over, and through swollen eyes saw all the money in the hole he'd made. More money than he could count, more money than he had ever seen before.

He lay back on the carpet, on the worn patch beside his mother's bed. He raised his hand and looked at his Death Watch.

It was wrong, he thought. It had always been wrong.

Jim knocked on the door again.

He took a step back and looked up at the house, at the top floor, where all the drapes were closed. He could feel the heat on his back. The fucking heat that was starting to get unbearable.

He banged the door, then glanced around at the deserted street. Everything looked so bright he could barely take it.

He tried the door. It opened.

The smell hit him first.

"Jerry?" he called out, drawing his gun.

He moved slowly along the hallway. He could hear the clock in the living room, the ticking louder than ever.

He stepped into the kitchen, saw the dishes piled high on the counter. He glanced at the refrigerator, at the photographs pinned to it. Jerry looked young, sad, even though he was smiling. His mother stood beside him, her arm tight around his shoulder.

He moved back into the hallway, then into Jerry's dark room. Everything was neat. He stepped back out.

The stairs creaked as he climbed them, his gun trained in front of him.

"Jerry? It's Jim. I just came over to check on you."

He saw one door closed, the rest open. He checked each room quickly, then swallowed as he turned the handle.

It was dark inside, the air asphyxiating. He placed a hand over his mouth while the other gripped his gun tightly, the metal cool against his skin.

He saw Jerry's mother in the bed, long since dead.

He saw a hole in the drywall behind, and piles of money inside.

And then he saw Jerry.

And he dropped his gun, and ran across the room.

He started CPR, and radioed for help.

He pumped Jerry's chest so hard and for so long that sweat was dripping from him by the time the medics dragged him off and took over.

28

Prom

"Wow. Furat, you look so beautiful," Elena said, as she snapped a picture of her.

Furat grinned. "Thanks. I got tired of waiting so I thought I'd come over and pick Manny up instead. Where is he?"

They looked up at the stairs when they heard Manny call down.

"Ma, can you go next door and tell Furat I'll be there in five minutes? I can't get my hair to cooperate at the moment—shit's trying to fly away or something. I've used some of that mousse from your room—it fucking stinks though. I smell like a whore, so I've had to put some cologne on my head to cover it up, but that's burning, so I might have to wash it all off and start over. But don't tell her any of that. Tell her I'm finishing my stomach crunches so I'll be ripped for tonight. Or tell her that Thalia started crying, wouldn't let me leave unless I read to her. Yeah, tell her that—she'll eat that up, see that I'm all sensitive and shit. Ma, you there?"

They watched Abe kiss his mother goodbye from the car. He walked toward them, a hand over his mouth, wearing his Brooks Brothers suit and his father's cravat.

He opened the car door and climbed into the back.

"What happened to the bird shit? We were working on that for weeks. By the way, I picked up some more seed," Abe said.

"My mother made me wash it. Fucking sparkling now."

"You look nice, Furat. Sorry again, by the way. I know I'm the third wheel," Abe said, finally taking his hand away from his mouth.

Manny looked in the rearview mirror and slammed on the brakes. The driver behind blasted his horn and just managed to swerve around them.

"OH MY GOD. You fucking brought it back. Your mother let you? Holy shit," Manny said, as he looked at the thick mustache on Abe's upper lip.

Abe nodded, smiling as he stroked it.

"This is going to be the best fucking prom ever."

"You think Jane will like it?" Abe said.

"Are you kidding? Once she sees you she's going to kick Dylan McDermott to the curb and drop her panties right there on the dance floor. She'll be carrying your child by the last dance, mark my fucking words."

Manny floored the accelerator and pressed the button to open Abe's window.

He sounded the horn all the way to prom.

Dylan McDermott stood in the center of his group of friends. They'd been drinking most of the afternoon. He glanced over at Jane.

Jane sat at a small table by the door, collecting tickets as people made their way inside, one of the many drawbacks of being Chair of the Prom Committee.

She looked back at Dylan and smiled, though he was starting to annoy her.

"How much longer, babe?" he called out.

She shrugged.

He turned back to his group, loosening his tie. "She'd better be worth the wait."

They all laughed. They always did.

"You really think you're going to bang her tonight?" Zac Evans said.

Dylan smiled. "I already booked a room."

Jane sighed, pretending that she couldn't hear them, pretending that her date wasn't such an asshole. She hadn't really wanted to go with him, but he was popular, and good-looking, and captain of the football team: qualities hard to ignore at high school. Her parents had wanted her to go with Abe, and, if she was honest, a part of her wanted to go with him too, but only as friends. She was much too busy to think about having a boyfriend, and, as cruel as it sounded, she didn't find him at all attractive. He was too tall, too thin, and too . . . *Abe*, to be attractive. Still, she had little doubt he would have been a perfect gentleman, and at least she would have been able to relax. Now she'd have to spend all night making sure Dylan hadn't spiked her drink with booze, hoping to get her drunk enough to accompany him to one of his father's hotels. She shuddered at the thought, before once again allowing her mind to wander to the end of summer, when she'd leave Tall Oaks behind and head out into the real world. No more Dylan McDermott, and no more bullshit high-school politics.

*

"What the fuck have we got here?" Dylan said, as Manny and Abe walked up to the desk.

Abe ignored him, self-consciously smoothing his mustache down as he did, but Manny stared straight at him.

"You got something to say, Romero? I thought you'd be wearing your little gangster hat tonight," Dylan said, smirking at Manny.

Manny shook his head. "No, I left it in your mother's bedroom. It fell off when I started fucking her in the ass."

Furat sighed.

Dylan smiled and started to walk over. He stopped in his tracks when he saw Mr. Brown, the vice principal, walking slowly toward them.

Manny handed the tickets to Jane, and held Furat's hand tightly.

Jane looked up at them, nervously.

"What's the problem?" Manny said.

"Didn't you see the notice?" Jane said.

"What notice?"

"They changed the rules. Mr. Brown said that only seniors can attend. It's supposed to be senior prom."

"What the fuck, Jane? I asked weeks ago and they said it would be fine."

Jane looked at Furat. "I'm so sorry. I don't make the rules."

"But she's not even started at the school yet. Come on, Jane, can't you make an exception? I've paid for the ticket and she's bought a dress."

"Please, Jane?" Abe said.

"I'm sorry. It's not my decision."

"Is there a problem here?" Mr. Brown said.

"Yeah, the problem is I asked weeks ago if I could bring Furat as my date and everyone said it was fine, but now we can't go in."

"You didn't see the notice?" Mr. Brown said.

"What fucking notice? Where?"

Mr. Brown fixed Manny with a hard stare.

"I don't care for your language, Mr. Romero. The notice was posted on the school's website ten days ago."

"Who the fuck goes on the school website?"

"Now I'm sorry, but there's nothing I can do," he turned to Furat. "Miss Al-Basri, I'll look forward to welcoming you at the start of the new school year."

Furat looked down.

"This is such bullshit," Manny said.

Furat tried to drag him away.

"What did you say?" Mr. Brown said.

"I said this is bullshit. This is why teachers are all cocksuckers, because you get drunk on your little bit of power. Making up shitty rules that we have to follow, because we don't have a choice. Well, I have a choice now; I'm done with this school so you know what, Mr. Brown, or should I call you Rusty? Nice name by the way, makes Abel sound good." Manny winked at Abe, who frowned back at him. "You know what, Rusty? You, and all of the other teachers at this shitty school, can go fuck yourselves. Because if my girl can't come in, then I'm not coming in either."

Mr. Brown stared at Manny for a long time, and then smiled—a smile that said "I've seen your grades. Good luck in the future." Then he walked inside, closing the door behind him.

Abe, Manny and Furat turned and slowly started to walk away.

"Just as well. We don't want terrorists in there, blowing us up," Dylan shouted.

It was a weak blow, though one which drew plenty of laughs from his friends, and felt like a bullet to Furat.

She thought of her mother, going with her to buy her dress and spending all afternoon helping her with her hair and makeup, even though she didn't really know what she was doing. And her father, taking hundreds of photographs when she finally emerged from her bedroom. And then she felt it, felt it more strongly than she ever had before. That she didn't fit. That people looked down on her.

Manny turned to her and tried to smile. Then he turned back to Dylan McDermott.

"Me and you. Parking lot."

They made their way across the grass quickly, toward the half-empty parking lot. Dylan McDermott smiled the whole way down. His friends slapped his back as he slipped his jacket and tie off.

"You don't have to do this, Manny. We should just go home," Furat said, gripping his hand anxiously and watching the crowd start to swell as word reached the kids inside the hall.

Manny stared straight ahead, trying to stay calm, though she could feel his hand shake in hers.

She glanced at Dylan McDermott. He was tall and muscular. She gripped Manny's hand even tighter.

When they reached the parking lot Manny tried to ignore the shouts, the jeers, and the general laughter at his expense.

"Are you okay, Manny?" Abe asked.

"Yeah. I'm good. Just got to remember my training."

"If anyone jumps in, I've got your back, man."

It might not have been that reassuring, seeing as Abe had once lost a fight to a girl in a wheelchair in the third grade, but Manny was grateful.

He stared at the large circle that had formed around them, watching the other boys; boys who would, no doubt, run rather than get their own hands dirty, baying for blood.

Dylan McDermott stepped away from the group and beckoned Manny over. Manny turned to Furat and smiled.

"If this doesn't go to plan, tell my mother I love her. Thalia, too."

She smiled, though he could see the concern in her eyes.

As Manny took his jacket off, he tried to ignore the ripple of laughter and wolf whistles.

"Hey, Dylan. Try not to get distracted by his tits."

There was a charge in the air, an electric feeling to the warm summer night.

He took a deep breath and tried to stop his legs from shaking. He'd boxed before, but if he was completely honest, he hadn't been very good. Despite what everyone thought, what everyone said, it was all bravado. He hid behind it often, though he wouldn't do that now. Now it was time to face up. He swallowed. He was in little doubt that he'd lose, though how badly remained to be seen. He fought the urge to run, then felt Furat squeeze his hand.

"Manny," she said, softly.

He looked at her.

"There's one thing I want you to do for me."

She pulled him close.

"What?" he said, nervously eyeing the crowd.

She leaned in close to him, close enough for him to feel her breath in his ear.

"I want you to win."

He smiled.

This time she spoke louder, not caring who heard. "Win, Manny, win."

Manny took another deep breath and turned to Abe, then threw him the keys to the duck-egg.

"Open the windows and put my *Rocky* soundtrack on. It's show time."

Abe ran to the car and disappeared inside.

As Manny stepped forward the noisy crowd was silenced by the deafening sound of trumpets blowing.

Some cocked their heads in confusion, others laughed as Manny started to bounce up and down.

Dylan McDermott grinned, walking toward Manny with his hands casually by his side, a confident look in his eyes.

Manny raised his fists and started to move from side to side.

Dylan threw the first punch, a hard right that Manny saw coming. He just about slipped to the side and the momentum sent Dylan sprawling to the floor.

Dylan jumped back up quickly, anger lighting his eyes.

Manny glanced at Abe who nodded back at him.

He thought of French John, and his mother and Thalia. His family.

And then, when Dylan McDermott took a step closer, he thought of his father—his father who hated him, who had walked out on them when they needed him most.

And as he watched his fist connect squarely with Dylan McDermott's jaw, and saw his eyes roll back into his head and his legs crumple beneath him, Manny realized that his father had left them for no other reason than because he was a selfish prick.

It wasn't because of Manny, because even if he didn't like football, or anything else his father deemed important, Manny could still hold his head up high, because he had stood up for the girl he loved.

And he had won.

After the crowds dispersed, and Dylan McDermott's friends reluctantly drove him to the hospital to be checked over, Manny stood in the parking lot smiling as Furat held his swollen hand in hers.

They heard light footsteps on the grass and watched Abe jog toward them.

"I know you told Mr. Brown to fuck off and everything, and I know that I came with you, and you can't go inside, but Jane has asked if I'll accompany her to senior prom after all. Mainly because you knocked her date out, but part of me thinks that it's because she likes me too. So I was wondering . . ."

"Just go," Manny said, laughing.

Abe started to walk away, and then turned. "Manny."

Manny looked up. "Yeah."

"That was awesome. You're awesome."

And then Abe turned and ran back toward the hall, back to his date, the prettiest girl in school.

"She's one lucky lady, Jane Berg. If he kisses her, she's going to feel that thing tickling her lip. Pure silk."

Furat laughed. "So how was it? How was your moment?"

"I won't lie. It felt good, but only because you were there to see it. That might be the best thing I ever do, my defining moment. And you know what? That'll be okay, because as moments go, it was pretty fucking cool."

She smiled. "Yeah, it was. Pretty fucking cool."

He raised his eyebrows. "I've never heard you curse before."

"I think you might be rubbing off on me. My parents will be thrilled."

"I'm sorry you didn't get the prom you always dreamed of."

"It doesn't matter. I wish we could have had just one dance together though."

"Wait here," Manny said, as he climbed into the duck-egg.

He walked back to her and took her in his arms.

She heard the speakers crackle and then Sinatra filled the parking lot.

"A throwback to my gangster days."

As the music played, they danced together, slowly swaying from side to side beneath a starry sky.

It wasn't the prom that she imagined, far from it, but right then, at that moment, she wouldn't have changed it for the world.

Three thousand miles away, in New York City, James Donnell-King, the editor of *National Amateur Photography Magazine*, opened another of the competition entry packs, relieved that he was nearing the last of them. He saw that it was from Jerry Lee, in a town called Tall Oaks. He flipped through the pages. He'd have his assistant read through them all in the coming weeks but he liked to open them himself, to feel the first shards of excitement as he turned to the back page, to look at the photograph in the hope that he might unearth something special.

He noticed that Jerry Lee had forgotten to sign it, so he didn't hold out too much hope.

But then he saw it.

He fell back in his chair, trying to make sense of what he was looking at.

He sat still, almost paralyzed.

And then, because he felt that to look at it any longer wouldn't be appropriate, he reached for the telephone and asked his assistant to find the number for the Tall Oaks Police Department.

29

The Beginning

Harry Monroe lay in his bed and stared at the small camera on his nightstand. It was surrounded by soft toys—monkeys, lions and other jungle animals—but he could still see it because of the green light on the base. A light he knew let his mommy see him even though it was dark in his bedroom.

She was sitting on the top step now; he knew that because he had heard her tell his grandmother about it. She'd started in his room, and then moved outside of the door. And then slowly, a step each night, she made it up the stairs. Further and further away from him. She didn't need to sit there, she could just go straight up. He wouldn't call out for her, not after she scared him so much the last time he did. And he had only called out to her that night because he heard the street door close. So he had said, *Mommy, is that you?*

And she had run into his room and screamed at him to go back to sleep. And then screamed at him because of all the mud on the new carpet, even though he could see that she was the one that had forgotten to take off her running shoes. He'd tried to point down at her feet but she had been too mad to notice. So he lay back down and burrowed down under his sheet, afraid to move.

He wouldn't make that mistake again—he wouldn't utter a word.

He tried to close his eyes, tried not to peek and see if the nightlight in the hallway was still burning. He clutched Ralph, his comforter, tightly. And then, when he had managed to keep his eyes closed for a long time, he heard the stairs creak as his mother stood up.

He let his mind drift to his father, who he missed so much. And when he thought of his father he worried that he would never come back for him. And when he worried he brought his fingers to his lips and bit his nails.

"Only dirty little boys bite their nails."

He opened his eyes wide and stared at the camera, his heart pounding and his body starting to shake. He felt the tears building in his eyes.

"Don't you dare start crying. Go to sleep."

She sounded mad, mad like she had been the other night when he woke up and felt the warm dampness beneath his body. She had come into his room that night, her eyes wild and red. And she had pulled him into the bathroom, pulled him so hard he thought his arm would come off, and she had thrown him into the tub. The water had been ice-cold and he had felt it bite deep into his bones. He wouldn't call out to her again. And if she came into his room he would scream: scream loud enough for the lady next door to hear and call the cops again.

"SLEEP. NOW."

He clamped his eyes shut, desperately hoping the tears wouldn't fall.

Jerry stayed perfectly still, the kind of perfectly still that had come with seventeen months of practice. He wasn't far off the ground, but with his weight on the branch, and the difficulty he had in getting on to it in the first place, he was afraid to move, though that wasn't the only reason he was afraid to move. He could see the boys by the clearing: the same boys that came into the Photo-Max and laughed at him; the same boys that threw eggs at him.

He tried to stop his hands from shaking.

He gripped the Hasselblad tightly. The case felt smooth against his fingers, the strap soft around his neck. He tried not to think of how much it cost, or how much Max loved it.

He'd taken some test shots with his own camera, but all he had been able to see was a blurry collection of the darkest shades of green. But the Hasselblad, with its advanced optical system and color rendering, made the images look like they had been taken in daylight. If he was ever going to get a picture of the red-billed cuckoo then it would have to be with the Hasselblad. He still didn't know for sure if the bird existed. He believed it did, because he believed Lisa's dad, who sounded just like his dad: a man so lost in his own mind that on the rare occasion he found his way out it was a time to be savored. Jerry's dad had told him he loved him exactly once in his life too, after the Vikings beat the 49ers in the 1987 playoffs. Jerry held onto that memory tightly, and it had helped him when his father said awful things to him, and his mother just laughed—it had helped him remember that deep down they loved him.

He stared at the boys, then closed his eyes when he felt the sneeze tickle his nose. Hay fever. He clenched his teeth tightly and tried to wriggle it away. But then it came. And it was loud. And then there was laughter and pointing, and he knew they wouldn't leave him alone after that.

The first rock they threw was no bigger than a coin; the second, the size of his fist. It struck him hard on the shoulder.

He fell through the air and landed heavily enough to have the wind knocked from him. He gasped for air. Then he saw another rock hit the tree beside him. So he clambered to his feet and he ran.

He ran as fast as he could; ran until the trees nestled so tightly together that the branches tore at his chest and face. But still he pushed through them. He ran so far and so deep into the forest that he could barely see the moonlight.

And then, when he could no longer hear them behind him, when he heard the sky roar above, and when he looked down and saw the cracked case of the Hasselblad, he sat down on the leaves and began to cry.

Harry woke suddenly, ripped from a dreamless sleep at an hour when darkness still smothered his room.

It took him a little while to focus. And then he saw it.

Sitting by the window, in his rocking chair.

He sat up and rubbed his eyes to make sure he wasn't imagining it, and then he smiled.

It was his father. And he was wearing the clown mask; the mask that he had worn when he dressed up for his third birthday party; the mask that Harry made him wear whenever he came to visit, because he loved it when his father became the Clown.

"Daddy," Harry said.

The Clown put his fingers to his lips.

Harry knew he'd better be quiet so as not to wake his mother. She would be mad if he did.

"Daddy," Harry whispered.

The Clown nodded.

Harry grinned. He tried not to make a sound as the Clown walked over to him and picked him up.

The Clown put his fingers to his lips again as he put Harry's coat and sneakers on him. Though it was still warm outside, Harry could hear the storm, the rain lashing against his window and the soft rumble of distant thunder.

He had to bite his lip to keep from laughing when the Clown opened the door.

They were leaving. His father had come to take him away.

Though the Clown had carried a big umbrella, Harry was wet through by the time they reached the cover of the tall oak trees.

It was dark but the Clown had a flashlight.

When they were deep in the woods, only the occasional raindrop making it through the dense cover, the Clown stopped and Harry stood shivering beside him, the mud soft beneath his feet. As his eyes adjusted to the darkness he could see the oak tree that had fallen, the huge hole its roots had left in the earth. He could also see a shovel, lying in the leaves.

"Daddy, where are we going?" he asked.

But his voice was buried under a crackle of thunder.

"Daddy," he said, this time quieter, because Daddy was taking his mask off.

Only it wasn't Daddy after all.

Jess looked down at Harry. He looked small. And he looked scared. She crouched down to his level, her knees sinking into the mud.

She wiped his tears away.

"Don't cry, Harry. I'm doing this for us, so that Daddy will come back to us."

She rubbed his shoulders, trying to stop him shaking.

"I need you to be brave for me. Can you be brave?"

He shook his head.

"You can be brave. You can, Harry. When Daddy hears that you're missing he'll realize how much he loves you, and how much he needs his family. He'll come back to us then, Harry, and we can all be together again. Would you like that—if Daddy comes home?"

He looked up at her, his eyes wide and sad.

He nodded.

She stroked his cheek.

"Daddy says that Mommy is different because of you; that she's not the same Mommy that he used to love. So if you're not there, just for a little while, then Daddy will love Mommy again. Would you like that? If Daddy loves Mommy again?"

He looked down at the ground, his tears falling into the mud, and he nodded his head.

"And then we'll come and get you, Harry, and we'll be a family."

Jess shone the flashlight into the deep hole. "Mommy's made you a little camp. That's what I've been doing, when I go out running at night. I've made you a little camp in the woods. You'll be safe down there."

He looked up at her. "Will you stay with me?"

She smiled at him. "Mommy will come back and get you soon, when Daddy comes home. I've left food down there for you. And you can keep the flashlight. And there's your sleeping bag too. The one that you took when we went camping, remember?"

He nodded.

"I'll cover it over, you'll be safe and dry until I come get you. What's the matter, Harry? Why are you still crying?"

"I don't want to stay in the woods. I want to come home."

She grabbed his shoulders roughly.

"There is no home. Look at me. Harry, look at me. There is no home without Daddy."

He started to sob, his cries loud and piercing.

She shook him.

"Harry, stop crying. You see, this is why Mommy had to wear the mask, because you're always fucking crying."

The cries grew louder, and soon the tears were joined by screams; screams that were so loud that they made her ears ring.

"HARRY," she shouted at him, struggling to make herself heard over the screams, and the thunder, and the wind that was starting to whip up the leaves.

He had his eyes closed, closed so tight that his soft skin wrinkled around them.

The screams seemed to run together—not letting up for a second. They raced into her ears and fought their way through layers of confusion and exhaustion and then they rattled her brain and flashed red in front of her eyes.

"HARRY."

Her own scream was easily swept aside by the soaring wave of his.

She shook him harder but he just kept screaming and sobbing.

She felt her breath coming fast. The fierce anger that had become so normal to her since Michael left coursed through her veins, burning hot, making its way to the surface of her skin and flushing her.

"HARRY."

She shook him again, long past the point of worrying if she was hurting him.

She tried to prize his eyes open with her fingers, but that made the screaming even louder.

And then, reaching through a thick fog of rage, her hands found the flashlight, its steel case cool against her red hot touch, and she brought it down on his head.

And then the screaming stopped.

Because Harry Monroe was dead.

Jess lay on his body for a long time. Not crying, not screaming—just lying there. When she finally sat up, she looked down at him and felt no remorse. That would come later, when she realized the cold enormity of what she had just done. But for now, she felt nothing.

As she picked up his small body and held him for the last time, she was lost in her own confused thoughts. She didn't know whether the moment really existed, or whether she was caught up in another nightmare.

And if it wasn't a nightmare, if it had really happened, she didn't know whether she would ever have the strength to live another day.

As she softly kissed his head, she didn't know if Michael would come back.

And as she knelt in the mud and said a last prayer for her son, she didn't know how she would be able to breathe without them in her life.

At that moment there were lots of things that Jessica Monroe didn't know. Like the fact that the last flash of lightning hadn't been lightning at all.

It had been the flash of a camera.

30

The End

Jess stood by the clearing. The air was still, the storm on its way. She rubbed the muscles in her neck. She closed her eyes, found the memories troublingly sharp now. She'd made it further than she might have had she not believed he would come back. It had been that thought alone that kept her from giving up—the thought that they would one day be reunited. She coped during the days: she searched, she ran. But when darkness fell she heard the screams, so she sought heavier distraction.

She might have been able to go on, for a while longer at least, but not now, now that she had found the papers in her mother's bureau, hidden from her eyes and locked away.

He wasn't coming back. They wouldn't be reunited.

Michael was filing for divorce.

She'd worked hard over the past months, to keep the story alive, to keep herself visible. She'd kept Jim close, she'd visited the station often, keeping track of the investigation.

The pressure on Michael had been intense; she had done all she could to keep it that way. The media had quickly turned him into a pariah, a man that didn't even have the good grace to support his wife through the most arduous of times. Jess had anonymously pointed them in the direction of the women he'd had affairs with; the kind of women that eagerly sold their stories. She'd knocked on every door in Tall Oaks, slowly watching sympathy turn to anger, until he was shunned by the whole town. She'd been invited in by his neighbors, cried out her eyes while they comforted her—neighbors that would no longer even say hello to him. Jess knew his latest girlfriend, Cindy Collins, had now left him, unable to cope with the hatred she felt whenever they emerged in public together, or the suspicion that swirled round them after Jess had called in the Aurora Springs tip. There were rumors that Michael had been involved, that he'd done something to Harry. She fanned their flames long enough to see his clients pull every cent from his hedge fund, keen to distance themselves from him. Her money was all that kept him afloat. Yet still, after all of this, he hadn't taken the easy option. He hadn't come back to her.

She reached for her cell phone and dialed his number.

"Did you know? I wonder if you knew. That's why you didn't help search for him; that's why you didn't help me. Was it because I did it before? All those times I told you Harry was sick, just so you'd come over and see me? That time I told you he'd run away? Have you been grieving alone now that so much time has passed? Why didn't you tell Jim that I'd lied before? Was it because of the money? Was it because you still loved me? Did you want to protect me? They all think you left because you didn't care about us, but I know that you did, in your own way. I couldn't just let you walk

away. I had to try and fight. I love you too much, Michael. I think that's always been the problem."

She looked up at the tall oak trees. They rose high above her, casting a shadow she stepped under gratefully. She knew the woods well—she'd run the trails since she was a teen, when Dr. Stone had first told her that exercise might help. It did, though not as much as the pills he prescribed.

She turned and walked slowly into the forest.

When she was deep, when she'd walked so far her legs ached and the trees closed in around her, she left the trail behind and used her compass to find the fallen oak tree. She gazed up at the base, at the clumped roots, ten feet high.

She kneeled on the spot where she had buried him, her knees on a bed of leaves.

She closed her eyes and cursed herself for it . . . for what she had done.

And she cursed Dr. Stone for being so easily fooled, so easily bought, for believing that she had her life under control again.

She cursed Jim for falling in love with her: a love that she knew well; a love that made you do unspeakable things all in its name; a love that made him avoid the questions he should have been asking, always going easy on her, always protecting.

And she cursed her mother, for not taking Harry away when she knew how much she was struggling. Alison had seen the marks on his body, marks she should have known couldn't possibly have come from falling from the statue in the park. She knew Jess was too scared to let him climb it. But she didn't know she was scared because a trip to the emergency room would lead to a series of follow-up questions she couldn't possibly provide an answer to.

And finally, she cursed God, for making her this way. For making her capable of hurting those that she loved and driving them away. Capable of feeling the same kind of love that Jim felt for her, only a hundred times more blinding.

She would tell Him when she saw Him—God—after she found her Harry and made him love her again. Because she was on her way to them now. Now that she had taken the gun that she had found in Michael's desk drawer; the gun that she held to her head.

When she pulled the trigger she hoped to see a flash of light, a last image of Harry and Michael. But when she fell backward, and she caught a glimpse of the reddening sky through the tall oak trees, she saw the Clown, and he was racing away from her eyes, moving so fast and so far that he disappeared completely.

And then she felt the first drops of rain on her face as the heat finally broke.

31

The Strong One

The summer passed by in a blur of news crews and noise.

They found Harry Monroe's body buried directly under the spot where they found his mother. The site was located a mile from the nearest trail, and three miles from the edge of the search area. Harry was buried deep, in a tract of woodland prone to flooding. The ground appeared undisturbed. All facts that had been of little comfort to Jim.

As word spread to the people of Tall Oaks there were tears of unimaginable grief for the little boy who had died such a tragic death.

Every single resident attended his funeral in a show of such unbridled love that the previously silent Michael Monroe broke down in tears and cried for his son, for not doing more, for not protecting him, for not changing the way he was, and most of all, because it was too late for his tears to make a difference.

Jim put the last of the tapes into the machine, lit a cigarette and pressed play. He'd listened to them all again, in order, the pieces slotting together to form a picture he struggled to look at.

He skipped forward an hour—there were lots of breaks, lots of tears.

"I didn't know he was dead. I just thought she was holding him. I mean . . . with the rain and the dark. I didn't know the storm would drive the red-billed cuckoo out of its nest. I didn't know what I'd captured in the background."

"And when you did?"

"I showed it to my mother."

"I can guess what she said."

"She needed me. She said I'd get into trouble. There'd be no one to care for her. But . . ."

"But?"

"But then she sent it anyway, and I don't even know why. I like to think that it was because she loved me, because she knew how much it meant to me to do the right thing. I knew I could've tried to get it back. I could have phoned the magazine. But I didn't really want to. I knew it was the right thing to do."

"And the camera? The Hasselblad? We found it in your dark room."

"I wanted to give it back, but Max came in early the next day, because Lisa called him and told him about Harry. I was going to explain, to pay to get it fixed. But he was so mad. He was pacing up and down, his face all red. He punched the wall. He made a hole in it. And he had already called the police. And the town was crazy, with Harry."

He could still hear the fear in Jerry's voice: the pain, the anguish.

"I know I should have given it to you."

"But you didn't."

"I couldn't lose my job, Jim. I had to pay for her medication."

"I get it."

"I saw Jessica Monroe. I thought that she must have known where he was. And she's the only one that really needed to know. I mean, she's the only one that really cared. She did what she did. I know that now. It can't be undone. It can't be taken back. I wish it could, more than anything, I wish it could."

He stopped the tape, ejected it, then slipped it into his pocket.

He glanced up at the clock, then walked out of the station.

It was pleasant out, still warm but the storm had killed the searing heat. He headed in the direction of St. Mary's, stopping only to drop the tape into the trash.

Jerry could see the cemetery outside, through the open door.

He sat alone.

It was here he had sat, along with the hundred others that had managed to get a seat, and said goodbye to Harry. And then the very next day he had sat alone, on the very same bench, and said goodbye to his mother.

He'd come back to the church daily since, during his lunch break.

He glanced up at the beamed roof, and then down at the stone floor. He looked at his chubby fingers as he lightly traced them over the wood.

The service hadn't seemed enough: a half hour to say a formal goodbye. He'd sung; stood alone and sung "Ave Maria" to his dead mother and Father Andrew. And to Lisa, who had sat at the back. His voice hadn't changed in twenty-five years Father Andrew had said. It was a gift.

He could still see a mark on his hand from where they'd put a needle in. It had been his weight that had saved him in the end. The sting might have killed a smaller man with such a severe allergy.

He didn't notice the other man until he was sitting right beside him.

"Hey," Jim said.

"Hi."

"You okay?"

Jerry nodded.

Jim leaned back and stared at the cross. "You've been expecting me?"

Jerry nodded.

"I thought I'd give you some time."

They sat in silence for a long while, the kind of silence heightened for Jerry by the weight of the words that might follow. He hadn't heard anything since he'd given his statement. And he had waited. Waited and waited by the window. Always watching and waiting.

"I've seen the magazine. That guy from New York called me a while back. He asked if they could edit the photograph."

Jerry nodded.

Jim followed his eye to the cross.

They looked up and saw Father Andrew walk through the door. He smiled at them and then disappeared into his office.

Jerry breathed slowly. His shirt felt loose. He'd lost four pounds. A start.

Jim watched an elderly woman stop by a grave, cross herself, and then move on.

"The store looks good," Jim said.

"Lisa did most of it. I didn't want to. I know I don't deserve it, any of it. I'm so sorry," Jerry said, wiping his eyes.

Jim put a hand on his shoulder.

"So what happens now?" Jerry said, quietly.

"Max isn't around to press charges about the camera. I filled out my report, didn't mention it. I said your mother mailed the application and that you hadn't even checked the card, didn't know what you'd taken . . ."

"Because I'm slow."

Jim looked down at the floor, at the dust lightly blowing across it.

"You lied," Jerry said. "Why?"

"Does it matter?"

Jerry took a breath, and then looked up at him.

"I've seen you sitting by Harry's grave."

"Yeah."

"Do you believe in heaven, Jim?"

Jim stood, shook his head.

"So that's that?" Jerry said.

"We all do bad things, Jerry, but sometimes we do them for the right reasons."

Jerry watched him leave.

He sat alone for a long time.

And then he glanced down at his watch. His new watch; the watch that simply told him the time. It seemed slower than his last watch, though that might have been because he didn't check it as often.

*

"So this is it. The end of an era," Abe said, as Manny helped load the last of the boxes into the back of the car.

"I can't believe your mother gave you the Volvo."

Abe smiled. "Yeah, well, I think that was mainly because they've taken her license away. Her eyes are getting worse."

Manny looked back at the house. "Yeah, she nearly ran Thalia down the other day, when she came to drop off the prom photographs. She parked in our front yard instead of the street. My mother was pissed."

"I wish you were coming with me," Abe said, his deep voice cracking.

Manny pulled him in for a tight hug and then kissed his forehead, softly.

"You took the hottest, most popular girl in school to prom. You've got a sweet Volvo, the finest mustache I've ever seen, and the kindest heart of any Jew I've ever met. The girls on campus will have to take a ticket and get in line for a ride on your cock."

Abe smiled as Manny slapped his cheek.

"I'll see you in a couple of weeks. I've got to get into town. I've got a job interview."

Abe raised his eyebrows.

"My mother's ragging on me again, and I need my own money. I got a girl to take care of after all."

Manny walked away, not turning back because there was a serious danger that he might cry, and he couldn't let Abe see that—he was the strong one after all.

He cut through the narrow alleyway and walked up his street, waving to his mother and Thalia, who were busy trying to repair the tire marks in the lawn.

Then he stopped outside Furat's house and helped her with her case. He loaded it into the trunk and smiled at her mother, who was sat in the passenger seat of the car.

"Are you excited?" he asked.

"I can't wait. I still can't believe we're going," Furat said.

"So things are okay now?"

She shrugged. "He called her as soon as he heard about Harry. I think it brought it home . . . you know?"

"What did she call the baby?"

"Mohammed . . . after my father."

Manny looked up as Furat's father came out the house carrying a case.

He nodded to Manny.

"Merhaba yakışıklı," Manny said.

"Please stop speaking Turkish to my father."

Furat's father shook his head, then got into the car.

"Call me when you get to Chicago."

"Of course."

"And get some good pictures of baby Mo. Tell him his Uncle Manny looks forward to meeting him."

Furat laughed. "Good luck with your interview. Try not to curse. I'll see you in a week."

She leaned forward and kissed his cheek.

"I love you, Manny," she whispered into his ear.

"I love you too," he whispered back.

As Manny turned onto Main Street, the sun lighting his path, he saw Jim crossing the street in front of him.

"You okay, man?" Manny said.

Jim stopped. "Yeah."

"It wasn't your fault, you know. None of it was your fault. I know what they're saying . . . but fuck them."

Jim nodded once, and then he walked back toward the station.

Manny carried on up Main Street, walking past Pizza Hut and nodding to Stan, who looked away quickly.

He passed the newsstand, saw the magazine with the bird on the cover; the one that everyone was talking about. His mother had a copy at home. He'd smiled when he read the dedication inside. *To Lisa.*

He stopped for a moment and said hello to French John, who was sitting with Roger outside the Tearoom. They were smiling and laughing, and then both jumped up to help Henrietta with their drinks. She joined them and the three sat together.

Manny crossed the street and looked up at the sign, still so new it had a sparkle to it.

He pushed the door open to the PhotoJerry, and walked inside.

Acknowledgements

Thank you:

Victoria, who has discovered that being married to a writer is even less fun than being married to a trader. Thank you for loving *Tall Oaks* (and me).

To my parents (and Yiannis) for the early reads and careful critiques, your support means so much.

Julie, the kindest most generous person I know. (Scoring major mother-in-law points here.)

To my brother, Toby, for the Buddha lunches when I come to town, and for loving Manny as much as I do. That Travolta line was for you.

To all at WME, especially Cathryn Summerhayes. Thank you for all of your support, and for enabling me to use the immortal line, '*Talk to my agent.*' I say it to my kids all the time. You should probably expect their call.

All at Twenty7 and Bonnier.

My editors, Joel Richardson and Claire Johnson-Creek. Being a complete novice I didn't really know exactly what an editor does, but I do now. They take a book and make it a million times better in every conceivable way. I am eternally in their debt.

Emily Burns, for championing *Tall Oaks*, and for laughing at my stupid emails.

Rob Cox – don't look me in the eye. (It's happening already.)

Nick Stearn, for the brilliant cover. All that's missing is a mosque (you have a button for that, right?)

Robert Woolliams – launch party in a strip club? I'll make some calls.

Team Twenty7 – you're the best. I'd be lost without our secret Twitter group. Delete. Delete. Delete.

Annabel and the team at whitefox.

To my friend Scott Curran, for the boogie shit.

Rebecca Bowen, for the author photo, though I can't help feeling like we should have gone with the topless-quill-smoke machine idea.

Caroline Ambrose and everyone at The Bath Novel Award. If you're an aspiring writer it's a great resource.

Lastly, and most importantly, to Siobhan O'Neill. I don't know where to begin so I'll just say thanks for everything. I wouldn't have got here without you.